A GOWN of THORNS

NATALIE MEG EVANS

First published in Great Britain in 2015 by
Quercus Publishing Ltd
Carmelite House
50 Victoria Embankment
London EC4Y 0DZ

An Hachette UK company

EBOOK ISBN 9781784298432

This book is a work of fiction. Names, characters,
businesses, organisations, places and events are
either the product of the author's imagination
or used fictitiously. Any resemblance to
actual persons, living or dead, events or
locales is entirely coincidental.

10 9 8 7 6 5 4 3 2 1

Publisher contact: Kathryn Taussig

kathryn.taussig@quercusbooks.co.uk

Also by Natalie Meg Evans

The Dress Thief
The Milliner's Secret

The Dress Thief was winner of the 2014 Festival of Romantic Fiction's 'Best Historical Read' Award, and shortlisted for the 2015 Romance Writers of America (RWA) RITA Awards and the 2015 Public Book Awards.

The Milliner's Secret was shortlisted for the 2015 Romantic Fiction's 'Best Historical Read' Award.

This story is dedicated to Naomi Bolstridge,
my 'Aunt Omy'

These events happened in the year 2003. Some of us instinctively know that the past is always with us. Those of a scientific disposition resist the idea – until denial becomes, in itself, unscientific.

Part One

July

Chapter One

She wheeled her suitcases towards the ticket office, blinking in the sunshine. After the train's air-conditioned interior, Garzenac station felt like a bread oven. There ought to be a warning sign: Redheads, do not alight here.

The train doors sealed themselves with a gentle *tsssk* and the RER Paris–Bordeaux began to move. Shauna Vincent kicked herself: *why didn't I research summer temperatures in the Dordogne valley?*

If she didn't get out of this sun, she'd cook.

The ticket office clock said it was just gone three p.m.: The train had come in a few minutes early, so Madame Duval, her soon-to-be employer, might not have yet arrived. Shauna checked her phone for messages finding only a belated text from her service provider, welcoming her to France. Her phone was down to one bar of battery, she noticed. She couldn't have charged it properly before she left home. Disturbing. She *never* forgot to charge her phone. Just as she never came out in summer without sun cream in her bag.

She'd bought a map of the Dordogne *département* during a brief stop-off in Paris, and had spent much of the four-hour journey searching for her final destination, a village called Chemignac. It didn't seem to exist. She'd been expecting a rural backwater, but not complete isolation. *Please* let it not be out of mobile phone range. For her sanity, she needed to keep contact with friends, and with the job market. Two weeks ago, the research post she'd believed was hers had gone to somebody else. The shock of it had soured her final days at university, and made the many months she'd taken over her master's degree feel like a waste of time. Actually, it felt like a bereavement and she'd accepted this last-minute invitation to France as a way of dealing with the rejection. But had she made a catastrophic mistake, landing herself in the back of nowhere?

In the station foyer, she looked for a kiosk selling bottled water but there wasn't one. Not even a vending machine. Just unmanned ticket barriers. The heat radiating from the station forecourt was even more intense than that of the platforms. Screwing up her nose at the whiff of melting tarmac, she scuttled for the shade of some Cypress trees. Sudden cool and the scent of balsam calmed her a little. Curious, in spite of herself, to investigate this unfamiliar environment, she pushed aside the feathery foliage. Her eye fastened instantly on a small, brown insect which was almost indistinguishable from the bark. Evolutionary camouflage in action . . . sometimes the more simple life-forms were, the more intricate their defences. Globs of resin were trickling down the trunk like melted wine gums and she wondered if her little insect might eventually be overrun by it and end up, millennia from now, transfixed as a fly in amber.

A horn blast reminded Shauna that Madame Duval might have arrived. She glanced around expectantly, but the car was hooting to get the attention of a delivery driver blocking the station concourse. The delivery man was scanning a parcel, his rear doors gaping, and didn't even look up as the motorist hooted again. A younger man in a faded green bush hat standing next to him did at least give an apologetic wave.

One by one, drivers who had collected their passengers began to edge away until only a red, open-top 2CV and a silver Mercedes remained. Shauna trundled her cases towards the Mercedes, the more likely make of car for Madame Duval, in her mind. A relation on Shauna's mother's side of the family, Isabelle Duval was a complete stranger. All Shauna knew of her was that she lived in a wing of the Château de Chemignac, but that long ago, she'd been a fashion journalist in Paris. She'd married a diplomat and was now widowed. Shauna was to take care of Madame's grandchildren. She was picturing a woman with impeccably groomed grey hair – Isabelle Duval was in her late sixties – x-ray thin, wearing a little black dress. All right, perhaps not black in this heat . . . ivory linen, gold bracelets shimmering at her wrists.

'Pardon!' A woman, sweating under the weight of shopping bags, cut in front of Shauna to tap on the Mercedes' window. As the driver lowered the glass, Shauna realised the car was a taxi. Not her ride, obviously. The only vehicles remaining were the delivery van and the topless 2CV. Hoping she wouldn't be kept waiting very much longer, Shauna unzipped the smaller of her suitcases and retrieved a cotton shirt. At least she could protect the back of her neck from the sun. She was fighting to get her arms into it when the young man in the bush hat strode past, the parcel under his arm. He glanced at her through mirrored lenses and she sensed a moment's interest, followed by a dollop of pity.

All right for him, literally taking the heat in his stride. Jet-haired and muscular, brown as tropical teak and with a day's growth of stubble, he looked local, though the washed-out t-shirt and low-slung Bermudas could have originated anywhere. Buttoning her shirt to her neck, she watched him approach the red 2CV and place his package in the passenger footwell. So carefully, she wondered what fragile object was inside. He then vaulted into the driver's seat without opening the door. At the turn of his key, music with a heavy bass flared out. Then he was off, hair flying away from his face to reveal dark sideburns and the fact that he was singing.

The delivery van driver finished his paperwork and moved off too, and that's when Shauna saw there was one, last vehicle in the car park. Its driver was holding up a sign reading 'Chemignac'.

'Oh my God,' Shauna breathed. Then, 'No, please, anything but that.'

Chapter Two

It was a two-wheeled cart, a white pony between the shafts. A woman the same age as Shauna – twenty-five or so – was perched on the box seat, reins held loose in one hand. She wore a red singlet and knee-length shorts that showed off endless, tanned limbs. The *de rigueur* sunglasses hid her expression. What looked like honey-brown hair was shoved under a baseball cap. Even the pony wore a sunhat of knitted, tasselled string, fitted around its ears. Every time it tossed its head, the tassels dislodged a cluster of flies. *Fifteen kilometres in the back of a cart?*, Shauna wailed silently. She wouldn't cook, she'd chargrill.

'What kept you? I'm Rachel, I run the tourist side of things at Clos de Chemignac. Thought you'd missed the train.'

The girl spoke French in a fast, bored style that Shauna struggled to follow. She'd once been pretty handy at the language, but had given it up in Year 10 in favour of sciences. After saying 'Sorry,' in English, she corrected herself: '*Je suis désolée*, I expected Madame Duval—'

'Get up, will you?' Rachel interrupted. 'This is the worst time of day to make a horse stand around. You can see the flies, can't you?'

Apologising again, though neither the time of day nor the flies could be considered her fault, Shauna heaved her suitcases over the tailgate. She clambered in, finding a place to perch a second before Rachel clicked her tongue and sent the pony forward at a trot. They continued at this brisk pace right through the town of Garzenac, giving Shauna little chance to get the measure of the place. It seemed to be comprised of old houses clinging to a hill crowned with a church and the ruined towers of an ancient stronghold. Every residence had closed shutters. Perhaps the town's folk were hiding inside, against the blistering heat.

Flashes of furnace-pink oleander reminded Shauna that she'd travelled south by a whole ten degrees' latitude since leaving the north of England yesterday. A headache was climbing the walls of her skull. Again, her fault as she'd lost her sunglasses. She'd been leaning against the stern rail of the cross-channel ferry, staring into the wake as the boat navigated out of port. She must have fallen into a trance, and her favourite Oakleys had paid the price.

As they bowled along a sunlit road, Shauna pulled her shirt collar as high as it would go. It really wasn't like her to be scatty or distracted. She just couldn't stop brooding about the plum post at Cademus Laboratories, snatched from under her nose by a girl half as qualified as she. A girl who happened to be rich, beautiful and socially well-connected. Shauna didn't object to a fair fight, but society girls with an inflated sense of entitlement made her angry to her soul. Had things worked out differently, she'd have been flat-hunting in the East Midlands, looking for a place to rent close to Cademus's glass-and-steel HQ. She'd have been shopping for work clothes and reading everything she could about her new employer.

Now, instead of working with a team of internationally renowned scientists, she was going to be an *au pair* to a Frenchwoman's grandchildren. She was heading to a corner of France as alien as the surface of Mars, with added heat and flies. She could have said no when her mother told her that a distant cousin was desperate for summer help, but she'd shrugged and said, 'Why not? Nobody else wants me.' In the same surly mood, she'd said 'Fine' when her mother warned her that the job was for three months. She'd bundled a random selection of dresses, shorts and leggings into one suitcase and filled another with study notes. Without brainwork, she'd go mad – if this heat didn't get her first. Wanting the reassurance of a familiar voice, she speed-dialled her mother. When her tiny screen flashed its 'No signal' message, Shauna called to Rachel over the pony's clip-clopping hooves, 'Do you get phone reception at Chemignac?'

'I wouldn't know. I don't bother trying.'

OK, I get the message, Shauna answered silently. *Or rather, I don't.* Giving up on her phone, she turned to face the back of the cart to avoid staring into the sun. Vineyards hugged every hill and dip, a this-way-and-that patchwork of emerald rows separated by strips of sun-parched grass. This was wine country, though the occasional pocket of strident yellow announced that somebody was growing sunflowers. She could be travelling into the heart of a painting by Cézanne. To her right, trees followed the course of the Dordogne River. To the left, the ground rose towards hills pock-marked with sand-coloured rock. Heat haze hung over everything and Shauna, her temples pounding, couldn't shake the sense of heading into a mirage.

'You'll fall in love with Chemignac,' her mother had promised. But Shauna knew all about false promises. Her mobile buzzed, finally picking up signal, and she found a text message from Grace Fuller, who had been her closest friend at university. Grace, who'd gained a first in physics, was working in a sandwich shop in Sheffield, the city where they'd both grown up. *I'm not the only one whose career has hit a roadblock*, Shauna reminded herself. Grace had written, 'Allo, allo? How are ze locals? Anywhere decent to go out? Anyone to go out WITH?'

'Doubtful on both counts,' Shauna texted back. 'Not sure destination exists. Have been picked up by bad-tempered time traveller. Message me every hour for the next three months in case I've been abducted.' She pressed 'send'.

No network, her phone told her. She tried 'send' again. And again until Rachel turned in her seat and shouted, 'See up there? There's Chemignac.'

At the end of an avenue of walnut trees, Shauna made out salmon-red roofs and what looked like a gatehouse with battlements. To one side, wrecking the symmetry, was a squat tower. Then Rachel cried, 'Allez, hue!' and the pony set off at a furious pace. Shauna's luggage bounced off the back of the cart. Furious, she roared, 'Pull up!'

Rachel did so and Shauna scrambled out, jarring her knees on the stone-hard driveway. 'I'll walk the rest,' she said curtly, though she was swaying as if she'd been spun on a fairground ride.

'Suit yourself,' Rachel tossed back. 'Through the big gate, into the courtyard. Madame Duval lives this side of the château. Look for a rose-pink door. Give the brass bell a good clang, she's a bit deaf.'

Rachel drove onward while Shauna went to rescue her luggage. The zips had held, thank goodness. Sixty pages of hand-written notes would have made an interesting addition to the scenery. Hopefully, the homemade elderberry cordial her mother had sent for Madame Duval was still intact. Mouth as dry as tumbleweed, Shauna approached her new home.   Château de Chemignac looked to be a hybrid of medieval farmhouse and fortress with its watchtower and encircling moat. Clay roof tiles shimmered under the four o'clock sun, and the sandstone walls had an iron-red sheen. The moat was dry, she discovered – grassed over. Walking beneath the castellated gatehouse felt like passing through border control. All the way up the avenue, she felt the eyeless watchtower questioning her. Had she been less exhausted, she'd have fled.

In the courtyard she looked around for a rose-pink door and instead saw an open-topped 2CV, ladybird red under a coating of road dust.

There were two doors of nail-studded oak on opposite sides of the quadrant, each with a brass bell with a rope attached to the clapper. No pink door to be seen. Choosing the nearest oak door, she rang hard and rehearsed her greeting: 'Madame Duval? I'm Shauna, Elisabeth's daughter. *Si heureuse de faire votre connaissance*. Please can I have a bucket of water?'

She heard footsteps and a grumbling male cough. Frowning, she glanced at the red 2CV. Was she about to meet the man with the mirrored sunglasses who liked Guns N' Roses? She was boiling-sweaty – thanks to Rachel – and in no state to face an attractive man.

The door was wrenched open and Shauna's smile dropped away as a figure in blue overalls demanded to know what she wanted. True, it was a man, but one whose lined face was dominated by a beaky nose and a bristling, white moustache. 'Who are you?' he demanded, glowering at her with ink-black eyes. 'Why were you trying to pull the rope off the bell, *hien*?'

'I wasn't! I mean' – *Je suis desolée* – 'I'm looking for Madame Duval.'

'For Isabelle?' The old man pointed at the door opposite. 'She isn't in, though. You're the English girl? We don't want you here.'

'I beg your pardon?' Shauna took a step back, but the old man seemed unmoved by her dismay.

'We don't want you. *Casse-toi, Anglaise!*' He slammed the door on her, though not before spitting a final missile, *'Rouquine!'*

Rouquine? Nope. Never heard that one before. Shattered, Shauna dragged her suitcases across the courtyard and rang the other bell. Squash plants spilled out of half-barrels either side of the door and fat melons grew in an open cold frame. A short hose was attached to an outdoor tap. Beyond caring if the water was suitable for drinking or not, Shauna filled her mouth. The front of her shirt got soaked but it felt wonderful.

After five minutes' wait, she abandoned her luggage and retraced her way through the gatehouse. Beyond the moat stretched acres of uncut meadow, the tall grass turning to hay, jewelled with wild flowers whose scent made her head buzz.

She could search for the employee, Rachel, or even the owner of the 2CV, but frankly, she'd had enough of French people for one day. She'd find a shady spot, she decided, and lie down. She took a shortcut to the meadow, slithering into the dry moat and climbing up the other side. Wading through the grass, her progress marked by bursts of pollen and topaz butterflies, she aimed for the margins of a wood. There the grass was shorter, greener, the air cool. She lay down, using her long-sleeved shirt for a pillow. Sleep would cure her.

Sleep came, but brought muddled dreams and the sensation of falling into a treacle-black vortex. She dreamt that bullets were zinging past her, fired from the ground where flames raged.

As she slept and the sun dipped, Chemignac's doves returned to their roosts under the conical roof of the tower until, without warning, they all shot up into the sky at once with a sound like whips cracking. Shauna woke.

In the stable yard on the château's eastern side, a man broke off from cold-sponging the sore, swollen legs of a white pony. He stared up into the violet sky, expecting to see a circling sparrowhawk or buzzard, but there was nothing to explain the panicking doves. He pulled a face, remembering coming here as a child to visit his father. In a bid to seem grownup and brave, he had insisted on sleeping in the tower room. The doves would often wake him, taking off from their niches as if the tower itself alarmed them. Or something in the tower.

Chapter Three

'Shauna?' A woman wearing a Boho-style turban over dyed black hair called her name as Shauna slowly entered the courtyard. She looked to be in her late sixties or early seventies. Could it be . . . ?

'Madame Duval?'

'Indeed I am!' A cotton kaftan, beaded at the neck, and colourful, ethnic earrings were far removed from the chic look Shauna had ascribed to Madame Duval. As she approached Shauna, she leaned heavily on an ebony cane and when she spoke again, her voice rasped as if walking were painful. *'Salut, chérie!'*

'Salut! I've come to work for you.' Shauna had woken in the meadow feeling strangely chilled – and with a jolt, like an electric shock. In her dream, she'd been about to plummet into gunfire

and though part of her mind had known it wasn't real, the scene had been terrifyingly graphic. Returning to the château had felt like swimming through celluloid. She must look wild-eyed, she thought, her hair full of grass seed. With the dying sun picking out its copper and bronze highlights, she probably resembled a traffic light. Red and amber.

'My dear, how rude you must think me, but Rachel said nothing of your arrival.' Madame Duval kissed Shauna on both cheeks, gripping her arm with her free hand. 'I saw the estate car parked near the stables where it's been since yesterday, so I supposed you had been delayed. Rachel did not tell me she had taken the pony and trap!' She pushed her turban higher up her forehead, as if to inspect Shauna better. 'How like Elisabeth you are, pink as a peach! She could never stand the heat, but I think it is more than that. *Oh, mon Dieu!*'

Shauna's legs gave way. Madame Duval bent as low as she could, taking Shauna's chin in her fingers. For the second time in that courtyard, Shauna felt that she was being studied ten layers deep. 'You have sunstroke! How could that happen?'

'Not sunstroke,' Shauna muttered. She felt safer sitting on the cobbles, and just lucid enough to explain, 'Heat exhaustion. My fluid and salt levels have dropped. I need water and electrolytes.'

'Electrolytes? I don't know . . . but you can stand? No? Wait here.'

Shauna flinched as a cacophony ripped the air. Looking over her shoulder, she saw Madame Duval with her arm inside the 2CV, the alarm yawping like a siren warning of chemical attack.

'Laurent! Laurent! *Viens ici, vite, vite,'* Madame Duval pitched urgently, repeating herself until fast footsteps could be heard, and a male voice shouted, 'What's up?'

Somebody else – the old man Shauna had met earlier? – added his voice: *'What the devil is this racket? Why is this girl still here,* la rouquine*? Who invited her?'*

Shauna tucked her head into her chest, wanting to avoid the old man's unnerving gaze. She kept her eyes shut even as a shadow fell across her, and a strand of hair tickled her face. The shadow held the scent of horses and citronella. Somebody was reaching down. Arms linked around her, and a moment later, she was being carried like a bride over a threshold and set down on a divan. Finally, she opened her eyes, and the room was spinning.

'You feel pain? Where – head, neck?' The voice was low, carrying a note of true concern and Shauna felt tears well up. It was the man from the railway station. She recognised his hair, longer than the current fashion with neatly-razored sideburns. His gaze held hers unblinkingly as if searching for something he might recognise. His mouth was beautiful, narrowed in concentration, a charcoaling of stubble around it. Something deeper than gratitude flooded her and she reached for his hand. Missed and grasped his wrist. His flesh was warm under its sprinkling of hairs, his pulse steady and unflustered.   'Have you had cramp?' He used the phrase *'crampe musculaire'*.

'No, but my head aches.' *My heart, too.*

'When did you last drink water?'

It took her a moment to assimilate his meaning, and to muster the correct phrases to answer him. 'Um, an hour ago. Maybe two hours . . . well, not since I was on the train.'

'You are dehydrated, do you think?'

He was asking good questions and he wasn't trying to stare into her soul, she realised. He was checking for dilation of the pupils. Whatever she was experiencing by being so close to him, he wasn't feeling it back.

'She asked for electrolytes,' Madame Duval interjected. 'Do you know what they are?'

'Salts, *tante* Isabelle, like magnesium,

calcium and potassium. I'll get some from the lab. Meanwhile, give her plain water and find a fleece blanket. She's flushed, but feels cold. More like shock than sunstroke, which is strange.'

'A blanket. *Oui, docteur,*' Isabelle Duval said teasingly, though with evident affection for the young man who was ordering her about.

Tante Isabelle? So this Laurent was Madame Duval's nephew. And yes, though he dwarfed his aunt, he had the same eyes, dark as a shot of espresso. When he gently unlatched Shauna's hand, and took her wrist to find her pulse, she glimpsed a bold tattoo on the underside of his arm. A thorn twig with barbs that would hurt if you got on the wrong end of them in real life.

Shauna blinked in confusion – she had the identical symbol tattooed on *her* arm, just below her left shoulder.

It took Shauna three days to fully recover, and four before she met the children she'd come to look after. Isabelle Duval tended her all that time, mortified at the part she'd inadvertently played in Shauna's rough reception. 'That wretched Rachel Moorcroft! I was going to ask Laurent to collect you from the train station because he had an appointment in Garzenac but Rachel volunteered to go herself.' Madame Duval was pouring peppermint tea. They were in her drawing room, the windows open to the breeze. The view was of lawns and rose gardens giving way to meadow and eventually, the massing fringes of the forest. 'I presumed she would take the big Peugeot, which she uses to pick up visitors to the winery. But no! She takes a horse and cart as though we are . . . what are those people?' Madame Duval's earrings shook as she struggled to find the word she wanted. Her hair, freed from its turban, hung in page boy bangs and she could have passed for a fairground fortune-teller. 'You know, those

Americans who do everything in the seventeenth century?'

'Amish?'

'*Exactement*. The pony cart does tourist rides, but never at the hottest time of day. Laurent found the poor little animal in a bad state and he is incandescent.' Rachel's job, Isabelle Duval went on to say, was to escort visitors on horseback rides through the vineyards and the woods. The girl had overstated her role when she described herself as 'running the tourist side of things.' Her domain was the stables. 'Chemignac is famous for its white horses, and though they make little money, they bring visitors in. People come to ride, and then buy wine afterwards! Laurent employed Rachel because she's English, like most of the guests, and he thought she would aid communication. Ha!'

Rachel was English? 'But . . . she sounded like a native Frenchwoman.'

'She's from London. Why must she speak French to you at all? Showing off! Or perhaps it was one of her not-very-funny jokes.'

Not at all funny, Shauna agreed. 'Why did she direct me to a non-existent rose-pink door?'

'To trick you into clanging Monsieur de Chemignac's bell. Poor *oncle* Albert! He was taking his siesta, and you know, he is nearly eighty. He is angry too.'

Yes, Shauna thought, *but not with Rachel.* She sipped the fragrant tea, ruminating on the fact that, through complicated degrees of cousinhood, she and that curmudgeonly old man were also related. What would Albert de Chemignac make of that? Not very much, Shauna decided.

Just that morning, Isabelle had drawn Shauna a family tree, showing that she and Shauna's mother were third cousins once removed. Isabelle's great-grandmother was Elisabeth Vincent's great-great grandmother. They'd hardly been aware of each other's existence, she had told Shauna, but that was hardly surprising as Elisabeth's mother had married an *Anglais* and moved to the north of England. 'But then, one day I get a letter. Elisabeth is coming to study in Paris and wants to meet her mother's family. I invited her to my magazine office by the Seine, then took her to lunch. She had a terrible French accent and was very shy.'

Nevertheless, Isabelle had taken to the red-headed Elisabeth and, though there was an age gap of twenty-three years between them, an enduring friendship had formed. Shauna had been astonished to learn that Elisabeth had met her husband, Shauna's father, right here, in Chemignac. 'They met in Ireland, I always thought.'

'No, no.' Elisabeth had joined Isabelle one summer at Chemignac. 'I think it was 1973'. She'd come to help with the *vendange*, the grape harvest. On her first day, she'd glimpsed a handsome lad among the vines. He was from Dublin, earning his holiday money as a harvest hand. *Un coup de foudre. Love at first sight!*

Isabelle said now, 'When you have drunk your tea, would you like to help me prepare the vegetables for dinner?' She reached for her stick. 'We're having Sobronade – a casserole of white beans, ham and pork – to my mother's recipe. The *petits sauvages* are back at six and will be ravenous.'

'Of course I'll help. Your poor grandchildren have had to tip-toe around because of me these last few days.'

'It is good for them. Good for children to learn to think of others. I wish I had mastered that lesson earlier myself. I was a wilful, horrible child.' Isabelle got up with a drawn-out 'ooooh'. She had broken her femur in a car crash two years before and the fracture had been slow to mend. Then, just a couple of weeks ago, as she was due to leave Paris for Chemignac, she'd tripped on a kerbstone and badly bruised her knees. No longer able to act as daily chauffeur to her grandchildren – her customary role during the long summer holiday – she'd sent a panicky email to Elisabeth, asking her cousin to cast around for an au pair. 'A nice girl who can drive on our side of the road, who can coach my brats in English and is free right away.'

Elisabeth had looked across at Shauna, seeing her daughter wan-faced and on the cusp of depression, and uttered the fateful words, 'You will fall in love with Chemignac. I did, years ago, and so did your father.'

Shauna followed Isabelle out of the drawing room, slightly swinging her arms, testing her balance. She felt fine, no lingering symptoms of heat exhaustion. Rest and peppermint tea had done the trick. Nor had that unsettling dream come back. *Better give mum a call*, Shauna thought as she waited at the kitchen table to be given a job. Isabelle had telephoned England to let Elisabeth know that her daughter had arrived, and was a little unwell. *I must let her know I've risen from my sickbed.* It felt strange to have gone four days without contacting the world outside. Grace was probably convinced by now that she *had* been abducted. Shauna also had no idea if Mike Ladriss, the senior professor of her university faculty, had messaged her. He'd promised to alert her to any suitable research posts that crossed his radar. Their last meeting had been deeply emotional – for her anyway – and she'd said things she now regretted. A friendly text from him would put her mind at rest.

'Where's the best place to get a mobile phone signal, Madame?'

Isabelle, standing in front of an open fridge, gestured vaguely. 'Garzenac, in the churchyard, the highest part of town. That is the only place my phone works, though Laurent uses a different network with a better range. Shauna, please call me Isabelle, not "Madame". I know I am old, but I don't like to feel it. Would you open the back door? It is so hot! These Dordogne summers kill me, yet I keep coming back.' Reaching into the fridge and almost to herself, she added, 'Nobody who loves Chemignac ever really leaves it.'

Opening the door onto the courtyard, Shauna breathed in the musk of ripening cantaloupes. Chemignac seemed pretty much immune to modernity, yet as a wine estate and tourist attraction, it must have a computer somewhere. Or at least a fax machine. Or maybe Laurent would let her borrow his phone? Would it be too pushy to ask? He hadn't called on her since that first evening, even though the back wall of his apartment was twenty strides away. He'd telephoned for updates on her condition, according to Isabelle, but that wasn't the same as coming to see her.

She found a way to introduce his name.

'Does Laurent run the vineyard by himself?'

Isabelle was dicing pork. 'He has two helpers
to do the work in the *clos* alongside him, though one
of them, Raymond, is often unwell. His back has
gone, poor thing. Hardly surprising as he's been
labouring since he was ten years old, and he's older
than I am! Oncle Albert also tries to help, but he
can't do much now, either. And of course there is
Rachel, and a couple of part-time stable hands, but
they keep to their own tasks. Come harvest,
Chemignac turns into a factory and we're flooded
with *vendangeurs*.' Harvest-hands, she explained.
'But Laurent thinks that if he rests, some pest or
disease will attack the vines and, you know, there
are ten hectares of them to watch. This month he
will clean and service every piece of equipment
because, when the grapes are being picked, you
cannot afford for anything to go wrong. And then
there is eternal paperwork – this is France! He

works through the night sometimes, and collapses into bed for three or four hours' sleep. He worries me.'

'Sounds tough,' Shauna said, settling down to scrape potatoes. Was it totally inappropriate to wonder if Laurent collapsed into bed alone? *Yes*, she decided, *inappropriate and a bit crazy.* Face it, she'd seen him twice and both times she'd been thoroughly over-heated. The occasional fantasy wouldn't hurt – so long as it stayed in her head. She wasn't ready for fresh hurt and she'd become something of a disappointment-magnet lately. During her third year at university, she'd fallen head over heels for a post-grad student. They'd moved in together, planning their future to the last detail to allow both of them to achieve their career potential while enjoying family life. Doctorate for her, a professorship for him, two children, a travelling sabbatical each, a mortgage, happiness, prosperity and a dog. Then, without consulting her, Jason had taken a job in America. A month in, an email. He'd met somebody else . . .

The one evil of technology, as far as Shauna was concerned, was that it made rejection easy. Fire off an email, job done. Whatever happened to sitting down with a person and looking them in the eye?

Watching Isabelle assembling her *Sobronade*, Shauna wondered if her mistake in life was too much planning. Plans hadn't stopped Jason going to the States. It hadn't stopped Shauna's father dying. Nor had it prevented Isabelle's widowhood, which, Shauna had gleaned, had begun some thirty years ago. 'Life is what happens when you're making other plans.' John Lennon hadn't even realised how ironic he was being when he said that.

For some reason, Shauna's eye was suddenly drawn to a narrow door in the corner of the kitchen. 'That leads to the tower,' she said without thinking.

Isabelle looked up from her casserole. 'How on earth did you know that?'

'I've no idea. Can I go up?'

'The children can show you, though they don't like it up there.' Isabelle explained hastily, 'Because they are outdoor beings. It's a lot of steps to climb, and there is only a bedroom at the top. The view is good, I grant you. If you like old rooms with cobwebs and sad memories, go any time. Me, I like my feet on the ground.'

'You never go up there? Oh, I'm sorry,' Shauna exclaimed as Isabelle tapped the crook of her walking cane. 'Nothing about you seems old, *tante* Isabelle. I forgot about your limp.'

'I wish *I* could forget it, but there. If I had not fallen, you would not be here. *C'est le destin.* Elisabeth's girl! Tell me, which shade of red is your natural hair?'

Shauna touched her short layers. 'Um . . . my real colour is what we call, "strawberry blonde".'

'*Blond Vénitien*? How pretty. You should let it grow out. But not now!' Isabelle added hurriedly. 'I mean, well . . . here it would fade in the sun.'

Shauna suspected that Isabelle might not have meant that at all.

'Grandmère, we're home!' The kitchen door was flung open.

'Well, I didn't think it was a visitation of angels. Olive, Nico, say hello to Shauna. She's on her feet now.'

Shauna laughed as two children clad in up-to-the-minute sportswear looked her up and down, taking in her short, print dress, pale skin and bright hair.

'You are wearing gold rings on your toes.' Olive stared, fascinated, at Shauna's criss-crossed sandals.

'Cool,' said Nico.

'I always think toes get neglected. Why shouldn't they have jewellery, too? Happy to meet you properly at last.'

Olive, twelve, and Nico, ten, were tall for their age. Brunette like their grandmother, their deep tans were accentuated by their white sports kit. They were chatty, too. Over dinner, they peppered Shauna with questions about British sports stars and pop groups. She tried to give useful answers, but when Nico asked which soccer team she preferred, Arsenal or Chelsea, she had to admit that she only cared about Sheffield United as that was her home team. And even then, she didn't care very much.

'If you don't watch soccer, what *do* you do?' Nico asked, bewildered.

'Read. Study. I dig about in forest floors and peer under stones to see what's crawling about beneath.' Laughing at their expressions, she explained, 'I studied biomedical sciences at university. I spent the last two years researching plant medicines for my MSc. Master of Sciences,' she translated. 'I'm taking a year out then I may go back to do my doctorate.'

'Are you a professor?' Olive asked, with a glint that might imply respect but which was more likely astonishment. People were often downright disbelieving when Shauna told them she was a scientist. Something about the pixie hair, the fact that she was barely five-foot-five and did not wear glasses. People had fixed ideas that female scientists resembled either Jodie Foster or Rosa Klebb from *From Russia with Love*. 'Not a professor, no. My ambition is to carry out research and work in industry. I don't see myself teaching.'

'Speaking of which,' Isabelle cut in, 'did Elisabeth mention that I wish you to give the children some English coaching each day?'

Olive and Nico issued a simultaneous groan.

'She did, and that's no problem, if you don't mind them ending up with a northern accent.'

'We all have a regional accent,' Isabelle laughed. 'I promised their mother they'd finish the holidays well ahead in their studies. Two hours a day, nothing but English.'

'What will we talk about?' Anxiety filled Nico's eyes.

'You can show me Chemignac and the vines,' Shauna suggested. 'I'd like to see them.' *And Laurent, just possibly.*

'They're boring.' Nico wrinkled his nose. 'Lumps of green with silly grapes on them. All of Chemignac is boring, apart from the horses.'

'My grandchildren are sports mad, as you must have noticed. But they can read and study when they set their minds to it.' Isabelle got up to cover a plate of food with silver foil, explaining, 'I'm taking this next door. Oncle Albert won't eat with me while the children are here. He cannot bear modern manners. Olive, go fetch some books to show Shauna. Nico, fetch the apple tart from the pantry. Shauna, help yourself to another glass of wine. It's a 2001 Sauvignon Blanc. What do you think? Not a bad year.'

It tasted exquisite to her, though to be fair, pub Chardonnay was the limit of her experience. Shauna watched the children doing their grandmother's bidding and knew she liked them. *Should have boned up on Arsenal and Chelsea, though.*

Olive came down with *Le Seigneur des Anneaux* – the French translation of *The Lord of the Rings* – announcing that J.R.R. Tolkein was the best writer in the universe, ever. Recognising common ground, Shauna said, 'Why don't we get hold of the English version and read it together?'

'Laurent has an English copy,' Nico piped.

'Repeat that in English,' Shauna commanded. They might as well start as they meant to go on. Nico struggled through the sentence, then reverted to French. 'Let's go find him. He'll be in the *chai*.'

'What's—'

But the children were already outside. They moved fast, Shauna was discovering, out of sight before she'd knotted a shirt over her dress and put on the straw hat Isabelle had dug out for her.

Shauna guessed the direction the children were heading in. Leaving the courtyard by a side gate, she found herself on a track lined with the spindle-shaped Cypress trees that were the predominant, vertical feature in this landscape of vines. Ahead stood a huddle of stone outbuildings and she saw the children dash into one. Presumably the *chai* – pronounced 'shay'. She found the door they'd left half-open. Breathing deeply as butterflies took off in her stomach at the thought of seeing Laurent, she stepped inside and – before she could catch herself – exclaimed, 'Wow!'

Built of venerable old stone, in keeping with the rest of Chemignac, inside the *chai* was as slick as any modern food-processing unit. Its walls were panelled with fibreglass sheets, and its concrete floor shone wet, evidence of a recent hosing. Hearing the pulse of water hitting a hard surface, she followed a snaking hosepipe. As she approached the source of the noise, she began to understand that Clos de Chemignac was no small wine-making concern - not if the ten or so towering silver vats were all full at once. A line of handsome oak barrels stole her attention next, but before she could examine them, she spotted the children. They were peering inside the porthole of what looked like a concrete bunker, their voices echoing over the hiss of water.

'Laurent!' they shouted. 'Laurent! Come out, we need you!'

Glancing over Nico's shoulder, Shauna got a spray of cold water in the face. Laurent was inside the bunker, which was a couple of feet taller than him – about the dimensions of a very small bedroom. Seeing her appear, he grinned. The first smile she'd had from him and it turned her blood to warm syrup. *Get a grip, girl.* He was absolutely drenched. Barefoot, too. Water spewed through the porthole onto the giggling children, and out of the sluice holes. 'Go turn off the tap!' Laurent yelled and the children ran to do as he asked. When the jet ceased, he asked Shauna, 'Have you come for a wash?'

Bereft of a witty retort, Shauna said, 'I'll pass, thanks.'

Olive skidded up to them, asking Laurent, 'Can we borrow your *Lord of the Rings*?'

'Sure. Though I thought you were too busy whacking the life out of tennis balls to read. It's in the bookcase by . . .' but the children had gone, like a pair of greyhounds. Laurent climbed out through the tank's porthole, wringing out the hem of his t-shirt. 'I hope you're strong now, Shauna, or they'll exhaust you.'

'I'm fine. Thanks for electrolytes, by the way.'

'You're welcome. I keep two stocks, one for my workers and one for my horses.'

'Which did I get?'

'They're pretty much the same, though the dosage is different.' Laurent's next smile crinkled his eyes. He waited for her to say something.

'Um, thanks anyway. For scooping me up when I fell –' Shauna could hear herself urgently filling the silence, 'and for lending the book. Or agreeing to, anyway. It's about nine hundred pages, isn't it? Should keep us all out of trouble. They're really nice kids. I just wish I knew more about soccer.'

'Soccer . . . you mean English football? Why?'

'For Nico's sake.'

'Oh, Nico doesn't care about football. He's interested in footballing stars.' Laurent began to wind up the hosepipe. 'Any sports stars, actually, because that's what they intend to become. Nico in tennis, Olive in gymnastics. Or show jumping, if that brings in the prizes faster. They could make it, I think. Their parents spend a fortune on their training.' It was said without rancour or judgement, but with an edge Shauna couldn't wholly translate.

'Lucky them,' she said, watching Laurent fix the hosepipe on to its bracket. Water belched out of the nozzle. 'Having such dedicated parents.'

'I think it's more to make up for sending them to their grandmother all summer. To make up for handing them over to an au pair.'

And she'd thought him so friendly! He said 'au pair' like 'serving-wench.' It made her defensive. 'I still say they're lucky. This is such a beautiful place.'

'Beautiful, but cruel.' Laurent took a broom to the puddles that had collected outside the concrete tank, sweeping them towards a drain. The hands that had felt her pulse and tested her temperature were tense and she kept getting flashes of his thorn tattoo. She wondered what he'd say if he saw hers.

'What's this container for?' she asked, rapping her knuckles against the tank's concrete side. 'The staff hot tub?' She winced. Always a bad sign when she made jokes.

Laurent seemed to take her seriously, even more worrying. Or was he just happy the conversation was back on neutral ground? 'It's a holding tank for white juice, and a vat for red. After we've pressed our main red crop, Cabernet Sauvignon and Cabernet Franc, we pipe it in there and let fermentation start. After the malolactic stage, we pump it into the steel containers. Malolactic means—'

'The conversion of mallic acid into lactic acid, which gives wine its pleasant flavour.'

'You understand viniculture?'

'No, I'm good at pub quizzes.' She left, not waiting to see Laurent's response. Outside the *chai,* she let evening air erase the goose pimples she'd walked out with. For a time, she watched the swallows darting between the roofs, hoovering up midges. In the lyrical trill of a song thrush, she heard an echo of her mother's promise: *you'll fall in love with this place.*

Elisabeth had fallen for green-eyed Tim Vincent among Chemignac's vines. *It won't work for me,* Shauna thought sadly. *I'm 'reyt bad' as they say where I come from, and all out with the world.* Laurent had just paid the price, getting his head bitten off in exchange for an innocent remark. She half-hoped he'd come after her as she trudged back to the château, but he didn't.

As she entered the courtyard, she saw a light flickering behind the shuttered windows at the top of the tower.

Shauna's bedroom was on the ground floor of Isabelle's wing of the château. Though night's shadows had never worried Shauna before, she couldn't succumb to sleep. Her snarkiness with Laurent went round in her mind until she was sick of the memory of her own voice. After what seemed to be hours of kicking her duvet, she drifted off, only to be jolted awake a short time later by the strangest of sounds. She sat up, her eyes trying to unravel the dark. Had she really just heard a gaggle of geese?

Her room lay on the meadow side of the château, and as she listened for a repeat, she imagined a white-winged advance, emerging from the wood. Chemignac's walls, solid and picturesque during daylight, seemed suddenly threatening. Scuffling mice and the occasional house spider were one thing. But in the dark, envisioning she was about to be surrounded by powerful necks and pecking beaks . . . it was truly disorientating.

Pulling her quilt up to her chin, she drew her knees to her navel and closed her eyes. A moment later, she was sitting bolt upright as the honking sound erupted behind her bedhead, seeming to come from within the wall itself. Geese, inside? Shauna held her breath, reminding herself that this was an old, old building. Its frame swelled in the day's heat and contracted as the air cooled. What she'd heard could simply have been the settling of dry timbers. Or even the doves under the eaves.

She wasn't convincing herself, though. During a holiday job on an organic farm in Wales, her morning task had been to let the geese out of their fox-proof coops and dole out the grain. The racket made by twenty-four Brecon Buffs flapping to be first to the feeders was engraved on her mind. The only way to solve this mystery so she could get back to sleep was to look. She groped at her bedside lamp. As the low-energy bulb warmed into light, she got up and flung open her door, stubbing her toe as she stepped into the hallway. Empty. Dark. Silent.

Muttering 'Weird,' she returned to her room, but not to bed. After turning off her bedside lamp, she opened her window shutters and leaned out, convinced she'd discover a sea of feathered fowl. A chrome-bright moon lit an empty landscape. Nothing moved on the silvery meadows.

'Maybe sound carries across vineyards,' she murmured. Then she jumped as a creature's cry sliced through the night. In spite of her clashing heartbeat, she stretched further out of the window to investigate. The sound came again and she released her breath. Owls hooting, playing catch among the winery buildings, by the sound of it.

Now thoroughly churned up, she gave up on sleep, pulling open a drawer and rooting for clothes with the light still off. Hauling on tracksuit bottoms and a jersey, shoving her feet into a pair of comfy loafers, she crept through the sleeping house and out through the kitchen door. The night air tasted of warm cakes and, as in the old carol, all was calm, all was bright. Something made her look up. Light flashed erratically behind the tower's louvred shutters. Muted light, as if a bulb were pulsing behind greased paper. Could somebody be up there, working in torchlight? Surely not. The moon at the peak of its transit told her it was around two or three in the morning. The children would both be fast asleep, Isabelle too. Besides which, Isabelle never climbed the tower, she'd said so. Albert? From what she'd seen of the old man, it seemed vanishingly unlikely that he'd attempt those stairs either. Laurent? But if he was still at work, wouldn't he more likely be in the *chai* or doing paper-work in his office? There had to be a simple explanation. A lightbulb about to blow? A perished cable sheath creating a short circuit or inadequately fused wiring?

Which might overheat and catch fire . . .

She headed back inside, obeying a reluctant need to investigate, only to find the door between the kitchen and tower firmly locked. Keys hung from a rack next to the refrigerator, but none of them fitted so she gave up, making a note to raise the matter with Isabelle in the morning. Fed up with worry and with her bed holding no appeal for her, she decided to take a walk and perhaps watch her first dawn break over Chemignac.

Owls screeched a welcome as she stepped outside and Shauna set off to see if she could get sight of them. She hadn't gone many steps along the Cypress tree track when she noticed the steady glow of light in the winery. So, her instinct had been right. She'd had a patchy night's sleep, and *somebody* hadn't even begun his.

Chapter Four

Opening the *chai* door noiselessly, Shauna peered inside and blinked in the glare of strip-lighting. Laurent had his back to her and she watched him move slowly along the row of oak casks. At each one, he bent down and she heard liquid trickle into some kind of container. He was syphoning wine from each barrel. Conscious that she was lurking, she scraped her foot and called out, 'Hello! Good evening – or morning. I'm not sure which it is.' She moved forward, anticipating his surprise. 'I saw lights and thought— have you been working all night?'

'I suppose.' Laurent frowned as if he couldn't work out how she'd manifested in front of him. A plastic test jar in his hand brimmed with red liquor and Shauna's nostrils caught fruit-filled, leathery richness. It affected her senses and she blurted out, 'I'm sorry I was rude earlier.'

Laurent shook his head. 'You were rude? To me?'

'I stormed out!'

'You did?'

So he didn't even notice her when she had a hissy-fit! But now she was close enough to him to make out the bubbles on the surface of the test jar, and their faint tremor which suggested Laurent's grip was not quite steady. Was he exhausted? His outer clothes, drenched several hours ago, had dried like shrink wrap against his body. She saw how muscular he was, though in the unobtrusive way of someone who fuels himself well, and burns it off in continuous manual labour. Her lovers had always been fellow academics, soft-limbed men, often hopelessly impractical. What would it feel like to hold this taut form in her arms, to rouse him and satisfy him, while teasing out the intelligence of his mind?

'Shauna?'

'Oh, sorry.' Her voice slipped gear as she explained, 'I made that catty comment about pub quizzes and slammed out. Well, not slammed, exactly. Stomped.'

'Ah.' Laurent's brow cleared. 'At the time, I did not understand . . . not sure I do now, but thank you for apologising. Not that you need to. Being lumbered with the dynamite duo would fray most people's tempers.'

'You mean Olive and Nico? I don't know why you're so down on them. They're great kids.'

'I think so too, but greater proximity has taught me that they're also demanding and needy. Please one of them, the other inevitably feels neglected. You have entered the terrain of emotional trip-wires.'

That didn't sound promising.

He bent his mouth in sympathy. 'Isabelle hopes you will make them happy, but my little cousins are fundamentally *not* happy. I should know, I recognise myself in them. You will try your best, but they will wear you out. Chemignac will wear you out.'

That sounded an even less-joyous prospect, but Shauna managed to laugh. 'I don't flinch at a challenge. I'll make it work.' Had she said the wrong thing again? His expression hardened and his reply slashed at her.

'Shauna, you're a stranger here. No –' he corrected himself, 'a *visitor* and you don't yet perceive the complicated strands that weave us together. You were offended when I called you the "au pair"?'

'Of course! You implied that the children were being palmed off on a lesser being.'

'Not at all!' Red liquid splashed on Laurent's feet as he raised his hands, forgetting he was holding a jar. He was still barefoot, Shauna noticed, and ruby tears rolled between his toes. 'It wasn't an insult, just plain fact. Nico and Olive spend all summer here because it suits their parents to be rid of them. Isabelle loves to have them, of course, but she is getting too frail to properly supervise them. Their parents naturally feel guilty, so over-compensate by filling their days with high-status training. Lavishing expenditure on them with a promise that one day, they will be superstars. It's not your fault and not the children's either.' He went on, '"*Au pair*" means "equal". In English, you use the word "peer" as in "peer group", no? The words have the same origin. I do not think of you as a lesser being. *D'accord?*'

'All right. I overreacted. Truce?'

'Are we at war?' His gaze softened, with concern. With question. 'Why are you gliding around at this hour like a wraith? Do you sleep-walk?'

She explained about the owls, choosing not to mention the mysterious geese right away. However, she did tell him about the electrical anomaly in the tower. Laurent looked as if she'd given him an unwelcome message.

'I'll check it out, though it's probably to do with the appliances in Isabelle's kitchen causing a voltage fluctuation. When the tower was wired in the 1920s, there weren't such things as fridges or electric ovens.'

'I suppose not.' It made sense, but didn't wholly cure her unease. In for a penny . . . she described the deafening noise that had woken her. 'Geese, believe it or not. I was convinced they were right outside my room.'

'In the house?' Laurent stared at her, then bit his lip in automatic denial. 'That's not possible.'

'I agree. I checked and they definitely weren't there. Not so much as a feather. I dreamed them, Laurent.'

He nodded. 'A disturbing dream and now you can't sleep.'

'May I ask why you're working all night?' She tapped his plastic jar with a fingernail. 'Testing it or drinking it?'

'Both.' He seized the change of subject. 'And I'd better finish.' Turning from her, he twisted the spigot of one of the casks, topping up his jar. He then held the phial up to the light, examining the gemstone colour. 'This is last year's blended Cabernet Sauvignon and Cabernet Franc, which we sell as "Tour de Chemignac". It's sat in oak for twelve months and I'm taking a random sample to find out if it's ready to bottle.' He moved across to a workstation where screw-top capsules were lined up. Shauna watched him decant a small measure of wine into each, then label them.

'Now the fun part.' He shared the remaining wine between two glass tumblers, handing one to her. 'I haven't worked all night. There's still an hour or more before the birds start singing.' His voice became reflective. 'I often forget the time and the dawn chorus chases me to my bed.'

'Sleep deprivation isn't healthy, not long-term.' She over-tipped her glass, flooding her throat as the notion of chasing Laurent to his bed took hold. After a twenty-hour day he must crash into sleep, his circadian rhythms all awry. No doubt he'd wake, ragged, at the blare of his alarm. Did he ever indulge in a lazy morning under the duvet? She raised her glass for another slug of wine.

'No, no.' Laurent touched her hand, slowing her down. 'It's a good vintage and I want your opinion.' He picked up one of the labelled capsules. 'Some of these will go to the lab in Bergerac for final analysis before bottling. The rest go abroad to my distributors so they can taste, and then buy. An Irish wine merchant rang a few days ago. One of their directors tasted *Tour de Chemignac* while he was on holiday nearby, and he's talking about ordering five hundred cases. Wine bars are springing up all over Dublin, did you know that?'

'No, though there are plenty in Sheffield.'

'So? Give me your thoughts.'

If she told him those, he'd probably blush, or run a mile. 'The wine? I like it.' It was every bit as intense and satisfying as its colour promised. She put her nose over the rim, to dissect its aromas, wanting to impress Laurent with her sophistication and intuition. Unfortunately, her scientist's brain was taking over. 'I'm getting . . . hang on . . .' could she risk saying, 'phenylpropene compounds'? That was exactly what she was picking up, though most people would call them 'clove and nutmeg'. *Come on, Shauna, let the poetry flow.* 'It's like opening a spice cupboard at Christmas. I think I can taste vanilla, too.' Laurent raised an eyebrow, inviting more, sabotaging her confidence. 'No – I don't know. You tell me.'

He swirled his tumbler under his nose. 'Seductively full bodied, bright to the palate with a long finish of smoke and, yes, vanilla. Spicy, as you say. That's down to the compound eugenol.'

She knew that. Now she wished she'd said it.

'There are hints of caramel and toffee . . .'

That would be Furfural and 5-Methylfurfural. She hadn't tasted those, though evidently, she and Laurent had studied the same food science modules.

Laurent rolled the liquid around his mouth before swallowing. 'A back note of coconut, which is derived from oak lactones.'

'From the casks?'

'Not really.' He surveyed the barrels, explaining, 'French white oak, irreplaceable. They date from my grandfather's time but they're exhausted. I don't mean they leak, they're just neutral as far as flavour goes. So, I use these.' He produced a bundle of oak staves that resembled a dismantled window blind. 'If you cannot bring the wine to the oak, you bring the oak to the wine. These slats go in the casks until the wine has the flavour and body I'm looking for.'

'You love your work, don't you?'

He didn't answer straight away. 'Love is too simple a word. I would do this even if I made no money from it. But love can tie you and limit you. It rubs sores in your flesh. So no, I would not say it is love. More, a life's voyage. How do you feel about your work?'

'Passionate. I could never imagine doing anything else, and nothing will keep me from it.'

He frowned, as if her ready answer unsettled him. 'I had a dog once,' he said, looking towards the door. She followed his gaze, half expecting a four-legged ghost to amble in. 'She was a Pyrenean Mountain Dog I called Saskia. I found her in the woods, when I was eleven. She wasn't much more than a puppy, tied to a fallen log with a cord that had cut into her flesh. There for days, I think. When I rescued her, she tried to climb into my arms. Now, that was love.' He smiled, though sadly.

'You kept her here?'

'I kept her wherever I was. Nobody dared stop me. She died ten years later. I went to America after that.' Memories were drawing him away from her. Suspecting they were talking of love in all its forms, she again navigated the subject to safer waters. 'When will you know if your *Tour de Chemignac* is ready to bottle?'

'Tomorrow. But now, shall we go to bed?'

Her throat caught. She couldn't get a word out. Laurent waited, his expression guileless, his thick lashes intensifying the smoulder of his eyes. She needed to say something. 'I don't – I mean, I think I need to know you better.'

His brows pulled together and he shook his head. 'I meant, to our *separate* beds. I apologise. When I'm tired, I stumble over my English.'

Her face caught fire. 'I really didn't think you meant it.' But she had. 'I mean, I was a bit shocked because I haven't – I mean, I don't – ' *Oh help, this was digging a mine-shaft.* 'What I mean is, I don't –
'

'Want to. Very wise. Go out ahead of me and I'll turn off the lights.'

They walked side by side back towards the château, she with her hands pressed to her flanks, he with his clasped behind his back. *We're doing a cracking impression of the Queen and Prince Philip*, she thought. Dawn had brought salmon streaks to the eastern skyline, while to the west, above the forest, stars still shone in the purple-dark. Shauna stopped, frowned. Was that a shimmering among the trees? It looked like torchlight, only dampened, as if the beam was being projected through muslin or transparent paper. She wanted to call it the *memory* of light. Laurent saw it too. He checked in his stride, but said nothing. In the courtyard, he murmured, 'Sleep well, Shauna,' and they went their separate ways.

The remainder of the week introduced Shauna to her new timetable, and Laurent's warnings resounded as she got the measure of the children's routine. After a hastily eaten breakfast, Olive and Nico would grab bulging sports bags and they'd all squeeze into the estate's runaround, a fuel-efficient Renault Clio. First call, a tennis academy outside Garzenac where the children took tuition and played in a competitive league. That gave Shauna three hours to herself and she could either drive back to Chemignac, or hang around. Anxious to avoid Laurent, having catastrophically misunderstood his invitation to bed, she spent the first few days visiting Garzenac's church, its ruined castle, wine museum and the chi-

chi gallery next door where the art prices were stratospheric.

She found the spot in the churchyard where her mobile phone worked, and had a short, broken conversation with her mother and an equally broken but giggly one with Grace. Ultra-cautious of the heat, she drank copious water and far too much coffee, and indulged in a local speciality – sticky walnut cake. Even so, those three hours hung heavy.

On day four, Friday, she came across an internet café in a backstreet and gave an exclamation of delight. Here was a neat solution. She could hire a couple of hours' online time each day, writing up the notes she'd brought with her, the aroma of fresh-ground Arabica tickling her nostrils. Monty, the café's British-born owner, was friendly, inviting Shauna to make the place her office. Judging by the empty tables, trade was slow.

That night, Shauna charged up her laptop and the next day claimed a blue-painted table and chair in the corner for her own. She began transcribing the jottings she'd made two summers ago as a volunteer goose-girl and all-round labourer on that Welsh farm. While Olive and Nico practiced their killer shots on the lower side of town, she worked undisturbed, breaking off for coffee and cake, and to check her emails. She responded to a message from an East Midlands lettings agency, as to whether she was still looking to rent a home. With heavy fingers, she typed, 'My plans have changed; my job fell through. Please take me off your mailing list.'

She scrolled down several days' worth of messages without finding anything from Mike Ladriss. Her professor had gone silent, it seemed. Quite likely, he'd had time to digest her angry reproaches at their last meeting. She took a breath and wrote an apology, giving him Clos de Chemignac's fax number which Isabelle had written down for her. 'Write to me on this number, assuming you want to, of course. I'm still in the job market; any efforts on my behalf will be appreciated. Kindest regards, Shauna.' She deleted 'kindest' and wrote 'warmest'.

After a salad lunch, she packed up her laptop and hurried off to collect the children, driving them back toward Chemignac, where she dropped them off at a riding centre within the nearby forest. Watching them walk through the centre's immaculate white gates, she swallowed a stab of envy. She'd been a not-bad rider as a girl, and missed the thrill of being on horseback. Such magical afternoons, hacking out with her dad through Ecclesall Woods on the outskirts of Sheffield, on heavy-footed horses borrowed from country friends. Muck-splattered and laughing, they'd race each other, leaping puddles and fallen trees. Tim Vincent had been an instinctive horseman – not a lesson in his life - and she'd learned through copying him. No denying it, her childhood was a universe away from Olive and Nico's. It had been happy and uncomplicated, until her father's death, anyway. For her, none of the stress of league tables and striving for medals; but then, she'd never had her eye on Olympic glory.

She found a patch of shade, intending to skim over her morning's work. Frustratingly, her laptop battery was low and the computer closed down on her after a couple of minutes. She locked it back up in the Renault's trunk and decided to explore a track she could see through the trees. It seemed the follow the course of a river. Lush, summer leaves filtered the heat from the air. The sadness provoked by memories of her dad mellowed into wistfulness. He'd have loved this walk – though, come to think of it, he might once have strolled through this forest with Shauna's mother. Young lovers, sipping at the prospect of a life together. *You'll fall in love with Chemignac.*

'All right, mum,' she acknowledged. 'It *is* beautiful here, but I won't be losing my heart.'

She stopped at a fork in the path. Which way now? Straight on would be safest, keeping to the river so she didn't get lost. Or she could take the stone bridge she could see through the trees to her right. It spanned the water, drawing the footpath away into a verdant backcloth. '"Stay on the path at all times",' Shauna quoted, mindful of Little Red Riding Hood and the dangers of dark woods. Though she was unlikely to encounter wolves; wild boar were the more probable danger. Then she started: there was a man standing on the bridge, staring down into the water. A man she recognised. 'Laurent?'

Though he made no answer, not even looking up, she headed in his direction. She knew the profile, the dark grazing of sideburn hair, the resolute jaw. Only when she was a few paces from the bridge did she hesitate. The clothes were wrong. This man wore a wool-weave jacket, like a farmer or huntsman, and serviceable grey-blue trousers.

Every tractor driver and field worker she'd seen since arriving in the region wore overalls of a similar shade. *Bleus de travail* they were called. Literally 'work blues.' The heavy combination of blue and brown was so unlike Laurent's casual style . . . he must be sweating! She called to him again but he moved off, taking the path up the slope with easy strides.

He continued to stay ahead of her, a charcoal-sketch slipping between the trees. After five minutes or so, an internal voice told Shauna to give up and retrace her steps before she became hopelessly disorientated. Yet he lured her on, pausing just often enough to make her believe she could reach him. Breaking into scout's pace – half walk, half run – she muttered, 'Fine. I'll play your game. Just don't drag me into the heart of the forest and disappear.'

The track was narrowing, now a pathway only in the most generous interpretation. Her footwear, loafers and ankle socks, was inadequate against stones and low-growing bramble. Laurent had melted away and Shauna dropped to a walk, needing to catch her breath. She turned this way and that, sometimes imagining he was hiding nearby, watching her. And then she'd hear the distant crack of feet breaking twigs. Well, she'd had enough.

How far had she wandered from habitation, from phone signal? A crunching sound warned her that something was advancing on her, treading through the dry underfloor. She prepared for Laurent to leap at her, shouting 'Fooled you!' Or maybe she was about to meet her first wild boar . . . were you meant to freeze or drop to the floor? Her captive breath burst out in laughter as a male blackbird hopped from under the skirts of a myrtle bush. How could something so small be so noisy? All it had been doing was pecking for grubs in the leaf mould. But perhaps it hadn't really been that loud. Fear was fiction's greatest muse, she reminded herself.

She peered up, trying to fix the position of the sun through the leaf canopy. She'd left her phone in the car and wasn't wearing a watch, and had no idea how long she'd been chasing Laurent. The kids would be coming to the end of their lesson shortly and they still had one last appointment to get to before the day's marathon was done. She picked her way back down the slope, skidding to a stop as she saw something she'd missed on her way up.

It was a cave, partly obscured by saplings, that yawned from the base of a sandstone outcrop. Its mouth was just high enough for her to pass through without dipping her head. As she stepped into the gloom, she thought she saw a shoe print. Too late to be sure; she'd stepped right on it. 'Laurent?' she called. Maybe he wanted to show her something he'd found. Cave paintings, maybe. This region was a cradle of Neolithic culture, and remnants of Stone Age culture had been found just a few kilometres from here. Or maybe he wanted to show her the living quarters of some rare lizards or bats. Most girls wouldn't be thrilled by that, but then, she wasn't most girls. A torch would have been useful to cut through the dense shadows at the back of the cave. She could have checked for more footprints in the sandy floor. 'Laurent?' No echo, so clearly the shadows were misleading. This was no deep cavern. If Laurent were somewhere ahead, he'd have heard her perfectly. 'I'm going to count to three, then leave.' She reached 'two' when a gust from the cave's innards almost toppled her, forcing her to shield her eyes from a dust-devil of fine sand.

Chapter Five

Something unseen passed through her, air filtered through ice. She backed away, then turned and ran for the exit, her shoes filling with sand as she stumbled from the cave and pelted down the slope. Her body seemed to split apart as she moved, her consciousness separating from her physical self. Her mind was clear while her body was numb; a bizarre and terrifying feeling. Clanging through her mind, the conviction that – 'They've got me! They were waiting!' A metallic sound filled her skull, followed by a scream that did not come from her own throat. She tripped and fell, sharp stones bedding in her palms which became quickly bloody. 'Laurent, Laurent, help me!' Her appeal was broadcast in fragments because she was shuddering, short-breathing. The only word to describe what she'd run through was *death*.

'Shauna? What the hell? What have you done to yourself?'

The hands on her shoulders felt real, as did the smell of olive soap and horse sweat as somebody crouched beside her and supported her. She rested the side of her face against a forearm, making out the shape of a thorn tattoo, and thought, *People died here. Running. Panicking. Head over heels in their own blood.* 'I – I found a cave.'

Her voice was dry powder. There was still sand in her eyes.

'What sort of cave?'

'Dark –' she made a feint of pointing. 'Up there.'

Laurent helped her up and wiped the grit from her cheeks with the front of his shirt which he freed from his belt. She grabbed the fabric, pulling him against her. 'You've changed your clothes,' she accused. He was no longer wearing blue, cotton drill trousers but boot-cut Wranglers, rubbed pale inside the thigh, and a polo shirt. Riding clothes. Two horses, white as cloud, stood a short distance down the path, shaking their heads as they were being stopped from cropping the grass. Rachel sat astride the smaller horse, holding the reins of a strapping male animal that Laurent, presumably, had just dismounted from.

'Is she putting it on?' Rachel's lip curled as she waited for Laurent to step away from Shauna. 'She spends more time on the floor than on her legs.'

'You should feel her heart pounding,' Laurent threw back.

'I'll take your word for it. You're practically taking her pulse with your tummy button.'

'Take the horses back to the yard.' Laurent spoke impatiently, as if irritated by Rachel's mockery. 'I'll help Shauna.' When Rachel cocked a disobliging eyebrow, Laurent's tone gained an edge. 'If you can't ride one and lead the other, just tie Héron's reins to a branch.'

'Laurent darling, I can ride and lead with my eyes closed. I've won so many prizes for driving four-in-hand I could give Charlton Heston in a chariot a run for his money. You walk Goldilocks home if you want. Bye-bye.' For all her boasting, it took Rachel a minute or more to turn the horses and get them walking away, two abreast. Even as they went, they snorted and shied, their ears laid flat as if something in the trees, or in the air, spooked them.

Only when Rachel was gone did Laurent speak again and this time, his voice carried an undertow of excitement. 'I've always known there was a cave in this part of the wood. For years I've been trying to find it.'

'You changed your clothes,' Shauna insisted stubbornly. 'You weren't on horseback before.'

'Before what? I worked until lunchtime in the *chai*, then checked the Semillon vines. Rachel suggested a hack through the woods – the horse you saw her on has been misbehaving lately. Sometimes it helps to bring a nervous one out with a well-behaved companion.'

'You were here,' Shauna insisted. 'In baggy trousers and a jacket. I followed you from the carpark by the riding school. Where I parked the Clio.'

He shook his head. 'You cannot have followed me. Rachel and I rode from Chemignac, over the meadows. We came from that direction.' He jerked his thumb, presumably indicating the château. 'I heard you shouting my name, and we left the main path to find you.'

'I saw you on a bridge. You were wearing a tweed coat and I followed you.'

'I've never worn tweed in my life!'
Accepting that she wasn't going to back down, he

examined the palms of her hands where traces of sand were mixed in with blood. He brushed them gently with the pads of his fingers and painstakingly picked the remaining pieces of grit from her skin. 'Can you show me that cave? Do you feel able?'

He sounded so fixed on it that she reluctantly started back up the slope. She stopped at the outcrop of rock whose face shone like cinder toffee in the afternoon light. No sign of a cave. All she could see was dense greenery, myrtle, wild vine, boxwood and fern, though she'd swear she'd seen it right here, between two bends in the path. 'We must have passed it,' she said, seizing the excuse to turn back. This place rippled with invisible violence, its untouched serenity a lie. Laurent seemed oblivious to the atmosphere, but to Shauna, it felt like a singing in the blood. 'It's gone.'

'If you saw it, it *must* be here.' Laurent walked on up the slope and out of sight just as his blue-and-brown lookalike had done earlier. When he returned to her, his expression was a cocktail of disappointment and doubt. 'Did you walk right up to the ridge, further than you think?'

'No.' Before he could ask again, she told him she must get back to the carpark. 'The children will think I've abandoned them.'

Olive and Nico emerged through the white gates moments after she reached the car. They'd been delayed, and the explanation was muddled. It sounded as though Nico had tried to make his horse jump a fence without being authorised and having seen her brother do it, Olive had leapt her horse over an even higher one. Shauna deduced they'd received a stiff telling-off from their instructor.

'You're idiots,' was Laurent's opinion. He'd accompanied Shauna to the carpark, and seeing how her fingers shook when she tried to unlock the Clio, had taken the key from her. 'You've no right jumping horses who haven't been properly warmed up first. That's how tendons and ligaments get pulled.'

'They were warmed up,' Nico came back sulkily. 'It was boiling hot in the sand school.'

Like Laurent, the children smelled of horse-sweat and expensive saddle leather. If they noticed that Shauna was pale and rather distant, they made no comment. It was Laurent they wanted to shower with the minutiae of their day's experiences.

'I have to go back to work,' he said, after he'd listened to several minutes' breathless telling. 'You have to go on to your next venue, no?' Without waiting for an answer, he pressed them into the back seat like a policeman confining a pair of suspects. Then he turned to Shauna who was at the driver's door, filling and emptying her lungs like a yoga student.

'Are you fit to drive? I cannot believe you have more crazy activity to cram into the day.'

'I'm fine, honestly.' She sank into the driver's seat, fired the engine and lowered the window. 'Next stop, Bergerac for two hours' gymnastics. Oh, and sorry about getting wobbly on you again. You probably think I'm certifiable, but I'm not normally this emotional. I'm suffering from Sudden Holiday Syndrome.'

Laurent rested his hand on the window sill, keeping her from driving away. 'Is that a recognised ailment?'

'It ought to be! Thing is, I've been studying flat out for five years. In what passed for spare time, I had to supplement my student loan with whatever jobs I could get. No time off other than the occasional weekend at my mother's.' When she'd arrive exhausted and sleep till Sunday. 'Now I feel as though I've fallen off a boat and washed up on a strange shore. I like Chemignac,' she said quickly, as hurt flashed in Laurent's eyes, 'but the world has stopped too quickly. Everything's different, all at once.' She tapped her head. 'Too much space up here and I'm filling it with weird episodes. Phantom geese, caves in the woods, lights in the tower – yes, I know,' she cut him short. 'Wires short-circuiting. You will have an electrician check it out?'

'Don't go up there, not without me. You hear?'

'I hear.' Wow. He meant it.

'I don't want you to get hurt, Shauna. I don't want more misfortune to rain on Chemignac.' He took her left hand from the steering wheel and brushed her cut and bruised palm with his thumb. After counselling her to watch out for farm vehicles hogging the roads between here and the D936, he stepped back. As she reversed out, she saw him take the path that would eventually lead him back to his vineyards. Dappled shadows soon absorbed him.

At the urban sports centre on Bergerac's outskirts, Shauna left the children to grapple with balance beam and parallel bars and went for a swim.

It was her chance to don a sports bikini and dispel her brain-fog with fast lengths of front crawl. The chlorinated water cleaned any lingering bits of grit from her hands and the exercise restored her. Arriving back at Chemignac just before six, she parked the Clio by the winery and walked with the children to their grandmother's kitchen door. She was spent, but she still had two hours of J.R.R. Tolkein to come, and language lessons via Middle Earth. The smell in the courtyard of roast dinner was divine, however. Letting the children run ahead of her, Shauna's eyes consulted briefly with the tower window. Behind the shutters, the glass was blank. Inert. 'I don't need to know what lies behind you,' she told the window. And that was true. She didn't need to know. But part of her wanted to, very badly.

Chapter Six

Sunday arrived and was declared sports free. 'By royal decree. Mine,' Isabelle announced. She and Albert went to mass in the village, driven there by Laurent. Shortly after their return, a taxi drew up to take Isabelle, Albert and the children to see relatives in Bordeaux. A four-hour round trip. The children grumbled, but their grandmother informed them that nobody got to do what they wanted all of the time. 'Being bored sometimes is good for the soul. It makes you think.'

The taxi doors clunked shut and everyone shouted goodbye to Shauna, except Albert. Alone in the château for the first time, Shauna knew exactly what she was going to do.

With more time – and daylight – in which to sort through all the keys, Shauna quickly found one that fitted the door to the tower. She must have overlooked it last time. Iron ground against iron, but the key eventually turned. The door needed a couple of hard pulls to open, suggesting that nobody had used it for some time.

Shauna looked in vain for a light switch. Unable to find one, she left the door open. The tower was almost circular, except where it linked to the building. Embrasured arrow slits were the only source of light in the lower part of the stairwell, but they were just about adequate. Stepping cautiously over a wooden trapdoor, wondering if it was a vestigial escape hatch into the moat, Shauna climbed the spiral stairs, tripping several times until her legs got used to the steepness. A rope hand-hold had been provided and she was thankful for it. The air smelled musty but at last she came across a window. Its hinges creaked as she pushed it open and from somewhere above, doves fluttered indignantly. Reaching the top landing, her thigh muscles burning, Shauna found another studded oak door. Locked. Damn. She hadn't thought to bring the rest of the keys with her.

She prepared to go down just as she heard footsteps at the base of the tower and a voice calling her name. A female voice, with a scornful echo. 'I'm up here!' Shauna answered, adding silently, 'and you can do the leg work.' She had a few things to say to Rachel Moorcroft. The girl was free with her contempt, her mockery, but how would she stand up to a bit of Sheffield straight-talking?

Rachel got the first word in. 'That grumpy old beggar Albert won't like you being up here. Were you hoping to poke about in the bedroom?' Pausing a few steps down from where Shauna was standing, she said in a sinister whisper, 'I bet the cupboards are full of mouldering skeletons of all the women

Albert didn't marry. Why can't the poor old stick just come out as gay? Anyway, shall we go in and raise some ghosts?'

'The door's locked.'

'Ta-dah!' Rachel opened her palm. 'I also know where they keep the keys. I saw you open the window and guessed you were sneaking up here.'

'Isabelle said I could come into the tower any time I liked.'

'Isabelle? Always "Madame Duval" to me. You *are* honoured. Laurent told me once that Albert was furious when Isabelle inherited the part of the château with access to the tower.' Rachel proffered the key, which Shauna took. 'But nobody actually owns it. For some reason the tower was left off the plans when the building was divvied up between the heirs – it's everybody's and yet nobody's, a vertical twilight zone. So it's not really for Madame Duval to give you permission to enter.'

'But it's not your business either, is it?'

'Well, if you put it like that. Only trying to be friendly.'

'Oh yes? I suppose 'friendly' means different things to different folk.' Shauna unlocked the bedroom door and walked in. There was just enough light to make out a wooden-framed bed and a wardrobe. The wardrobe being broad enough to house all Shauna's possessions, with room for her to get in alongside. And there was the window, its panes begging for a clean, its shutters clenched against the day. Flinging them wide, Shauna heard a thud. She turned in time to hear a key turn and knew from the callous chuckle on the other side of the door that she was locked in.

Chapter Seven

No reason to panic. With its huge bed, this was a snug enough place to await her eventual release.

'If you like old rooms with cobwebs and sad memories . . .' Shauna wasn't bananas about sad memories, but cobwebs fascinated her. Cobwebs were manifestations of perfect geometry, and spider silk was among the strongest fibres in nature. She peered at a web stretched across two panes of the window. One day, spider silk would probably be used to make parachute harnesses and body armour.

She saw Rachel crossing the courtyard and shouted, 'If you're hoping I'll die of terror, you've picked the wrong victim!'

Rachel's reply was a teasing wave.

Shauna looked about her temporary cell. Ghosts did not exist. Sadness did not hang around like a bad smell. Memories were real only in the sense that they altered brain chemistry or created tension in the body. There was nothing to be afraid of.

The bedroom was circular of course, with cleanly plastered walls. A stone lintel suggested that the tower had a second window, this one on the side facing the meadows and the woods. She couldn't look out of it, however, as a picture hung in front of it, one with a heavy frame, depicting a scene of wading cattle under a gloomy sunset. The rest of the furnishings were of dark wood and probably several hundred years old. After all, you wouldn't make a regular habit of hauling wardrobes and beds up and down tower stairs. They might even have been made up here. Testing the bed for comfort, she sneezed. Dusty. A whizz round with a duster wouldn't go amiss.

A mirror on a wooden stand threw back a misty reflection when Shauna stood in front of it.

This had been a woman's room, she decided.

The outlook over the courtyard extended beyond the roof of Laurent's apartment and on to a garden. Well-tended, laid out in neat rows and squares. Laurent's handiwork? When did he find time? Beyond the garden, the vines began, lush *parcelles* planted with different grape varieties, the whites on the cooler slopes, the reds where the sun shone hottest. The only man-made structures between the château and the horizon were two modern barns, green metal roofs wobbly with heat haze. They must shelter the horses, Shauna decided, though she saw no sign of them grazing in the paddocks.

Tearing herself from the window, she tried the door in case Rachel had somehow failed to properly lock it, but it was immovable. OK. She'd snooze till the family came home. It crossed her mind that nobody would know she was up here, and that banging on the floor would rouse nothing but more dust. If they failed to hear her shouting from the window, they might think she'd run away. She could die of thirst. But she doubted Rachel's prank would go as far as that. *Now, what about those skeletons in the cupboard . . .*

She opened the wardrobe expecting nothing but dead moths, and her mouth dropped open. A treasure trove lay before her. Not your average old tat on a hanger, but sinuous, full-length vintage gems.

'Knew it was a woman's room!' Shauna fetched out a flapper dress heavy with iridescent beads, black and hot pink. Holding it against herself in front of the mirror, she couldn't resist humming the tune to the Charleston. It would be the right size for her too. Modern dresses were usually too long.

She returned the flapper dress to the rail and took out another, then another. Silks with padded shoulders and small waists. Plunging, cross-over V-necks that must have revealed a lot of candlelit bosom. A velvet coat with a majestic satin collar, hand-stitched to look like astrakhan fur. Another gown in plum satin, a matching taffeta jacket with black reveres. And finally, a dress that took her breath away.

Shauna was not a clothes person. She liked natural fibres and unusual colour combinations. At university, when short of cash – which was most of the time – she'd shopped in the teenagers' section of chain stores. The dress that held her spellbound now was a sleeveless tube of finely pleated silk, each pleat as fine as a harp string. It had a draped neck and a waist-tie. Simplicity incarnate. She took it to the window the better to see it and discovered that silk cords strung with glass beads had been sewn to the side seams. Such fine craftsmanship, you'd think the fabrics had been fused together. When the hem touched the floor, the pleats splayed out like a pool of melted ice-cream.

Part of its distinction was its colour – intense amethyst at the hem, lightening by stages to silvery lavender at the neck. Shauna stroked it, cooing with pleasure. Then, driven by an urge she didn't question, she quickly shed her clothes and slipped the dress over her head.

The scent of patchouli wafted about her like smoke. Beloved of her hippie parents in their younger days, patchouli oil also had a long history as a moth repellent. The strong smell told Shauna that this dress was misted every now and again to protect it. Knotting the belt around her waist, she went to the mirror.

Her reflection stunned her. The natural elasticity of the pleats defined her curves, moulding like rows of vines to the contours of the land. She could be a statue of Venus. The rich colour transformed her, adding translucence to her skin. Even her short hair seemed sophisticated, the violet hues drawing out its richness.

Shauna stared as her face changed before her, growing leaner and far more beautiful. Unable to blink or move, she felt an unbearable sadness swelling through her. Tears began to course down her cheeks. *Where did this grief come from?* It wasn't to do with a stolen research post or the loss of a university lover. It didn't stem from her feverish attraction to Laurent . . . no, it came from a cause more terrible – and without remedy. The woman in the mirror flared her eyes back at her in desperate appeal. When fingers touched Shauna's wrist and a face joined hers in the glass, she screamed like a jungle-creature.

'Shauna? It's me, Laurent. Shauna, wake up! Look at me.'

She reached for him, gasping, and he helped her to sit on the bed. She must have held her breath to the point of fainting. No wonder she'd begun to hallucinate.

'I saw Rachel leave the tower. I thought you

might be locked in.' Laurent sounded angry, but in that quiet way that detonates at some later date. 'It's not the first time she's done something of the sort.' He cupped her face. 'You're so pale. Do you have some kind of condition we should know about?'

'No. I'm well. And I'm sorry,' she whispered. 'I shouldn't have come up.'

'I should have been with you. Maybe you came up the stairs too fast?' He crouched in front of her, his hands wonderfully, humanly warm against her skin. He stroked the draped silk at her neck, like a harpist drawing notes from his instrument. 'Nobody ever puts on this dress,' he said in a low voice. 'It's known as "The Gown of Thorns" and has a history we hide, even from ourselves.' He stood up, though with visible reluctance. 'And I should warn you, my oncle Albert retains strong feelings about it – and this room.'

'Why?'

'Old quarrels, guilty secrets. Every family has them.'

'Mine doesn't!'

'No? Then you are fortunate.' Laurent walked to the door, turning brusque as he said, 'I'll wait outside while you change, then I'll escort—' he stopped abruptly.

Shauna turned, twisting the satin bed cover into a starfish pattern. 'What is it?' she asked. 'What are you staring at?'

He was looking straight at her left side, at her bare arm. 'You have our symbol. That tattoo . . .'

She shrank into herself. Inexplicably, she felt naked and the tattoo, which she'd always celebrated, felt dirty. She couldn't fathom why, but if he stayed, looking at her like that, he'd drag some dreadful truth from her, the way a chef drags the guts from a fish.

In one movement, she stood up and pulled off the dress. Hearing Laurent's unfettered gasp, she feared her gamble had misfired. Then she heard the door click quickly shut. 'I will wait here for you,' Laurent said from the other side of the door.

At the same moment, a thousand kilometres away in a hospital ward in Dakenfield, in England's West Country, a patient woke abruptly from a dream. No ordinary, vapid dream. She'd *really* held a man's hands, felt them covering hers, dry and strong. She'd lost herself in his gaze because his eyes could smile and pledge themselves, even when the mouth stayed stern. Without warning, his eyes had blurred, tears flowing, then blood –

That's when she'd woken.

'Nurse!' she called, hating that she sounded as if she had a broken reed in her throat. Pain stormed into her pelvis and legs, diabolical pins and needles. She needed morphine, though she knew it would make her sick. 'Nurse, please.'

'Coming.'

Don't say you're coming then not come. She called more urgently, adding a scream because they made you a priority if you threatened to wake up the ward. Later, see-sawing between sleep and lucidity, she called to the girl in the blue tunic, 'The man who was here, bring him back, dear. I must tell him that I was wrong. I should not have done what I did. I have to tell him, so he can forgive me.'

'There, there Antonia, only a bad dream.' The trainee nurse spoke in a soft, automatic voice as she read the notes at the end of the bed. Moving to the pillow end, she checked the insertion point of the drip in the age-spotted hand. 'You're imagining things. You had a nasty fall, Antonia. We're putting you back together.'

A second, older voice reproved: 'The patient has asked us to call her Miss Thorne. It says so on the notes.'

Giving herself up to the befuddlement of

morphine, Antonia tried one last time – 'Bring Henri to me. He *has* to forgive me.' She knew she'd begun speaking French, and likely, neither the trainee nor the ward sister would understand her. 'I should never have put on the Gown of Thorns. I was warned. It wasn't mine to wear.'

Chapter Eight

The following week rattled past for Shauna, the only surprise a sharp downpour early on that briefly flooded the road into Garzenac. Her days were forming a recognisable shape. Isabelle was becoming a real friend, delighted to hear her grandchildren's English improving rapidly. Two hours of conversation expanded to four, after which Shauna would fall into bed, into blessedly dreamless sleep. Beyond her forays to the winery, she'd still seen very little of Clos de Chemignac. The wildflower meadows remained unexplored, the horses elusive. She hadn't bumped into Laurent again either, nor Rachel, though she'd seen both of them at a distance. Isabelle told her, quietly, over breakfast in the middle of the week, 'Laurent has given Rachel her notice. I don't know why, but keep away from her for a while.'

'Laurent dismissed her? I thought your uncle ran this place.'

'Albert?' Isabelle glanced up from trickling honey on to rye bread. 'Albert no longer owns any portion of the château, nor of the wine business. He sold out to Laurent's father years ago. I'm a shareholder, but I leave everything business-wise to Laurent. He makes the decisions here, not Albert.'

'Tough for Albert, I should think. I take it he was the younger son?'

Isabelle made a face. 'The fourth son, actually. My father, Henri, was the eldest and the two who came after him perished in the war. They joined the Free French Navy and died at sea. Albert . . . well, Albert was an afterthought. He was born nearly twenty years after my father.'

'Let me get this right –' Shauna screwed up her eyes, visualising a family tree. 'Your father Henri was Laurent's grandfather?'

'Exactly, and Laurent's father was my brother. My papa died during the war too, when I was just eight years old, and my little brother was three. It had a terrible effect on us all. As the last of four brothers and the only one not to fight for his country, Albert became a little . . .' Isabelle made a face, 'I don't want to say "strange". A little unpredictable.'

I can vouch for that. Shauna hadn't forgotten Albert's ferocious welcome, nor had she yet looked up the word 'Rouquine.' Actually, she wasn't sure she wanted to know its meaning. 'He unnerves me. I think he intends to.'

Isabelle acknowledged it. 'I might as well tell you as I know you won't gossip. Many years ago, when we were all still young, Albert tried to set up a rival vineyard, not far from here. He didn't get on with my brother, who owned the larger share, and thought he could do a better job. But the venture failed and Albert lost everything. Without telling us, he'd used his stake in Chemignac to take out bank loans. The first we knew of it was when a sober-looking official arrived with a clipboard, to make a list of Albert's assets.' Isabelle pressed her hands to her temples, as if the memory still brought a sweat to her. 'Thank heavens, my brother managed to raise enough to clear the debt, otherwise we wouldn't have a family business now. That was how my brother acquired Albert's share of the family fortune, and why it now belongs to Laurent.'

'So Albert is a kind of lodger?'

'Yes, though you wouldn't think it from the way he talks to us all. He had nowhere else to go, but here. He is bitter still, as if the fiasco was everyone's fault but his. The kinder Laurent is to him, the more he resents it. He punishes us all, because he tried to escape Chemignac and failed.'

Escape? Laurent had described his home as 'Beautiful, but cruel.' Isabelle had once mused out loud, 'Nobody who loves Chemignac ever really leaves it.'

'Madame, what's wrong with this place?'

'Wrong?' Whether deliberately, or because she was growing hard of hearing, Isabelle answered a different question. 'It might have been a slight birth defect. Albert was the last child of aging parents. His mother was fifty hours in labour and it killed her.'

Shauna flinched at the thought of it. 'That would scar anyone.' Recalling Rachel's facetious reference to Albert's sexuality, she asked casually, 'He never wanted to marry?'

'Albert is not comfortable with women.'

'English women in particular, I notice.'

'All the English, I'm afraid! He says there are too many cars on our roads with "GB" on the bumper. In truth, Albert can never forgive your Winston Churchill for pulling his troops out of France in 1940, leaving us to the mercy of the

Germans, nor for forcing us to scuttle our ships at Toulon.'

'He's still reliving the war? That's over sixty years ago!'

'To Albert, it is yesterday.'

Conversation ceased as Olive came in to tell them that they needed to be at tennis half an hour earlier because Nico had a tournament match. 'He has to warm up. He must win, it's a grudge-match.'

The following Sunday, July 13th, brought sultry air which sent Isabelle to her bed with a migraine. Olive had an invitation to spend the day with a friend in the village, and zoomed off on her bicycle. That left Shauna to entertain Nico, who was in low spirits, grunting moodily at every suggestion she made for his entertainment. *Had this been a normal home*, she thought, *he'd have stayed in his room playing computer games,* but these, she'd learned, were restricted to two hours a week. Sports, fresh air and books were what their parents ordered.

'Come on, spit it out, Nico,' Shauna said when she could no longer bear the sight of him kicking his chair leg. 'What's up?' He was a bit young for girl trouble or adolescent angst.

Nico shrugged. 'I didn't play my A-game on Wednesday.'

'Your A . . . oh, you mean you played badly? There's always another day.'

Nico threw her a look of utter contempt. 'No, there isn't. I lost the match. I'm out of the tournament.'

'We can't always win everything, Nico.'

'I can. At tennis, anyway.'

'Not even Pete Sampras wins every game. And what about Lleyton Hewitt? He won Wimbledon last year, then bombed in the first round this time. How do you suppose he felt?' Unsporty as she was, Shauna always made a date with

Wimbledon. She'd watched the 2003 men's finals with her mum and Grace, the pleasures of strawberries and sparkling wine amplified by the brilliance of a newcomer called Roger Federer.

'That's a grand slam tournament. I lost in the poxy junior league.'

'And so did they, once.'

'How do you know?'

'I don't,' she admitted, 'but everyone loses sometimes. I of all people should know.'

Curiosity flickered in Nico's eyes. 'What did *you* lose?'

'In April, I applied for a post in the research department of a big corporation in the Midlands, about seventy miles south of where I grew up. I'd have been working alongside a Nobel prize-winning scientist, studying the potential of plant acids to destroy cancer cells. My dream job, with a proper salary for the first time in my life. It would have shoved me several rungs up the career ladder.'

'But you didn't get it.'

'Worse than that. I got it. They said I was the outstanding candidate. I finished my master's degree, gave up my flat, began packing to move. Then, on my last day at Uni, I got an email saying that my application had been re-evaluated and the job offer withdrawn.'

'Why?'

She blew out a painful breath. 'Money. Politics. So you can trust me when I say I understand how you feel. I've also had to start again, and it's not the first time it's happened. Tell you what – lob me one thing you would like to do today that is in my power to grant, and I'll do my best.'

He shrugged, looked mutinous, then mumbled, 'Go riding with Laurent.'

'Right. On a horse?'

'Obviously, not on an elephant.'

'Are you sure he'll agree? It's hot out there

for riding.'

'He'll say yes if you ask him. He likes you.'

'Really? I mean, no, he doesn't. He doesn't know me.' When Nico shrugged, Shauna couldn't help asking, 'What makes you think—?'

'When Olive and I took you to the *chai*, he was cross with us for leaving you to find your own way. Then he made us repeat your name three times so he got it right.' Nico reached for his baseball cap and headed for the kitchen door. 'It's obvious he fancies you. And anyway, you've got the same tattoo.'

Grabbing her straw hat, Shauna dashed after Nico. 'How d'you know about that?'

'Olive and I saw you getting out of the swimming pool in your bikini. If you don't want people to see it, you should swim in a wetsuit.'

No sign of Laurent in the stable yard. Shauna
followed Nico into the closest of the steel barns.
Strolling down its central walkway, she thought - *At
least now I know where he keeps his horses!*
Indoors, in ventilated comfort. Stalls each side of
the corridor were occupied by the same breed of
white pony that had pulled the trap. Grey-pink noses
poked through U-shaped grilles. Hay nets had
obviously just been filled, because the predominant
noise was of molars chomping. The horses were
bedded on some kind of fibre that smelled sweetly
of eucalyptus. Presumably, the addition of
eucalyptus oil was to deter flies.

The second barn housed animals of greater
stature and she thought she recognised the one
Laurent had called Héron. They were all greys too,
with short, muscular necks and a bluish marbling to
their coats. 'Are they Percherons?' Shauna asked as
they emerged into the sunshine, still without finding
Laurent.

'No –' Nico threw out a breed name she didn't catch, then shouted, 'Rachel! Where's my cousin?'

Rachel was sprawled on a plastic chair outside a wooden building with a sign on the door stating that it was the stable yard office. In a cropped top, shorts and knee-length suede riding boots, with a genuine-looking Stetson shading her face, she was enough to make a ten-year-old boy's eyes ping out on stalks and Nico's duly did. Shauna, less impressed, eyed the cigarette lighter dangling from Rachel's neck on a leather thong. The girl surely didn't smoke near the stables?

'Last time I saw Laurent,' Rachel drawled, 'he was in the south *parcelle*, communing with his *Cab Sauv*.' Rachel returned Shauna's look. A long stare that mirrored that of the tabby cat curled by her chair.

'Thank you.' Shauna was tempted to walk on without alluding to their last meeting, but Rachel's manner grated and she added, in English, 'And thanks for locking me in the tower. I'll return the compliment one day.'

'Be my guest, but don't leave it too long. I'm off, once harvest is over. Did Isabelle mention that I've had an amazing job offer? A country club in California. Three thousand dollars a month, and more days off than I get here.'

'Congratulations.'

If Rachel heard the edge Shauna put on the word, she made no sign, saying, 'Spend too long in a backwater, you rot. What I keep telling Laurent. My face is here, Nico.' Rachel pointed at her cheekbones, turning her headlamp stare on the boy, whose eyes had indeed slid down to the cleavage bursting from the crop top. He blushed and hurried away.

They found Laurent between rows of vines, on one knee, pressing the grass with his knuckles. '*Salut.*' He stood to greet them, pushing his bush-hat back off his brow. 'I will have to mow, at least on these southern slopes. That rain has brought on a flush of grass.'

'Can you leave it a day?' Nico entreated. 'Mowing's boring.'

'He's hoping to go riding with you,' Shauna said, colouring because Laurent's glance had reminded her that the last time they'd been in each other's company, she'd torn off a dress in front of him. She pretended to be fascinated by a vine laden with clusters of hard, green grapes. She'd expected them to be further along than this. Velvety magenta and sweet. Eager for neutral ground she said, 'They look ages from being ripe.'

'Cabernet Sauvignon is always quite late. Six weeks to go, depending on the weather.'

'You've been spraying?' The lower foliage

was tinged with blue residue that had also dripped on to the grass. It matched the stippling on Laurent's forearms and finger ends, and she imagined him going bush-to-bush, inspecting leaves for hidden grubs or signs of rot. 'Maybe I can help—' she broke off, remembering Nico's teasing; he *fancies you.*

No, he doesn't, she silently answered. Just because she got a tumble dryer stomach when she was near him didn't mean a relationship was either sensible or feasible. To reinforce it, she said the unsexiest thing she could think of: 'You treat them with copper sulphate, I presume?'

Laurent nodded, still with that unreadable curve to his lips. 'Every ten days or so.'

She'd have liked to stroll along the rows with him and at the right moment, turn the conversation to what she'd experienced in the tower. What they'd both experienced, if her intuition was correct. But Nico was sticking to his agenda.

'You always take me out riding when I'm here, Laurent.'

'Today, mowing is a boring necessity,' Laurent replied. 'Straggly grass encourages pests and if it rains again, it might be days before I can do it. So, here's the deal.' He brushed grass off the knees of his long, grey shorts. 'Help me and we'll ride afterwards. It's too hot now, anyway.'

'Don't the horses graze in summer?' Shauna asked.

'They do, all night. It's more bearable for them.' Laurent turned again to Nico. 'You can earn your ticket by helping me hitch up the new mowing attachment, and walking alongside as I go up the rows. You can be my second pair of eyes and emergency cutter.'

'I'll drive the tractor,' Nico fired back. 'I know how.'

'I doubt it, living in Paris. Anyway, my insurance won't cover you.'

'Who cares?'

'I do. If you had an accident, I'd be up before a judge. *Ça alors,* you think I have time to negotiate?' Nico had opened his mouth to argue. 'Listen, my father wouldn't let me handle the controls till I was sixteen, and it drove me mad too. In five years' time, I'll teach you.' He patted his young cousin on the shoulder in a gesture which clearly meant 'shut up' then threw out a sweetener. 'You can ride the tractor for a few rows beside me, *if* your walking and sheering lives up to my hopes.' Laurent lifted Shauna's straw brim. 'You should go back to the house. This job's hot and noisy.'

'I'd like to help. My walking might live up to your hopes too.'

After a slight recoil, Laurent's gaze warmed. 'I have a feeling it will, but I have to keep my eyes on the job, or I might drive over the vines. So, no distracting me.'

'Can I have a go on the tractor too, if I'm

good?' She saw the change in his stance, his throat moving above the neckline of his work-worn t-shirt. Why was she flirting? Opening a door marked 'danger'? 'What I mean is, I'm competent with machinery. I've ridden quadbikes and driven Land Rovers on rough terrain.'

'The tractor responds only to brute force. I believe your touch would be too light.' He was flirting back, and belatedly cautious, she stepped back. 'What I really mean is, I'm getting used to the heat and I'm smothered in factor forty. I can help, if you want me to.'

'All right, but you'll need insect repellent, too. Go to the house and spray, and bring back bottles of water, enough for all – oh, *Dieu*!' Nico was running off. Laurent muttered, 'I'd better get to the tractor before he does. He probably knows where I hide the key.'

Returning fifteen minutes later with a rucksack bulging with bottled water and slices of melon in cling film, Shauna found Nico seated on a small tractor. It was a basic machine, without a cab, and antiquated to judge from its dented panels. The contraption whose drive-shaft Laurent was attaching to the rear looked virtually space-age in comparison. Laurent shooed Nico off the seat and fired the ignition. He let it run for a minute or so then turned it off. 'So, this is a mulching cutter,' he said. 'The blades reach right under the vines, but they won't cut everything because the rows are not equally wide. Where I miss a weed or a clump of grass, you two cut by hand. All right?'

'Sounds easy enough.'

'It's tiring.' He handed Shauna a pair of short-bladed sheers, an identical pair to Nico. 'The mower shoots out stones and twigs, so walk with a row of vines between us. Don't ever come up behind me. If you need me, run to the top of the row and approach me from the front. Got it?'

It was easy enough to start with, the stroll in the sunshine she'd hoped for, though the mower and tractor at full throttle were a deafening combination. The vines were level with Shauna's eyebrows and all she could see of Laurent were flashes of fabric and bare arm. The foliage canopy, supported on tight lengths of wire, was busy with flies, bees and butterflies. Not a wild landscape, she thought, but nurtured and perfect in its way. Most of the grape clusters hung below waist level, giving her an intimation of the work ahead in picking them. She saw the virtue of Laurent's labour-saving monster whose rubber bumpers caressed the feet of the vines while its blades reduced grass and weeds to fine cuttings, leaving a diesel vapour trail.

'Missed a bit!' Shauna yelled, then said, 'Oh, hang on, that's me.' Kneeling, she used her sheers on a straggle of grass, then ran to catch up with Laurent. Some twenty rows later, they stopped for water and melon. Shauna lay back with her head on her rucksack.

'You can retire if you like.' Laurent flung his melon peel over his shoulder. He'd taken off his shirt and his nut-brown torso gleamed wet – using bottled water, he'd sluiced off the copper sulphate residue that the machine had stirred up. When he leaned forward to smack a horsefly on his ankle, Shauna saw that his shoulder blades were flecked with grass cuttings.

'What about you?' Her voice made an involuntary key-change. 'Will you take a break?'

'No chance. Look up.'

She did, at a sky dappled with greyish clouds. 'Altocumulus,' she said. 'Isabelle said there was thunder in the air. She's gone to bed with a pressure headache.'

'I doubt that's the only reason,' Laurent said. 'She's right, though. Storm later, though probably not till after dark. Nico will get his ride.'

'I'll help you finish off here.'

'I appreciate it, Shauna. Nico, are you fit to go on?'

'When may I go on the tractor?'

'For the last ten rows. Shauna, do you want to try driving?'

Her leg muscles felt like sponge, but having talked up her rough terrain skills, she answered, 'Definitely.'

Three times she stalled the tractor. 'Hard down on the clutch,' Laurent instructed. 'Go off in first gear, never mind the noise it makes, then into second gear, but don't come too fast off the clutch.'

On the fourth attempt she got it. 'Slowly, keep a consistent speed and whatever else you do, drive straight!' Laurent bawled at her. He kept alongside for a while then dropped back and she was on her own. Her hat disappeared over the back of the tractor. She made it to the top of the row of vines with all the concentration of a child riding her first bicycle. She swung around the headland at the top of the avenue, and headed down the one beside it, laughing with the joy of mastering a new art. Laurent let her complete four rows before waving her to a stop. 'Bravo!' he congratulated as she put the tractor in neutral and turned off the engine. Her whole body was shaking with the effort of controlling pedals and steering and her ears were booming. He held out his hand to help her as she stepped unsteadily onto the grass. For a second or two, he held her and then lightly kissed the top of her head.

'Go find your hat. I'll finish off because I go faster and I want to take my labourers to lunch. With luck, we can eat and go for a ride before the storm breaks.'

Half an hour later, they crammed into the red 2CV. Laurent drove them to a pizzeria in Garzenac whose wood-fired oven produced the biggest, most loaded pizzas she'd ever seen. They shared two, and a generous salad. Laurent ordered coke for Nico and two glasses of red wine for them, saying, 'This is a neighbour's Cabernet Franc. It only just missed being given its *appellation d'origine controlée.* They can't export it, so we get to drink it here.'

'Do you export yours?'

'Last year, I sent thirty thousand litres of red and nearly as much white overseas, mostly to Britain, Germany, Japan and Hong Kong. Before I took over, our whole *vendange* went off to a local cooperative, to make blended Pays de Bergerac wine.'

'Now you press it at the château?'

'Yes. Vinify it, bottle it and market it, too. It's hard work and so much can go wrong in a season. But I wanted to take Chemignac back to its time of greatest pride, when my grandfather Henri was in charge, before the war changed our family's fortunes. Not everyone approved.'

'But you're stubborn.'

'I prefer "focussed". The best way around obstacles is to look beyond them.'

Albert is an obstacle, she conjectured. *Bitter over the mistakes that lost him his birthright.*
'Before mechanisation, how did growers keep the weeds down?'

'Some didn't, and got poor yields.' Laurent swirled his wine, checking its body, its clarity. 'Others would go out with a *binette*,' he mimed using a long-handled tool. A hoe, she guessed. 'Or let sheep roam around the vines, nibbling everything down.'

'Including the grapes?'

'The vines would be trained higher, or maybe the sheep had shorter necks. There is a new breed so small, they can wander among the vines.' His expression changed, suggesting he was confiding something close to his heart. 'I'm thinking of importing a few because I want to produce wine more sustainably. It is the future, I think.'

'Going organic?'

'Not everybody agrees.'

'*Écolo!*' Nico crowed derisively, helping himself to more pizza. 'Granola.'

'He's calling me a granola cruncher,' Laurent said in English. She'd not really noticed before, but he spoke English with an American inflection. 'A muesli eater. In England, is that what you call people like me?'

She laughed. 'Not these days. Muesli's gone mainstream. "Tree-hugger" is a good translation, though I've never understood why it should be an insult. I've wanted to hug more trees than people.'

He held her gaze. 'Then it would be frustrating to meet you in the forest.' Raising his glass, he gave her a silent toast, then turned to Nico, asking in French, 'Did you understand any of that?'

'Most of it,' Nico answered. 'You fancy her. I've already told her.'

Back at Chemignac, parking in the stable yard, Laurent invited Shauna to ride out with them.

When she told him she hadn't ridden in ten years, he said, 'I've a good-natured mare trained to take all levels of rider. We'll take it steady.'

She was tempted, but Nico's face told her that he, at least, hoped for a fast ride and that her presence was not in his plan. 'I'd love to another time, Laurent. I'm going to rest, then maybe take a walk in your woods. Not to hug trees,' she said, spoiling the effect by blushing. 'To explore. Turn over a few stones.'

'Wear proper shoes,' he told her. 'And socks because we have snakes, though you're unlikely to see one. Follow the paths and keep the château on your right at all times. As you discovered before, it's easy to strike off at a tangent.' He looked up, frowning. 'Better get on with it. The weather's thickening up.'

After a shower, Shauna changed into a short, sleeveless dress of printed cotton, tied a shirt round her waist, then dug out the trainers she'd brought with her as a last-minute addition. As she was rooting out a pair of Olive's tennis socks from the laundry room, she heard the muttering of radio commentary, and followed the sound to the kitchen. Isabelle must have got up. She might be wondering where her grandson was. The kitchen was empty, but the table was piled with linen napkins, all of the same deep violet shade. There was a bundle on the ironing board. Shauna smoothed one out and saw the embroidered initials, 'H & M-L de C'.

Henri and Marie-Louise de Chemignac,

Isabelle's parents. The same initials were carved over the gatehouse, with the date of 1931, marking their marriage. 'My mother came from church in a carriage drawn by white horses,' Isabelle had told her. 'My father paid a mason to entwine their names in stone. Romantic, ha?'

These napkins were probably part of a trousseau, the table linen and sheets a bride brought to her new home. Painstakingly fashioned, stored lovingly, to be fished out every now and again, hot-ironed and doused in insect-repellent . . . the air smelled of lavender and patchouli . . . because even romance needed an underpinning of practicality. Embroidered beneath the napkin's cypher was a thorn twig, identical to Laurent's tattoo. No surprise, really. He was Laurent de Chemignac, after all. But what about *this* coincidence? She tugged at her dress, contorting to examine her own tattoo. A sprig of blackthorn, *Prunus Spinosa*, three spines each side. Or, if you wished to be mystical, it was the *straif* of Irish legend, symbol of war, strife and – so her mother had assured her – eventual victory. She'd had it inked below her shoulder on her twenty-first birthday, in memory of her dad. He'd worn the same symbol on the back of his hand. His had been blue-black like the sloe-berry, the fruit of the blackthorn.

'Isabelle?' Shauna called. The ironing board was fixed at a low height, suggesting Isabelle had done her ironing seated. On the floor, the kitchen calendar lay discarded. Today's date was ringed in black, an aggressive 'X' striking it out. Disturbed, Shauna went up to Isabelle's room and put her ear to the door. She wasn't sure if she could hear breathing or not, but felt she didn't know her hostess well enough to poke her head inside and check.

Instead, Shauna dashed off a note. 'Nico with Laurent, I'm out for a short walk, will be back in an hour or so. Hope you're feeling better. Happy to prepare supper – let me know.'

She went out by the front door, threading

through rose bushes to the moat. There, a narrow footbridge led to the meadows. Shauna crossed them, aiming for the woods. A saffron sky was streaked with violet-grey. Beautiful, but ominous – as was a distant rumble of thunder.

She'd gone a little distance when something made her look back at the château. The doves were on the wing again and she wondered if they sensed the on-coming storm. Interesting . . . the window on this side of the tower glowed yellow but she couldn't tell if there was electric light behind it, or if the glass was reflecting the sinking sun.

She became aware of a figure behind the glass, a slight, dark shape, seeming to stare down at her. Whoever it was must have taken down the oil painting that hung over that window, otherwise they wouldn't be visible. It certainly wasn't Albert. Nor Isabelle, who had several times insisted that she rarely went up into the tower. The figure was too insubstantial to be Rachel. Olive wasn't due back from her friend's house until nightfall. Nico was riding with Laurent. So who was it? Forgetting everything she'd ever said about superstition and apparitions being the failure of logic, Shauna turned her back on the tower and ran towards the woods.

Chapter Nine

'On the 13th July 1943, on this spot these men of
Chemignac fell, killed by German Gestapo agents.
Michel Paulin, Luc Roland, Henri de Chemignac.
Murdered alongside them were men of the British
SOE, Maurice Barnsley and George Sturridge. Their
resistance furthered the cause of liberty and
freedom.'

A bunch of roses and vine leaves lay against
the base of the stone, itself a rough boulder. One
face was cut smooth and inscribed by a mason.

Shauna had ignored Laurent's advice and left
the path, enticed by a splash of colour shining
through the greens of walnut trees and holm oaks.
She'd emerged into a broad clearing and discovered
maize growing tall among patches of blue-flowered
chicory. It was the silken tassels of the maize bathed

in early evening light that had caught her eye. That was when she saw the boulder, planted at the clearing's heart. She re-read the inscription, her heart picking up speed. Isabelle had said that her father, Henri, had died during the last war, but hadn't explained how. Shauna had simply assumed that he'd been killed at sea, or fighting in a regiment.

Executed for fighting with the Resistance. Here, on this spot, five men. Five clean shots or a bloody massacre? *Oh my God . . .* the date sunk in. Today was July 13th and exactly sixty years since the atrocity. *Now* she understood the mark on Isabelle's calendar. And maybe Isabelle's migraine? Shauna crouched, reading the card on the bouquet. It read simply, '*Jamais oublier, jamais pardoner*':

Never forget, never forgive

A head broke off one of the roses. She put it back with the others, but it rolled free, so rather than leave it, she buried it in the neck of her dress.

Then she cried. Not gentle tears, but tearing sobs. She then sat down on the ground, and leaned against the stone, passing into a kind of coma. Roused by a blue flash overhead, she realised that the sun had sunk and the storm had struck.

In her hospital bed in Dakenfield, a patient plucked at the cannula taped to her left hand. A nurse saw her, and tried to calm her.

'You must keep your drip in, Miss Thorne.'

'No – I have to go and find him, or it'll be too late to tell him I'm sorry.' They upped her morphine.

The first crash of thunder split open the sky, releasing a violent downpour. Within seconds, Shauna was drenched. Nature was in turmoil. The wind in the branches sounded like an express train blasting through a tunnel full of dried peas. She struggled to find the path in the sudden darkness, blinded by periodic bursts of lightning.

Thankfully, the storm was as brief as it was turbulent. By the time Shauna found her way and was walking towards a chink of twilight, a lull had descended. Her dress was dripping. It felt like wet bandage against her skin. At some point, she'd lost the shirt she'd tied round her middle. Her trainers and Olive's socks were mustard brown because the path had turned into an alley of mud. She trod on one of her laces, tripping and falling in the muck as a pale shape filled the void between the trees. It was an outline stolen from myth. A woodcut of a knight, broad shouldered with a tapering waist, astride a horse that seemed to be made of moon-mist. Only the picking of heavy hooves through puddles and the rhythmic percussion of the creature's breath as it came closer proved it was no vision.

'Shauna, is that you?' The voice was gravelly with exasperation, and she quailed, ashamed of being so easy overwrought, of getting lost *again.* Getting soaked and muddy.

'Laurent! I found something . . .' she scrambled to her feet as he rode up alongside her. His face, glistening with rain, was stern. Something hard in his manner doused her desire to share her discovery of the memorial stone. To avoid his eye and hold off whatever rebuke was coming her way, she leaned against the horse's shoulder. Its muscular flanks were heaving and heat radiated through its wet-satin skin. Laurent must have pushed quite hard to get here. As for Laurent, though he held the reins slackly, there was tension in his hands. His fingers opened and closed on the leather. She wondered if the storm had rattled him – or if it was the sight of her in a bedraggled dress. 'I would have found my way back eventually.'

'You went off the path, yes? You ignored my warning?'

'Not really.' *Yes, really.* 'It got dark on me, and then the rain came down and for a while I couldn't see my hand in front of my face.' It struck her then that he was alone. 'Where's Nico?'

'Home, ages ago. I called on Isabelle to check you were all right, and found her in a bad state. Linen napkins all over the floor, as though the storm had blown through the house—'

'Why were they on the floor?'

He didn't answer that. 'She was convinced you'd been struck by lightning, or worse. In your note, you told her you were going for a short walk, that you'd be back to help with supper. When you didn't arrive and the storm burst, she was terrified some harm had come to you. It wasn't fair to put her through that.'

He was right. 'I'm sorry. Time got away from me, but it was thoughtless. Laurent, I saw something—'

'Today is a difficult enough day for her.'

'I know. I found a stone—'

But he wasn't going to let her say it. 'I went back to the stables and got Héron and told Isabelle I'd find you even if it took all night.' His voice cracked, betraying something more than plain anger. 'You climbed the tower without permission, you've strayed into the woods – I can't look after you all of the time. If you won't take care of yourself, you should leave Chemignac before it's too late.'

'Too late for what?'

He put a hand on her shoulder. Not a gentle one. A constraining grip, as if he feared she might walk off. 'Can you get up behind me?'

'Not really.' The horse towered over her, easily sixteen hands.

He made the horse sidestep, and swung off its back. 'Hitch your dress up.' When she made no move, he put his hands on her waist. 'Let me lift you. Don't be afraid. Héron won't go anywhere.'

In the end, she bunched her dress around her waist, wishing she'd at least worn shorts and not cotton briefs, and let him lift her on to the broad back. There was no saddle, for which she was glad.

Laurent led Héron to a tree stump suitable as a mounting block and clambered onto the horse's back, behind her. They rode out of the woods together at a trot, water splashing up as far as Shauna's waist. Conscious of her bare limbs, she gripped Héron's thick mane, glad of the muscular body behind her while at the same time trying not to merge with it. Once in the open meadow, when the horse broke into a canter, she was glad of Laurent's arms around her. Years hunched over books and computer screens had sapped her confidence as a rider.

'Don't tense, Shauna.'

'Doing my best.' For such a sturdy creature, Héron was surprisingly smooth-gaited and she soon got the rhythm, letting go of the shocks of the day. Later, she'd make Laurent tell her about the memorial stone and the circumstances of his grandfather's death. But she wouldn't mention the wraith at the tower window. It would be humiliating to be told she was nuts or terrifying to be taken seriously.

Security lights came on automatically as they trotted into the stable yard. The tabby cat padded out from one of the barns while horses neighed and called out to them from some distance away.

'Are they out in the paddocks? The other horses, I mean?' Shauna was gabbling to divert Laurent's attention from her legs, which looked luminous under their spattering of mud.

'Yes, now the storm's passed. Anyway, they don't mind weather, they're hardy Camargues and

Boulonnais.' He dismounted and Shauna slithered into his arms, apologising for her filthy state, for leaving streaks on Héron's flanks.

'Did you roll down a slope?'

'Yes,' she admitted. 'The paths were like soggy cake.' She wriggled her dress down.

'Our summer storms are violent. Tomorrow, I'll worry about mildew on the vines.' A gruff note in his voice suggested he knew he'd spoken roughly before. He kept Héron's reins in one hand, his free arm around Shauna. She counted the seconds. What was coming . . . another telling-off, or the same polite withdrawal that she'd experienced before from him? She wasn't sure she could take another confrontation. When he was angry, he was irresistible.

'What is this?' He took the rose from the front of her dress. She'd forgotten about it - it must have worked its way out of her cleavage as she rode home. 'Stealing from my garden?'

'I . . . no . . . I mean . . .' She *hated* people thinking she was underhand.

'Shauna, you can gather them all, if you wish. You may have anything of mine that you want.'

'In the forest, I thought you'd decided to wash your hands of me.' She spoke carelessly, sounding more like Rachel, 'everything a joke', than her fragile, serious self.

'I was afraid that I'd lost you. Afraid that I had been careless with you. Driven you away. Afraid that Chemignac had done its worst. I could not bear it.'

She stared up at him then, defeated in her desire to appear unmoved. When he bent and kissed her, she opened her lips, offering no resistance or argument. The perfect first kiss. Explorative, respectful, tender. The growth of beard Laurent always ended the day with stirred something powerful inside her. Had the horse not pushed his nose between them, impatient at being kept standing, she'd have wound her arms around Laurent's shoulders and left him in no doubt how she wanted this to continue.

He gave a regretful laugh. 'Héron wants his grass.' He led the way to the paddocks which were shrouded in dense dark, their occupants discernible only from the snorting welcome they gave their friend. Hanging back, Shauna heard Laurent speaking softly as he led the horse into the field, and then the jangle of metal as he took off the bridle, a clank as he shut the gate behind him and finally, the thunder of hooves as the horses merged into their private, night-time world. Laurent found Shauna's hand. 'It's selfish of me to want to keep you here but—' he broke off. 'What is the matter?'

She was gazing up at the brilliant, full moon. Sadness knifed through her, and in a voice that was entirely unrelated to hers, she said, 'I shall never see the moon over Chemignac again. It is over.'

'Shauna?' Laurent put his hands on her arms, digging in when she failed to respond. 'What do you mean? Talk to me.'

She ripped away from him. 'I can't stay. I have to go home.'

'Of course, Isabelle is so worried. It's selfish of me to keep you.'

'I mean, to England. I should never have come. I'm not suited to this – I can't help them.'

'Them?' His grip tightened. His breath shuddered. 'You sense them too? Shauna, do you see or hear them or – ?'

They were interrupted then by a window opening above the stable office. A spectral figure loomed out and it took Shauna a moment to recognise Rachel Moorcroft, wearing a bathrobe, hair wrapped in a towel-turban. Rachel called out, 'Time was you'd lurk after hours with me, Laurent.'

Not wishing to hear how the conversation might develop, Shauna tore away towards the château, working out what she could say to Isabelle to release her from this contract. From this place, without delay.

As she entered the kitchen, the sight that greeted Shauna banished any such ideas. Albert de Chemignac was leaning against the worktop, his face disturbingly elated. Nico sat sobbing on the floor in a sea of violet napkins. Isabelle lay on the cold tiles, her stick across her body. She was breathing short and fast. Olive had the landline receiver shoved against her ear, wailing, '*Elle est gravement blessée! Tu devrais venir!*' Shauna gathered that Olive was entreating one or other of her parents to come to Chemignac, without delay.

She knelt beside Nico, asking gently, 'What happened?'

'Grandmère was making supper. She went into the pantry to fetch something and fell. We helped her up and she got this far and collapsed.'

'Has anybody rung for an ambulance?'

Nico looked blank, so Shauna tried Albert. 'Monsieur? Has anybody called the emergency services?'

The old man's eyes found hers. Never before had she sustained such focussed hatred. 'You took Laurent away from us this evening. This is your doing.'

Shaking her head in frustration, Shauna said, 'Nico, Laurent is back now, probably hanging Héron's bridle up in the harness-room. Go fetch him.' She hauled the boy to his feet, shooed him out, then detached Olive from the telephone. A moment later she was speaking with Madame Barends in Brussels. Isabelle's daughter was clearly distraught at being so far away. 'I'm calling an ambulance for your mother,' Shauna told her, 'but I think you should prepare to come here. I'll stay with the children until you arrive.'

As Shauna hung up, Laurent came striding in, just ahead of Nico. She watched Olive move towards him, like a moth to a lamp. *They need him so badly*, she thought. *He is Chemignac. I am not, and never can be. Something about this place petrifies me and as soon as I can, I will leave.*

But 'soon' did not come, and she did not leave.

Isabelle had not re-broken her femur, but in falling she'd sustained a second-degree sprain to her left knee. It was the fact that she'd gone into shock that caused the hospital to keep her in for three days' observation. By the time she came home in a wheelchair, her daughter had arrived. Daily activities were suspended as Madame Louette Barends drew up a routine of feeding and bed exercise, interrogating her mother repeatedly on the exact circumstances of her fall.

'One answer is never enough for my daughter,' Isabelle croaked pitifully to Shauna, a couple of days after her return from hospital. 'Only when she hears the same thing three times does she accept that it might, just possibly, be true.'

Once Louette was satisfied that her mother's recovery was under control, she fell to cleaning the house. Shauna did what she could to help, reading to Isabelle and keeping her company while Louette emptied cupboards, ran brooms along the beams and cooked immense meals which, even with the addition of Albert and Laurent at the table, were rarely consumed in one sitting. The children clung to their mother like baby primates. They'd thought their grandmother was going to die that stormy evening, and Shauna empathised with them. She knew how devastating it was, that first encounter with human mortality.

Louette babied the children until the end of the first week of her stay, then informed them that the drama was over. If Grandmère was well enough now to sit outside, it was business as usual – which meant a renewal of English lessons and sports for Olive and Nico, and chauffeur-duties for Shauna. For Louette, it meant six hours a day in the winery office, catching up on the work her mother's accident had interrupted.

'Thank God I have a flexible contract,' Louette told Shauna when she came in one evening after a long stint at the office computer. Reaching into the fridge for a bottle of Sauvignon Blanc, she added, 'Thank God too that this is still a vineyard. Can I pour you a glass?'

'A small one, thanks. What is it you do, Madame?'

'Oh, call me Louette. I work for the European Parliament, translating French documents into German and English. No shortage of work' – Louette raised her glass, giving a wry laugh – 'but there's a queue of eager new graduates offering to do what I do for less money, so I can't afford to miss a deadline, not even for an injured mother. What a stroke of luck you're here. *Maman* says it's destiny, her way of saying she adores you.'

After that, how could Shauna ask to break her contract? It was simply assumed she'd stay on at Chemignac. Louette agreed to remain until the end of August, five weeks away, after which she was needed back in Brussels. 'Our home is in Paris, but we always get co-opted to Brussels for the summer. My husband is currently on loan to one of the European commissioners and he dislikes living in rented accommodation. He detests even more going home to an empty flat. He is not a "new man", my Hubert.'

'I suppose your children must miss you,' Shauna suggested. It was Laurent's theory that Monsieur and Madame Barends off-loaded their children too readily, compensating with an expensive package of sporting self-improvement.

Louette Barends seemed to give the idea genuine thought. 'They've never said so and you can see, surely, how they love their sports? Besides, Paris is horrible in the heat – have you ever been there in summer? Thick with tourists and you can smell the car fumes even in the suburbs. No,' Louette said decisively, 'they're better here.' They would all return to the capital in early September, she added, in time for the new school term. 'But you must stay for the harvest, *petite*, because my mother isn't going to mend quickly. I think we can presume that she won't be in any condition to cook for the workers, and organise the *fête de vendange*.'

'Won't she go back to Paris with you?' Shauna had somehow assumed that Isabelle would return to her flat by the Seine once the holidays were over. 'I thought she only ever spent summer here.'

It seemed there was no chance of it, not before October at any rate, because Isabelle had let out her apartment on a four-month contract. Louette explained, 'Renting it to wealthy foreign visitors doubles her annual income. And she won't come to stay with us because we live out in Neuilly-sur-Seine, which she hates. Suburbia, you see? For *maman*, only the city or the countryside is worth bothering with. The middling places, where most people end up, don't exist for her. But this is good, no? For you, I mean. You must experience a wine harvest at least once in your life, Shauna. I believe you have no job to go home for? So – stay for the *vendange* and get a sun tan. You are very pale.'

Though Louette's father, the late Monsieur Duval, had been a diplomat it was clear Louette didn't take after him. She must know that most redheads did not tan; they either burned, or, by keeping their sun exposure to a minimum, achieved what could best be described as 'a healthy glow.' Usually because their freckles joined together.

As a teenager, Shauna had tried everything to get the California beach look – creams, oils, bronzing spray. The results had usually been something between gravy browning and marmalade. Once, she'd turned herself bright mango, and had spent a whole weekend rubbing herself with cut lemons in a desperate bid to bleach herself back to normal. She'd gradually come to terms with her DNA and these days, celebrated her pigmentation. The implication of 'pale' was that she was unwell or even anaemic.

She bit her tongue, however, and observed Louette, who had put down her wine and was leafing through her mother's telephone contacts book. Louette presumably favoured her father's side of the family in looks, being sandy-haired and large-framed. She made the most of herself with chic, Parisian clothes. And though she shared none of Isabelle's panache, she had a brusque, can-do attitude that got things done. She proved it moments later by saying, 'I need to find a local woman who can come in each day and clean. I can't do it and work, and it's not your responsibility, *petite*. You're doing a fantastic job with the children.'

'Will your mother accept a cleaner?'

Louette gave a throaty chuckle. 'She'll hate it but face it, it'll be months before *maman* can lug a hoover upstairs, or stand on a chair to polish the window glass. She needs help and I think I know who to call. Don't say anything to anybody just yet.'

Shauna promised and her feelings towards Louette softened. Tactless and bossy she might be, but who else could chivvy Isabelle into eating properly and doing painful physiotherapy every day? And the alteration in the children was astounding, too. The relentless pursuit of sporting excellence was downgraded to mere enthusiasm. They gave up their riding to spend more time with their mother, and Nico was heard to say, when he and Olive crashed out of the mixed tennis doubles, 'It's only a game.'

The next morning, as she walked to the car ahead of the children, Albert de Chemignac stepped out of one of the winery buildings and called roughly, 'You, this is yours.'

He thrust an A4 brown envelope at her, letting go of it too soon so she had to lunge for it. 'In future, collect your letters yourself,' he muttered. 'I'm not your postman. Why should I, *hein*?'

She gave a nod that was neither acquiescence nor intended as a thank you, and walked on. Damn it, she wished she could stop being intimidated by that man, but the sheer force of his hostility got through every time. Getting into the Clio and putting on her seat belt, she examined the envelope, suspicious that it might be booby-trapped in some way. She doubted Albert could engineer an explosive device, but she could quite see him hiding a loop of barbed wire or a bag of razor blades inside her package.

She quickly saw that it was her mother's handwriting on the front, and ripped open the flap. Inside was a copy of the quarterly journal produced by her university faculty. All Shauna's post was being forwarded to her mother's house, and Elisabeth Vincent had sent it on, thinking Shauna would like to read it. Shauna wasn't certain that she did want to. She'd written several articles for this same journal in the past, and had been its assistant editor, a coveted post for science graduates. Its glossy-paper smell, the cheery note her mother had paper-clipped to it, brought a lump to her throat. Had she not been in full view of the *chai*, and expecting Olive and Nico to arrive any moment, she'd have given way and sobbed. Instead, she breathed down her home-sickness, and put the journal on the passenger seat to read later. 'What am I still doing here?' she murmured, though she knew the answer. She was showing loyalty to people she'd grown to care about. And she was hoping for a reprise of a certain kiss . . . perhaps the better question was, 'Why did I ever come here in the first place?'

Seeing the children loping towards her with their sports kit swinging from their shoulders, she fired the engine. As the stereo burst to life, the car filled with Céline Dion singing 'Destin'.

Destiny? No way. Shauna believed in self-determination, not fate or celestial alignments. If she was to enjoy her enforced stay at Chemignac, then she'd better persuade Albert to be less beastly and engage in some straight talk with Laurent. Simple, ha?

A few days later, an opportunity arose for the latter. Shauna offered to wash up after supper so Louette could help her mother to bed, then spend some time with her children. Laurent had eaten with them and he offered to dry the dishes. Standing next to him at the sink, her stomach knotted up. She felt she was about to go on stage to deliver a keynote speech to a difficult audience. Just say something. *Anything.* But what? Whenever their elbows bumped, Shauna jumped as if an electric current had passed between them. On the final occasion, she gulped, 'Sorry!' and he answered with exaggerated politeness, 'That's perfectly all right. I don't mind you touching me.'

And then he took a step to the left, so they wouldn't bump again.

Did she mind touching him? Was he crazy? She'd thought of little else since their kiss in the stable yard under that wondrous, full moon. But . . . its erotic potency had become strangely sullied. Rachel's interference and Isabelle's accident had removed its innocence. She couldn't shake the thought that, had they not lingered in the moonlight,

Isabelle would have been helped sooner. The children would have been spared a long spell of distress in the company of Albert. Albert, Laurent had said after the event, was no use in an emergency. 'Like a hare in the headlights, he freezes. It's as though he cannot assume responsibility for anything.'

Shauna could have put it more strongly than that. It hadn't been panic in Albert's face when she walked into the kitchen. He'd been feasting himself on Isabelle's crisis. That old man was full of hate, dangerous to be around. The last thing she needed was to grow any more vulnerable. Caring for Laurent, wanting his touch, his kiss, made her just that. Vulnerable.

The clink of crockery as she and Laurent washed and dried their way through the mound of dishes made the silence between them almost unbearable. Shauna's teeth clenched. Laurent kept clearing his throat. They finally let go what was on their minds at the same moment. 'Laurent, I have to know—'

'Shauna, this can't go on—'

'You first,' Laurent said.

'Why does your uncle hate me so much? And don't say, "He doesn't like women". That doesn't go halfway near it.'

'He hates the English.'

'Because we buy property in the Dordogne? Or because he thinks we left you high and dry during the war?'

'Because in 1943, an Englishwoman came here to Chemignac. An SOE agent.'

'SOE?'

'Special Operations Executive, Churchill's agents of sabotage. She was called Yvonne and parachuted in to be a courier. She was a go-between for the Resistance fighters and other British agents – she carried messages, handed out money, arranged drops of ammunition. Women were used that way because they could move around the countryside without attracting suspicion. Men were more likely to be searched, or arrested for evading forced labour. It was very dangerous, regardless. If they were caught—'

'They were shot.'

Laurent put down his tea cloth. 'The lucky ones were shot. Spies were interrogated, tortured, sent to prison camps. Female agents were often sexually abused as well. Few survived.'

'Yvonne?'

He shrugged. 'Nobody knows. Her British colleagues, Barnsley and Sturridge, were shot by the Germans. Their bodies were recovered from the forest.'

Shauna faced Laurent. Her inner eye homed in on a glade bathed in light the colour of corn syrup, a rock in its centre like the kernel of a peach. 'I tried to tell you before, I found a memorial in the forest. Your grandfather's name was carved on it,

along with Maurice Barnsley and George Sturridge .
. . and two others, I think.'

Laurent nodded. 'Local men, Michel Paulin and Luc Roland.'

'All from the Resistance?'

'The French were. The Englishmen were Yvonne's colleagues. They were dropped in together.'

'So, isn't it likely that she died too?'

'All that's known is that she disappeared. Certainly, her story is buried pretty deep. But Albert believes she turned traitor and betrayed the Resistance cell she was sent to help.'

'Including Henri de Chemignac.'

'Yes, including his brother. And Albert does not forget.'

Never forget, never forgive.

'It's more than just hating Englishwomen,' she said. 'It's about hating an entire race and a whole gender. Albert sees something in me that he can hardly bear. I suppose I can take comfort from the fact that it's not personal.'

Laurent touched her hair. 'Actually, it is. Yvonne was a redhead. Albert refers to her as "That perfidious *rouquine*". Don't look so unhappy! None of this is your fault. It's *our* family's history, *our* grief.'

And I'm sharing it, she thought. From not knowing what to say a few minutes ago, she now wanted to tell Laurent everything. 'As I walked to the woods the evening of the thunderstorm – it must have been about five o'clock – I glanced back at the tower and saw somebody looking out at me. A girl, I think.'

'Who? Olive?'

'Not Olive. She spent the whole day in the village. She didn't get home till nearly dark – she had to wait for the storm to pass before she cycled back. And I'm pretty sure it wasn't Rachel.'

'No, it couldn't have been. She was escorting

a group ride. They got caught in the downpour and had to turn back, so she spent most of the evening refunding customers' money and hosing mud off horses' legs. Besides, I told her not to come into the château again, unless invited.'

'She could have snuck inside.' This was playing Devil's advocate, but Shauna wanted to test all possibilities.

'But she wouldn't have found the key,' Laurent insisted. 'I showed Isabelle a new place to hide it.' Throwing down his dish cloth, he walked to the middle of the room and reached up, finding a split in the beam from which he pulled a short, black key. Shauna recognised it as the one for the tower bedroom.

'Could Isabelle have gone up there?' she suggested.

'Be serious. Isabelle couldn't climb those steps, even before her fall.'

'Somebody was up there, staring across. At

me, or past me, I'm not sure. I felt – miserable. And frightened. I ran.'

'You weren't seeing a person, Shauna.'

'It was no mirage. You won't convince me otherwise.'

'I'm not trying to.' He opened the tower door and was halfway up the stairs before Shauna had dried her hands. She caught up with him, gripping the rope handrail in the darkness. She wasn't ready for this.

Laurent let them into the top room and turned on the light, ushering her ahead of him. The first thing she saw was the violet silk dress laid out on the bed like a surrendered female form. Hadn't she hung it away? Maybe not, as she'd been in such a hurry to leave last time she was here.

'Which window, Shauna?'

She gave him a blank look. 'Sorry?'

'Which window was the figure standing in front of?'

'Oh.' She made a slow turn, in no hurry to answer. She felt Laurent was waiting, like a magician about to pull an unpleasant rabbit from a hat. His appearance was different tonight. He was wearing a cotton sweater, the sort preferred by yachtsmen, and chino trousers. He'd come to supper once in a t-shirt and shorts, and Louette had sent him home to change and shave. Ever since, he'd made more effort. Tonight, his hair looked very black, his complexion unusually drained. And he was tense, his arms wrapped around his body.

'I saw her there.' She pointed to the picture of wading cattle. The window behind it faced west. Its glass would catch the setting sun.

'You're sure she was at that window?' When she affirmed it, he asked, 'You saw her from the lawn?'

'From the meadow, but I have good eyesight,' she said, her irritation rising. It was hard enough to admit to being spooked, without an interrogation on top. She explained how the sudden racket of doves taking flight had made her turn. 'Girl or woman, I'm not sure, but she was staring out towards the woods.'

Laurent lifted the picture off its hook and Shauna saw the outline of a window frame. An outline only. Its centre was filled with stone blocks which, judging by the condition of the mortar, had been in place for many years.

She swung between bewilderment and mortification. Self-evidently, she couldn't have seen a window. Yet she *had*, so what did that say about her mental state? She'd always been the cool logician, the girl with the sceptical, white-coated mind. *She had seen a figure . . .* through blind stone. So – she was guilty of self-delusion and Laurent had brought her up here in full knowledge. 'Thanks for the humiliation. You and Rachel are one of a kind.'

He raised his hands. 'I needed to show you this, but believe me—'

'Right from day one you've played games, the pair of you! "Let's pick her up in a pony cart and give her sunburn!" "Let's lock her in the tower, see if she gets the screaming jimjams!" You and Rachel had something going, didn't you?'

He shrugged, resisting the direction of the conversation, but giving in as she continued to glare at him, her jaw set. 'Yes, we did, but it's over, dead as roadkill, and we have never discussed you. Never. Ah, no!' He caught her as she tried to push past him. Her need to return to ground level was urgent and she struggled with him, elbowing him in the chest.

Laurent locked his arms around her. 'Race down in the dark, you'll go headfirst. Shauna, listen.' He put his lips to her ear. 'Come back to me.'

Like a kettle coming to the boil and clicking off, the pressure subsided in her head. She flopped against his chest. Her lungs hurt as if she'd cried for a week. 'Am I going mad?'

He gave a grim laugh. 'No more so than any of us at Chemignac. Look, I'm going to turn off the light now but I won't let go of you. Follow me down. Hold tight to the handrope.' In the second before he extinguished the light, she looked back into the room.

'I ought to hang up that dress.'

A click, and darkness. His voice rasped, 'Leave that hellish rag alone.' He stopped, saying in his normal voice, 'I mean, it's fragile. It can't take too much handling. We'd better go down and put away those dishes, or Louette will accuse us of sloppy workmanship.' He all but pulled her out of the room.

Part Two

August

Chapter Ten

She wasn't sure if Laurent was avoiding her, but she was avoiding him, making sure she was out as much as possible. He stopped eating with the family, excusing himself on the grounds of a heavy workload. Not altogether untrue as Raymond, the elder of his two vineyard workers, was again on sick leave, this time with a herniated disk in his spine. Laurent was also interviewing candidates to take over Rachel's position. And though nothing specific was said, there was a feeling among the adults that Laurent was having to monitor Rachel's work closely as, with her departure only a few weeks away, she was slacking.

Louette commented on it over dinner one

evening. 'August is supposed to be the month my cousin gets a little time off, but I've never seen Laurent so harried. He can't look after vines *and* run stables. I knew the first time I met Rachel that she was trouble. She has the coiled look of someone waiting to steal the best piece of meat off your plate. Laurent should hire a temporary manager.'

Albert answered morosely, 'You never take time off in this business. Always watching the grapes, the weather . . .'

'The weather does what it does,' Isabelle put in. 'No point watching it.'

'*Véraison* is the most crucial time,' Albert jabbed the table. He could no longer be of much use in the vineyard, Isabelle had told Shauna, as he suffered from arthritis and hip dysplasia. It didn't stop him hobbling among the vines nearest the house though, expressing his opinion of Laurent's methods. He was particularly put out by Laurent's decision, some years back, to seed grass between the vines, rather than plough the strips each season. Albert insisted that the grass sapped the vines' energy, but Laurent's answer was simple. He didn't want his vines to grow too vigorously. He wanted them to put down deep roots, to draw minerals from deep in the soil. It was also why he added very little fertiliser. 'Make them search for their own food,' he'd said during his last appearance at the family dinner table, 'and they will be healthier and reflect the *terroir*.'

Albert's response had been scathing. 'I grew up using my eyes, ears and nose. You young people rely too much on machines and science-lab toys.'

Shauna had listened, struck anew by the difference between the two men. Laurent had acknowledged his uncle's opinion and answered his criticisms in a way that suggested a profound study of the subject, whereas Albert just rammed his fist down. *My way or no way.*

They'd bandied about terms like *terroir*,

which she learned meant the unique character of the soil, its minerals and the hours of sunshine it received, all of which established the flavour and character of a wine. Tonight, she'd have liked to ask what *véraison* meant, but, as ever, Albert's presence affected her like a wet sack over her head. She sometimes thought he only came to meals for the pleasure of making her uncomfortable.

When the cheese was brought out, Shauna asked Isabelle to excuse her. 'I've got the fidgets. Do you mind if I go out for a walk? Leave the washing up for me.'

'Nonsense, the children can do it. Or Audrey will do it in the morning.' Audrey Chaumier, who was Raymond's wife, had been Louette's choice of daily help. She now came in every day to clean and her efficient, genial presence helped neutralise household stress.

'Are you heading towards the woods or . . .' Isabelle's eyes gleamed, though with mischief or pleasure, Shauna couldn't tell, 'to the *chai*?'

Shauna wasn't sure where she'd end up. If she happened to bump into Laurent, well, *c'est le déstin*. 'I thought I might roam among the grapes.'

'Then bless them as you pass,' Isabelle chuckled. Her spirits had mended since her fall, though her damaged joints still pained her. 'They need all the prayers they can get. Sunshine, plenty. Rain, a little. Pests, none.'

Shauna found Laurent on one of the southwest-facing *parcelles*, his white shirt jumping out of the topaz light. Walking towards him, uncertain what she would say, she let her mind fill with the sounds and scents of early evening. For once, birdsong trumped the buzz of insects. The air smelled of wild mint released by the heat of the day. It was the perfect temperature and she'd walked out in a dress with spaghetti straps and a silk crochet shrug protecting her shoulders. A beautiful evening, a flawless scene. Vineyards reached away to a lost horizon that no longer felt threatening because she now understood the patchwork. Each *parcelle* was cultivated to catch the sun, and must follow the slopes and valleys carved out after the last ice age. Extraordinary, to think that the movement of melting ice floes twenty thousand years ago should affect the acidity of a bottle of Sauvignon Blanc in 2003. The vines' colour palette had intensified from her first view a month ago. The grape clusters were bigger. The greens less sour-looking, more translucent.

'Heuh!' Laurent came towards her and she picked up her pace, anxious to read his expression before it was too late to invent an excuse for being here. He wasn't smiling, but at least his eyes were welcoming. 'It's too early to pick, you know.'

'I do know,' she answered. 'I need to ask you something.'

'Go ahead.' A small pair of scissors was tucked into his belt and he carried a plastic beaker.

'What does *véraison* mean?'

A weak reason for interrupting him, but Laurent seemed pleased by the question. 'It's the moment of ripening, the moment of truth, when you know you will have a harvest in six, seven, eight weeks.'

'Has it come, your moment of truth?'

He made a non-committal sound. 'The weather cooled off this week, as you noticed, but the forecast is for another heat wave. Give it a day or two and I will know. These are Muscadelle.' He showed her the beaker, half full of gooseberry-green orbs. 'For sweet wine. I won't sample any of the others yet. No point questioning what cannot speak to you.'

She drew a breath and came to her real reason for wanting to bump into him. 'I'm sorry I was a bit hysterical the other night, in the tower. I'm not mad – well, ninety-five percent sure I'm not – just overwrought. I must have imagined the figure at the window. 'Course I did. And the window itself, too. It's all been . . . I mean, the weird business with the cave and then Isabelle's accident, and of course, finding that Resistance memorial and reading your grandfather's name on it. . . It's shaken me more than I realised.'

'Walk the forest tracks in southern and western France, you will find many such stones. But I don't think you are an idiot, or mad, and I'm sorry if I seemed brutal. Perhaps we were both overwrought.' He waved away a wasp zig-zagging close to Shauna's hair, and then rested his hand against her neck. 'Louette says you're staying for the harvest. I'm glad.'

'She wants me to. Isabelle won't cope with the *fête de vendange* this year. Not without extra hands. Not sure mine will be much use, but if necessary, I can beat eggs into submission. My omelettes were famous when I shared a student house.'

'Only stay if you want to. We can always hire in more help for Isabelle.'

'I – I've said I will stay. I want to.' Did she? Yes, because she'd learned in the space of ten breaths that she could never be happy away from this man. 'And I'm sorry for being snide about you and Rachel. I believe you when you say your relationship is over –'

'It isn't.'

She gasped, the pain shockingly savage.

'Because it was never a relationship.' At last, he smiled. 'I'm going to the *chai*. Want to help me?'

'Of course. Help with what?'

'Something completely pointless but very interesting.'

Being diligent – or was it 'pedantic'? – about learning new words, Shauna had established that the *chai* was traditionally the place where wine was stored. Laurent used the term more loosely. His *chai* was where his presses were located, and his vats and oak barrels. He also bottled his wine there. When the harvest kicked off next month, the new grapes would be brought in on the back of a trailer and pressed. Fermentation and every other process happened in this vast, barn-like building. Laurent had explained, 'In every other business it would be called a factory, but that's not a word wine-growers like.' This evening, he led her past the main door and into a small side building, where he spread his arms wide and said, 'Welcome to my laboratory.'

Like the *chai*, the lab was pristine, its stone walls blasted clean, the mason's chisel marks as sharp as if they'd been made yesterday. The stone must have been sealed too, as there was no dust. Laurent pointed to a partition wall, telling her that the winery's office lay on the other side – it was where Louette went each day and where, at the moment, machinery was buzzing. 'Sounds like a fax is arriving.' These days, most people used email, but she supposed that Chemignac was an electronic backwater. 'Do you want to check it?' Shauna asked.

Laurent listened until a series of beeps established that it was a short message. 'I'll give it a miss tonight. You wouldn't believe the paperwork I have to deal with. Everything has to be recorded and officially stamped, usually in triplicate. I can't walk across a room without filling out a form. So now I'm going to show you my latest labour-saving device. Or "laboratory toy," as Albert would call it.' Laurent set his beaker on a countertop, then reached into a base cupboard, bringing out a cardboard parcel that Shauna recognised.

'You collected that at Garzenac station,' she said, 'the day I arrived.'

'And I saw you, all hot and bothered. Had I realised who you were, I'd have taken you home with me.'

'Instead you left me to Rachel's tender care.'

'I saw her before I left, harnessing the pony, and assumed she was picking up guests. Some of them like to arrive in old-fashioned style, though not usually in such searing heat. Rachel has a nasty side. I'm inured to it, but I'm sorry you had to discover it. It's partly why we never had a deep or lasting relationship.' From the package, Laurent pulled out a tubular object. It was shaped like the neck of a clarinet.

She leaned in to look. 'And this is?'

'A refractometer. In the cupboard you'll find a garlic press and plastic containers. Would you mind?'

Armed with a very clean garlic press and a sterile beaker, she followed Laurent's instructions, squeezing juice from a couple of Muscadelle grapes.

Laurent flipped up one end of the refractometer and told Shauna to pour a drop of juice on to its exposed glass. 'Just a little.' Moving to stand under a skylight, he tilted the instrument a couple of times then invited her to look. 'The liquid is caught between twin prisms, you see? You know how a prism works?'

'It splits light into its component wavelengths. Pretty basic physics.'

'So, the light passes through the juice and the angle of refraction tells you the concentration of sugars.'

'Sugar content affects light refraction. I see.'

'Read the gauge. It's just above zero so we won't bother marking it down, but in a few days, we will do this again.'

'And judge how fast the grapes are ripening?'

'And predict the vintage. Each day, I compare this year with last, and all the years since I've been running Clos de Chemignac.'

'Neat. That's really impressive.'

'I'm impressed by you, too.' He wiped down the surfaces they'd used with ethanol spray, then cleaned the refractometer with a solution designed for surgical instruments before putting it into an ultrasonic cleaning machine. He was deadly serious about his environment, she realised. Scientifically literate, focussed *and* sexy. No wonder she grew short of breath when he was near. He set the timer on the cleaner. Forty-four seconds. 'You have a remarkable grasp of physics and chemistry,' he told her.

'I should do. I studied it for five years and have a BSc in biomedical science and a Masters' in medicinal plant science.'

The ultrasonic machine pinged the end of its cycle. With an odd look on his face, Laurent emptied it, put the last items away and shut the cupboard door. He turned to her, a groove between his brows. 'You're not a canine reflexologist?'

'A what? Good God, who said I was that?'

'Rachel.'

'Laurent, think about it . . . reflexology on dog's paws? I don't generally like Rachel's humour, but that's a gem. It's only mildly less crazy than being an equine reflexologist.'

He made a face. Then laughed. 'OK, I fell for that one. Though I tell you what, somewhere in the First World, there will be a canine reflexologist.'

'Bound to be, but not me. I'm a scientist. Does that worry you?'

'No, and it answers a few questions. I was puzzling for days how you knew all this stuff. I thought maybe I had left a wine science reference book at Isabelle's!'

'"All this stuff" was in my A-level chemistry curriculum. I lied about being good at pub quizzes.'

He wrapped his arms around her. 'Welcome to Chemignac, Madame la Scientifique.'

'It's good to be here.'

'And you will stay?'

'For the harvest.' Seeing the doubt in his eyes, she added, 'I don't break promises.'

He kissed her, bunching her hair, his other hand pressing into her waist. She gave everything to the kiss, lifting herself on tiptoe, discovering how soft his hair was, how hard the wall of his stomach. When she reached inside his shirt, hanging loose over his waist band, she discovered that his chest hair thickened between his ribs, grew sparser over his breastbone. She'd once watched a news report of a violinist reunited with a stolen instrument. The girl had tucked her violin under her chin in stirring tenderness and Shauna now felt the same – reunited with a part of herself. Being in love, expressing physical intimacy, was Shauna's art, her creative outlet. During her single years, she'd piled her loving instincts into her studies. At last, she could break away and fly . . . longing swelled under the urgency of Laurent's hands, his lips – which broke from her mouth to skim down her neck – to caress the curve of her shoulder. He spoke her name with such smoky intensity, she swayed. And then he stopped. 'We need to speak about this.'

He gently pushed aside her silk shrug to reveal her thorn symbol. With a groan of frustration, she pulled the garment off, angling her shoulder so he could see the tattoo plainly. 'It's the *straif*. It's Irish. It's co-incidence, Laurent.'

'It's the de Chemignac badge. It's ours.'

'Well, you can't have this one, it's attached to me.'

He turned her so they were looking at each other. He bent his right arm to exhibit his own tattoo. 'I need to understand why we share this mark.'

'Nothing to understand. My father wore the symbol above his knuckle. He was an Irish folklorist. A musician and poet, and a specialist in Celtic languages. In the ancient Ogham script, this symbol means "strife". When I was twelve, he died very suddenly. Nine years later, I had it inked on to myself because I was coming up to my graduation and it hit me – he should have been there and I needed him with me.' She spoke fast, to get the explanation done before tears came. 'I hadn't even heard of Chemignac.'

'Come, see this.' Laurent led her out of the lab, across a yard paved with limestone, stopping at a circular wall inside which grew a blackthorn. Its tortured trunk hinted at great age. A sparse crop of unripe sloes peppered its branches. He picked one off, gave it to her. 'Bitter tasting on the tongue, until the October frosts. The name "Chemignac" comes from an ancient word older than the French language and means "crooked one".' He gestured to the tree. 'There were thorn trees here before there were vines and we have a family motto: "Tend the vines or the thorns will return".'

'They have,' she said, stepping up on to the

low wall, ignoring the barbs against her bare shoulders. 'My mother's maiden name was Thorne. I'm Shauna Thorne Vincent. Careful how you handle me, Laurent de Chemignac. As for the tattoo: I'll ask Isabelle to invite my mother here, and she'll tell us if my father's mark had anything to do with your family. Agreed?'

His answer was to lift her down and kiss her until the sun slipped below the horizon. He led her to a fold of the meadow where they lay in the grass. At first, they gazed up at the moon, as yet barely visible against the sunset. As it gained definition, and the shadows thickened, they turned to each other. Removing their clothes, helping one another without embarrassment, without coyness, they gloried in the readiness of their flesh. They made love, knowing it was love, though the why and the how eluded them.

In the winery office, Rachel Moorcroft finally allowed herself to turn the light back on. She'd whacked the switch when Laurent and Shauna came in, hardly breathing for upwards of forty minutes while they held their mutual admiration party on the other side of the door.

'Madame la Scientifique!' Rachel mocked. She'd been using Laurent's computer to send emails to her friends, assuming he'd stay out among the vines until dark. He'd swallowed her line about the 'amazing job offer' in California, so she didn't want it known that she in fact had no job to go to, and was sending her CV out to all the recruitment firms specialising in leisure and holiday employment.

Rachel has a nasty side . . . too right. Laurent should know better than anyone as they'd seen every side of each other during the months they'd been lovers. Crashing together like cymbals whenever they could get away – two honed, hungry bodies, equally matched. So they'd never had a relationship, ha? What, when you put it under a microscope, was a relationship? Weren't relationships what people reached for when white-hot sex fizzled out and neediness took over? There'd come a moment with her and Laurent when the flames had flickered down and she'd caught a glimpse of the future . . .

Laurent had wanted her. Of course he did. She could pretty much crook her finger for any man, any time. But the primal, self-protecting part of her knew he'd never commit. Whatever he was looking for, she didn't have it and for the first time in her life, that mattered. Still, she'd done what she always did. Given him the elbow before he could do it to her. It had been harvest time, two years back, and a Spanish temporary worker had been her willing decoy. Laurent had shrugged and moved on, but she'd always thought he'd come back to her.

Instead, he'd sacked her. 'Locking a girl in the tower room, a guest of my aunt's, too! You went too far, Rachel.'

'Can't you take a joke, Laurent? She didn't mind.'

'Shutting people up and running away is too close to sadism for my taste. You're dangerous, Rachel – to Shauna, to me, to Chemignac.'

Bloody, holy Chemignac had always been her true rival. Though Shauna Vincent, who only had to step out in the sun or touch a drop of rain before she had to be rescued, was running a close second. '"I have a BSc in biomedical science and a Masters' in being a know-it-all and fainting",' Rachel's whining impersonation of Shauna gave way to her own, private-school guttural. 'And I've got first class honours in sticking the spanner in other people's spokes.'

The fax that had come through as Laurent and Shauna walked in was one page long; hand-written in confident scrawl, signed 'Mike'. The crested letterhead belonged to LJKU, Lancashire

John Kay University, which sounded to Rachel like Nerd Central. 'Mike' was presumably 'Professor M. Ladriss, Head of the Faculty of Biomedical Sciences'. Try saying that after six vodka-and-limes. Rachel read the fax through again, soaking up every phrase.

Dear Shauna,

I've been texting you but getting no answer, then I remembered you'd provided a fax number. Major changes here - the senior research post at Cademus Labs has come free. Allegra Boncasson doesn't want it. She left me a message saying she doesn't need the experience or the money. Certainly, she doesn't need the latter as her father is one of our country's less scrupulous banking fat cats. I'm furious, as you can imagine. You accused me on the last day of term, during our painful interview, of kow-towing to financial interests and backing

Allegra for the post. Wrong – I backed you, but did not know then that Sir Christopher Boncasson had slipped Cademus £100,000 for research into skin-cell regeneration, no doubt to hide some of his obscene bonuses from the taxman while giving his daughter a leg up. I know I can trust you not to share this with anybody, by the way. Come home NOW. I can hold the job open a while, but not forever. Mike.

Rachel's first thought was to make confetti of the message, until it occurred to her that Shauna would fly after this chance, forgetting her promise to stay till the end of harvest. With her departure, Laurent might change his mind about her, Rachel's, future here. It might be in her interests to give this fax to Shauna and let ambition and fate take its course.

On the other hand, tearing it up and depriving Shauna of her big chance would feel very good indeed. Which option? Studying the letterhead's pompous, mock-heraldic crest, she thought, why not choose a third possibility? *Let's give Shauna Vincent something that ensures she always remembers her time in Chemignac.* After half-an-hour of online research, Rachel added a few lines of her own to the page, writing at the top, "For the attention of the Legal Advisor". She then dialled the fax number of Boncasson Banking and Finance Plc, which she'd found on their website. Pressing 'send', she sat back and rocked with laughter.

Dakenfield. They'd moved her to a recovery ward. New staff, new inmates. They tutted when she called the occupants of the other beds 'inmates'. Miss Thorne had insisted they reduce her morphine levels and though the penalty was grinding discomfort, her brain no longer felt like warm jelly. She was desperate to be allowed home. The need to be back among her books, her music, her furnishings, was becoming a fixation. From her hospital bed she could see the night sky. The institutional window had a broken blind and so during sleepless nights, she could plot the journey of the moon. A three-quarter moon had lit the deaths of Henri and the others, and had enabled her to escape. She hated a waxing moon. That bold, blank stare taunted her. Seemed to say, 'You got away all right. Pity about the others.'

In his apartment in the château, his table awash with old black-and-white photographs, Albert de Chemignac studied the face of Yvonne, the woman he'd desired and hated. The woman who had surrendered to Henri within hours of meeting him.

The girl looking after Isabelle's grandchildren – Albert couldn't pronounce her first name – was English like Yvonne. Red-haired like

Yvonne. Green-eyed like Yvonne. Had she been a little taller, she could have *been* Yvonne. Like Yvonne, he wanted her away from here before memories swarmed, like wasps from a ruptured nest.

On the steps of the tower, a figure climbed barefoot through the dark, drawn by the overpowering desire to slip a violet silk gown over her head and feel it settle against her skin. A hexed thing imbued with sadness and grief. But irresistible.

Out in the meadow, Shauna and Laurent lay serene in the night air. The strident calling of owls criss-crossed in the woods, and among the nooks of the winery. Shauna said at last, 'I ought to go in. They'll wonder.'

'When the next owl hoots, we'll get dressed.'

From that moment on, the Chemignac owls were strangely silent.

Chapter Eleven

Another Sunday. Shauna woke at dawn, as she often did now that she and Laurent were lovers. She reached for him, finding empty space. It meant he'd returned to his own bed, in his own apartment. Or more likely, he was at work in the vineyards or the stables. Sighing for the day they could legitimately be together, she got up to fling open her window.

The sun was rising. Unwilling to waste the watercolour mist, she took a fast shower, then threw on one of her jazzy, short dresses. She added a fluffy cardigan and leggings. The sun would grow intense later, the air humid, but at this early hour there was a bite in the air. At the back door, she swapped her trainers for Olive's sunflower-patterned wellington boots. Under her arm, a folded tartan rug. Dressed as if for a folk festival, she took the route out through the gatehouse.

The meadows between the moat and the woods were straw-coloured now, the grass pearly with cobwebs. Azure chicory stood to attention above the grass, the last remnants of summer. Laurent had his hay cut late to allow the flowers to seed, and sold the crop to a neighbour for sheep fodder. His seasons were relentless, but at least Laurent always knew where he'd be one month to the next. *Where would she be*, she wondered, *when spring arrived, and the flowers returned?*

The undefined status of their relationship and the presence of the children, combined with Albert's cast-iron views on sex before marriage, had induced them to keep their feelings for each other under wraps. Louette Barends, coming to the end of her enforced stay at Chemignac, was too busy to notice other people's affairs. Not only was she juggling translation projects, she'd started organising the *fête de vendange* – scheduling Audrey Chaumier and other local women to do the cooking that was beyond Isabelle this year.

Only Isabelle had detected the new chemistry between Shauna and Laurent, and she'd caught on to it within hours of their first night in the meadow. At breakfast the following morning, she'd waited until Louette had left the table before saying lightly, 'Did your promenade among the vines put that glow in your eye, Shauna? Or something more?' The children had been out of earshot, brushing their teeth in the bathroom. '*Chérie,*' Isabelle had continued, 'it is none of my business. After all, you are old enough to be married with a family. So all I will say is, have caution. After Nico, Laurent is my favourite young man in the world and I know already that you do not give yourself away lightly. I could not bear to send you back to Elisabeth with a broken heart.'

'You don't think it can work?' Shauna hadn't bothered denying it. Her feelings for Laurent were so boundless, so fresh, that sharing them with this woman felt natural. And there was no time for coyness. Doors were banging, the bathroom taps were on full blast. The children would be upon them any moment. Olive was loudly complaining of a dirty lace in one of her tennis shoes, blaming Nico for pinching her pristine, white one and replacing it with his. At any moment, they'd race into the kitchen, demanding adult mediation. Shauna asked, 'Why does it have to be a broken heart, Isabelle?'

Isabelle had chosen her words carefully. 'Laurent has not a good track record of long-term commitment. Oh, he has a kind nature, I am not saying he is a . . .' she fumbled for the word she wanted. 'What is that magnificent English term for bad men in *Bridget Jones's Diary* . . . ?'

'Um, philanderer?'

'No – "fuckwit". Shush, don't giggle, the children are coming. You see' – Isabelle spoke fast – 'Laurent's parents divorced when he was tiny and for years, his mother kept him away from his father and Chemignac. He wasn't able to return until his tenth birthday when he was at last able to express his feelings to his mother and gain her permission. I don't wish to criticise her, but she kept Laurent from his heritage and taught him that marriage is a battle-ground. He is marked by it, as that girl Rachel found out. You know he and she –' Shauna nodded, 'I know.'

'You had a happy childhood?'

'It was amazing. Perfect, till dad died.'

'A heart attack, your mother said.'

'Out of the blue, aged forty-three. It flattened Mum for a few years.'

'*Ah, pauvrette.* Perhaps *you* can teach Laurent what steady devotion is and give him a fresh perspective, but do not invest too much too soon. You have your career to think of.'

The children had rushed in just then, Olive pulling Nico's hair. 'Shoelace-gate' had escalated dangerously. Isabelle banged her cane on the floor to get their attention, then asked Shauna to kindly fetch a box from the dresser drawer. It contained a wad of white laces, which, Isabelle explained, she ordered every summer from a sports wholesaler. 'So there is no cause to steal each other's, you wicked savages!'

Chastened, the children replaced their laces then followed Shauna out to the car. That conversation with Isabelle had not been renewed.

So . . . another hot, August Sunday. Shauna desired Laurent more each day and knew he was becoming intrinsic to her happiness. Not a comfortable state for someone with aspirations to one day head a pharmaceutical research lab. When had she last belly-ached about losing that gilded position at Cademus? Or checked for a message from Mike Ladriss? And what about those notes she'd been so avidly writing up? These days, whenever she found herself at Monty's café, she ate cake and toyed with a crossword. Or smiled into space. Monty had even commented on it, 'Lost your mojo, love?'

'No,' she'd laughed. 'I seem to have found it.'

As for Laurent, he came to her each day with the same urgency and intensity, his frown-lines smoothing out whenever their paths crossed. They'd snatch hours together; horse riding early in the morning, or eating lunch in his apartment, listening to music. As a sweetener to the driving rock music he liked, he dug out his father's vintage LPs from the 1960s and 70s, and dusted off an antiquated gramophone. Often, they'd cook and eat listening to tracks by the Eagles, Johnny Hallyday, Sylvie Vartan. But their favourite time was night and moonlight.

She skirted the meadow, not wanting to flatten the grass so close to its mowing. Humming the riff from Guns N' Roses' "Paradise City" she followed the edge of the wood until she found herself on a patch of land she'd never seen before. As she'd not crossed any ditches or opened any gates, she assumed she was still within Chemignac's bounds. After following a winding brook for some minutes, she reached a meadow, low-lying and narrow, like an abandoned motorway. It was striped two shades of green and sang with the malty sweetness of new cut hay. The trill of larks proved it to be Laurent's land. Unlike many of his neighbours, he'd banned lark traps on his estate and these ground-nesting birds were colonising his meadows. It struck Shauna that she could have walked into any era of history. Not a modern landmark or building in sight. Finding an area of mossy green, she lay down, tucking the tartan rug under her head. She intended to meditate. To unlatch her mind from the intoxication of love and try to find a way forward that honoured her feelings and Laurent's while keeping her professional ambitions alive.

Sleep closed in on her fast. A sleep so deep, it sucked her from the earth into limitless space. Into another consciousness . . .

Chapter Twelve

Yvonne

Inside the Halifax bomber it was airless and clammy, the roar of engines scouring the insides of her ears. It couldn't be long, surely, until the pilot circled over the dropping point?

For over four hours, she'd perched on the edge of her seat, trussed so tightly in her harness that her shoulder blades felt pulled out of alignment. Beneath the man's camouflage jump-suit they'd issued her, she wore a brown check cotton skirt. It was tucked between her legs like a schoolboy's shorts. Beneath that, a rather seductive pair of Parisian silk knickers, but no girdle or stockings because nylon and silk was off the Frenchwoman's shopping list these days. Her ankle socks had been made in a Lyons hosiery factory before the war. The rest of her outfit consisted of a beige blouse, a knitted brown *gilet* and a tan, belted jacket, cut twelve inches longer than anyone was wearing in London. She hadn't worn so much brown since she'd played a woodland creature in a school performance of *Goldilocks and the Three Bears*. The jacket disguised the belt around her waist, concealing several thousand French francs, a number of forged ration books and clothing stamps, maps and some spare radio crystals. The crystals were for a wireless operator who was lying low in Bordeaux.

The heat inside the plane climbed until it was all she could do not to rip off her flying suit and helmet. She'd put her hair up in a bun and the grips were digging in. Glancing at her two SOE colleagues, Jean-Claude and Cyprien, she thought, *why is it that being female is always a handicap, whatever you're trying to do?* Jean-Claude, the oldest of the three of them, was asleep, his mouth open. Handsome, pouty Cyprien was staring down at his fingers. They were the fingers of a trained wireless operator. Once he'd been taken to his safe house, he'd transmit messages back to London. Messages she'd bring him. Until he got caught, that is. Wireless ops usually got caught, their signal giving away their locations. God, she thought to herself, what are we doing? Cyprien's lips were moving – reciting Shakespeare to himself? An actor before the war, Cyprien knew reams of it and claimed it calmed his mind. *Just don't quote any once we're on French soil.* She transmitted the thought and, to her fascination, Cyprien looked up and scowled.

She jiggled her helmet to relieve her scalp. If only they'd let her cut her hair short! But apparently, French women were wearing theirs longer now. Her handlers had tutted over its colour, too, muttering that she'd stand out among the dark-complexioned Dordogne population. She'd offered to dye it black and they'd looked at her as if she were mad. Did she not realise that luxuries such as hair colourant had vanished in France? What would she do if they couldn't extract her in a few weeks, as arranged, and her roots began to show through?

Their solution had been to give her a fake identity that fitted her complexion. She was no longer Antonia, a former teacher of French and Physical Education from the Derbyshire peaks. Until she returned to England she was Yvonne Rosel, born in Caen, Normandy. 'Lots of Normans are carrot tops,' her handler had explained.

'Titian-gold,' she'd corrected him coldly. Her rich hair had been an indivisible part of her personality since she'd been old enough to recognise herself in the mirror, and nobody was going to demean it with the word 'carrot'. Though right now, she'd have shaved it off if she could.

She hadn't noticed the sergeant going up front to speak to the pilot of the Halifax, but he must have done because he was suddenly yelling at them that they were over the town of Tulle, reducing height.

'Ten minutes, gentlemen and Miss.'

Yvonne's stomach responded with a shallow contraction. So. This was it, assuming no disasters or eleventh-hour changes of plan. How she regretted tucking into eggs, bacon, tomatoes and steak at lunchtime. *Feet together parallel to the ground,* she repeated, drumming the landing sequence into her brain, though quite honestly, if she hadn't learned how to parachute by now . . .

She was jumping in Cuban heeled lace-ups and before take-off, they'd bandaged her ankles tightly to keep the shoes on as she dropped. And to prevent her ankles breaking as she hit earth. To quell her rising fear, she patted the zip pockets of her jump-suit, checking papers, compass, torch and knife were still there. She bent her leg to ensure that the little spade was safely lodged against her calf.

That was for burying her parachute if the reception committee failed to show up. They'd better not fail. She went over the code phrase again that her French comrades would use to identify themselves: *Je préfère une alouette à un moineau. I prefer a lark to a sparrow.*

She took her place between Cyprien and Jean-Claude. Cyprien would go first with his radio set attached to his harness. The powers-that-be had decided that she, the lone female, should be sandwiched between resolute males. As if, by virtue of being a woman, she was the most likely to refuse to jump. Her bet was, if any of them funked it, it would be Cyprien.

'Five minutes, gentlemen and Miss.'

The dispatcher – the airman responsible for getting them out of the hatch, hurling them if need be – was performing a last-minute check on their harnesses and deployment bags. He attached the static lines that would open their 'chutes for them.

'*Au revoir, Antonia. Bonjour, Yvonne,*' she muttered. And then the hatch was open, icy air blustering in. Nothing beyond but blank darkness, until the plane began to turn and bank, and she saw a perfect half-moon. And far below, pin-point fires. She counted five, arranged in the shape of a capital 'L'. The drop zone. Her teeth slammed together with cold, because the temperature had suddenly plummeted from steam bath to icehouse.

The dispatcher threw out various packages with parachutes attached. These contained armaments for the Resistance circuit that operated around Garzenac. Sten guns, disassembled. Hundreds of rounds of ammunition, muzzle grease and a couple of Sten silencers. *Any moment . . .*

'I am Yvonne Rosel,' she murmured, 'Mademoiselle Yvonne Rosel.' Some four thousand feet below, the French *résistant* contact assigned to her was waiting. His code name was Écharde, which meant 'splinter', an amusing co-incidence since her real English surname was Thorne. Already, the dispatcher was clapping Cyprien on the shoulder, checking that his wireless set was secure in its pack. A moment later, he was gone. The hand came down on her shoulder and she thought—

Actually, no time to think. She jumped, with a piercing cry as her body drank in the freezing air. For a moment she was spread-eagled on her back like a frog dropped from a heron's beak.

The static line deployed and her 'chute flared open, halting her freefall. She was finally dangling upright in the nothingness, laughing. Laughing like the daredevil, fun-loving redhead everyone on her training course believed she was.

It was a pure, clear night and the terrain below began to make sense. Ponds and streams shone silver. Forest was easy to distinguish from fields. Grey stripes, like corduroy fabric, suggested vineyards. *Hmm, a glass of red would be just perfect*, she thought. Trifling thoughts fled as something sharp cut behind her back. That was when she realised that sparks were flashing far below, spitting like a welder's torch. Anti-aircraft fire? *They're firing at the Halifax,* she thought. *Or are they firing at us?* In that moment she knew – with absolute certainty – they'd been betrayed. She was dropping into an ambush.

Suddenly, the ground was coming up fast and she was in the blind zone, where the ground blots out all light. *Feet together, parallel.* She hit the earth and rolled, letting the movement absorb the energy of her landing. And it was a textbook landing, though bruising because the little spade dug into her shin. Ignoring the pain, she scrambled up, registering the fact that she'd come down in a dry meadow. And into a full-scale battle. *Where was the reception committee? Where was Écharde?*

She launched into the routine she'd practiced,

releasing the straps of her parachute, bundling it up. She saw Jean-Claude land and roll, his canopy sinking over him like a jellyfish. But she didn't see him get up, and when she called to him, she got the worryingly high-pitched reply, 'I'm stuck!' *And where was Cyprien?* Where the bloody hell was their welcoming committee? The darkness was alive with barking machine guns, their muzzle flares illuminating white faces and metal helmets. Answering fire came from the other side of the field.

Abandoning her parachute, she ran, bent double, and tripped headlong over something on the ground. Getting to her feet, she discovered she'd fallen over a radio backpack . . . Cyprien still attached to it. Putting an arm under his shoulders, she lifted him from the waist and loosened the straps that tethered him. He whimpered. His upper torso was blood-soaked. *What the devil was she going to do now?* Carry him on her back? Where to?

And then a hand clapped down on *her*

shoulder. 'Hsst! Yvonne?'

She squirmed round to find a man crouching just behind her. *Écharde?* His beret was pulled low, his face pasted in mud or coal dust. Was that the flash of teeth? He could smile? 'Identify yourself,' she commanded angrily.

'*Je préfère une alouette à un moineau.* Your welcoming committee. Bonjour, Madame.'

'About blasted time. There's an injured man here and poor old Jean-Claude is stranded somewhere.' She pointed. 'He's over there.'

The man gave orders in rapid French, and several dark figures slipped away towards the gunfire. He'd spoken in heavy dialect, so she supposed he was a farmer or a *vigneron*, a wine grower. Agriculturist by day, enemy of the German occupiers by night. More appreciative of the risk he was taking, she softened her voice. 'Are we betrayed?'

'Yes, and surrounded on three sides, but

we're holding the ground nearest the forest.' A thin moustache defined his smile. The humour in his voice even as he described their danger suggested someone who enjoyed a fight and knew how to win.

She answered in kind. 'I don't intend to perish on my first night here, you know.'

'Indeed, I would not allow it, Madame. What would you think of us? It is the *Milice* firing on us, incidentally. French police collaborators.' His tone curled with scorn. 'My men are thinning them out. So, ready to run?'

'Of course. Help Cyprien, I'll bring his wireless set.'

'On three, pelt towards the trees. If we split up, hide. Stay hidden all day, until darkness returns, then make your way to Chemignac. Ready? One, two—'

'Hang on. Chemignac?' During those instructions, her companion's accent had changed to one she was familiar with from her time in Paris, studying at the Sorbonne University.

'My home, Madame.'

'Are you the Comte de Chemignac?'

She got no answer. The outline of his features
beneath the beret suggested strength and mature
discretion. Of course he would not say who he was
in ordinary life, and she should not ask. But
something overrode the rules that had been
drummed into her. 'Tell me, will you! Are you the
Comte de Chemignac?'

'I am.'

'You're Écharde?' Was the splinter about to
meet the thorn?

Had the splinter met the thorn?
Shauna opened her eyes, then shut them quickly
against astringent sunshine. Morning had blossomed
while she slept. While she dreamed. She lifted
herself on her elbow, blinking. 'It's you!'

Laurent agreed that it was him. '*Bonjour, mon ange.* You were talking in your sleep, of Écharde. That was the code name my grandfather used when he was in the Resistance. How do you know it?'

'Mm? It popped into my dream. How long have you been watching me?'

'A few moments. I wasn't sure if you were in conversation with me or somebody else.'

She screwed up her face. 'So – does that mean you're the Comte de Chemignac too?'

'Unfortunately, yes.' A distance away, church bells tolled for mass. Laurent was on one knee beside her, a Basque beret pulled low on his brow. His expression was grave.

'You didn't tell me.'

'I don't tell everybody. Certainly, I don't introduce myself that way.'

'I'm not everybody, Laurent.'

He brushed that aside. 'You named other

names in your dream. Can you remember?'

'I was in a plane, padded up like the Michelin Man and sick as a dog. I had to jump. I'd trained for it and there were two men jumping with me . . .' The dream lingered, sharp as a just-watched movie. 'Cyprien and Jean-Claude. Not their real names, though. Those were code names too. Leaping out was a relief because I was free of the horrible, rattling noise and my back stopped hurting. Oh, and the moon looked wonderful. Only, later, I realised people were firing at us from the ground.' She shut her eyes again, experiencing the weightlessness of being suspended under a canopy. 'I thought I'd be shot to ribbons and was furious more than frightened because it meant the Resistance had cocked up. Or some bastard had betrayed us. I was helpless as a trussed chicken . . .' She sat up. 'What's that noise?'

It was the horse, Héron. He was a few paces away, tearing greedily at the grass with big, soft lips. His bridle was knotted around his neck. 'Did you come to find me?'

'We often gallop this field, Héron and I. He saw you and shied. I thought an elf had landed from heaven, or an angel in rubber boots.' Laurent got to his feet and reached out to haul her up.

'Elves don't descend from heaven. They're earth-bound.' Unlike her, it seemed. She'd *been* Yvonne, her shoulders in spasm because of over-tightened parachute straps. She'd gagged inside that shuddering fuselage, while envying Jean-Claude's ability to sleep through it all. Real, visceral emotions. Floating downward, feeling she could catch a corner of the moon . . . then the sting of bullets, scarily close. Where had it all come from? She'd never been a fan of spy stories or war films. 'Figments of a febrile imagination,' she said, more to convince herself than Laurent. Then she admitted, 'In that plane, I had intense feelings for the men I was jumping with. Not love. I admired Jean-Claude, and also pitied him because I knew that if he was ever cornered by the enemy, he'd be lousy at running or fighting back. Cyprien – well, he was a pain in the backside. A poseur who objected to being sent on a mission with a veteran and a mere woman. But, really, he was only a kid . . .'

'What makes you say that Cyprien was young and Jean-Claude, old?' Laurent asked. 'How do you know?'

'Because it was *my* dream. I'm allowed to make up the characters.' She tilted her head back and cupped his face. A face as exquisite as the carved heads in the nave of Chemignac's church. 'Actually, "old" is pushing it. Jean-Claude was only in his fifties, but that's late in the day to be—' she'd been about to say 'Throwing yourself out of Halifax bombers' when the absurdity of the detail hit her. Why a Halifax? Actually, what the heck was a Halifax, apart from being a town fifty miles from her native Sheffield? 'Don't look at me like that.'

Laurent's face tightened, pallor undermining his tan. He said, 'When will you accept the reality of these experiences, Shauna?'

'I won't, because they're not real. I've already confessed, I'm going a little bit crazy because I'm taking a break after five years of solid slog, not to mention a couple of major emotional upsets.'

'In the forest, you discovered the memorial to the men of the Garzenac, the murdered ones.'

'I told you I did.'

'And saw that two of the names were English.'

'Maurice Barnsley, George Sturridge.'

'Whose code names were Cyprien and Jean-Claude.' He ignored her intake of breath. 'They were dropped into this meadow in July, 1943, only just escaping an ambush that awaited them. Cyprien, who was twenty-one, suffered a bullet injury. Jean-Claude was unharmed but for a wrenched ankle.

They were parachuted in to aid the Resistance circuit of which my grandfather was a leading member. My grandfather - *Écharde*.'

'A thorn in Yvonne's side,' Shauna added, without thinking.

'Perhaps. Cyprien was a pianist.'

'He wasn't, he was an actor. An egotist. Heart-rending profile, middling talent.'

'Why has your voice changed?' Laurent narrowed his eyes when she denied it, then explained, 'Radio operators were called 'Pianists'. Because of their fast fingering. Jean-Claude was a talented photographer. His role was to take pictures along the Bordeaux to Limoges railway line, its depots and tunnels. Nobody knows why, though it was probably to aid the saboteurs that SOE intended to send in later. The men lasted two days before being murdered in our forest. How do you know their names, Shauna?'

'I don't.' Ice entered her blood. The answer

that sprung to mind was irrational.

His gaze dug deep into hers. 'Perhaps you read their story before you came here?'

'That would explain it.' Though, she had to admit, this region of France had simply not figured in her life before this summer. 'I could be experiencing what they call "recovered memory". Mum or dad might have told me stories of their time here when I was little.'

Laurent made a doubtful movement of the lips. 'The story of Chemignac's resistance was buried after the war. The memorial was only put up fifteen years ago, thanks to a local man. You know him I think. Monty Watson.'

'Monty who runs the internet café?'

'He came here in the '80s to renovate a farm on the other side of the hill.' Laurent jerked his thumb towards the rising land behind the château. 'He became obsessed with the story of Garzenac's resistance. He interviewed all the old folk in the surrounding villages, digging out those who remembered the war years. A slow job, gaining their trust. He tried once with oncle Albert.' Laurent gave a sardonic laugh. 'From eye-witness accounts and reports drawn from local archives, Monty pieced together how the victims died, but he never nailed exactly why. Chemignac finally honoured its heroes, but Monty couldn't get his memorial placed in the square at Garzenac. It had to be the forest or nowhere.'

'He didn't know why?' Shauna knew. 'They dropped out of the sky into blazing machine gun fire. Which means that somebody informed on them. Somebody living right here betrayed them.'

Laurent held her gaze. 'Turn over a stone, Shauna, and you usually find something unpleasant. Vital pieces of the story are missing. People knew there was SOE involvement, but nobody could recall who the Englishmen were until Monty Watson got access to documents released by the

British Ministry of Defence. That was ten years ago, in 1993. Fifty years after their deaths! Did you not notice that Barnsley and Sturridge's names were carved later than the others'? Their chisel marks are much clearer.'

She hadn't noticed, having read the inscription in syrupy, pre-storm light. She did the maths. 'My dad had been dead for over two years by 1993, so he couldn't have told me about the men.' Nor could her mother who had been nowhere near London – or indeed France - these last twenty years. Shauna still resisted Laurent's implication that she was somehow downloading supernatural knowledge. There had to be a sane explanation. Ah, she had it! 'Isabelle and my mother have been writing to each other for years. I'm sure your grandfather's memorial would have been a huge event to Isabelle. She told mum, mum told me and I filed the memory.'

Laurent shook his head. 'Isabelle never

speaks of what happened to her father. He brought those British agents back to Chemignac and it was his last action. It was his death. Isabelle was only eight years old. Can you imagine knowing your papa had gone out into the darkness, watching for him day after day, believing he would come back, only to hear adults whispering that he had been shot? She believes she heard it happen. She was being put to bed by her nursemaid, and they heard distant machine gun fire. She remembers scrambling to the window, seeing the sky lit by a summer moon. Tante Isabelle hates the month of July. She lives through her sadness every year, drawn back here, but she rarely speaks of it.'

'The roses at the memorial . . . "*Never forgive, never forget*".'

'Not hers. She could not walk so far. She marks the anniversary in her own way. Alone.'

'She had a migraine . . . well, she said she did.' Shauna cast her mind back to the linen piled in the kitchen on July thirteenth. Had Isabelle been keeping her mind off her memories? Someone had later thrown the cloths onto the floor, as if in disgust or despair. There were hidden currents in this place, and within this family. Arriving from Garzenac in the pony trap, Shauna had imagined herself crossing an invisible boundary, entering an unreal landscape. She'd blamed it on dehydration.

It *had* been dehydration. 'I don't know how I came up with Cyprien and Jean-Claude - Barnsley and Sturridge, call them what you will . . . wait a minute. Albert was at home with his brother in 1943. He was too young to go into the army at the start of the war. That's what Isabelle told me.'

Laurent nodded. 'He didn't join up.'

'Then perhaps he mumbles about the past, and I overheard him.'

With a shrug, Laurent strode to Héron. The horse lifted its head, still chewing grass. Laurent untied the reins, turned and said in a voice throbbing with vexation, 'You can explain away a dream, and even a girl at a blocked-up window.'

'I'm convinced now there was no girl.'

'But you cannot unsay those names. Nor can you explain why you have my family's crest tattooed on to your shoulder.'

'I told you that was for dad—'

'And tell me why, when you put on another woman's dress, you slid into a trance?'   'Stress. Heat. Inhaling patchouli vapours.'

Giving a snort, he vaulted onto the horse's back and set off at a trot.   'Anyway, what's the dress got to do with anything?' Shauna shouted after him. When he replied with a dismissive wave, she grabbed her blanket and ran after him. This, she supposed, was their first quarrel. Trust her to pick a man who had a horse. Forget slamming doors. This man could gallop off, while pelting her with clods.

She panted in pursuit, resenting Héron's effortless stride, wishing she'd chosen different footwear. Olive was a well-grown girl and her boots were a size too big for Shauna. 'Bad science, Laurent de Chemignac!' she yelled, hoping to shame him into slowing up. 'A few unrelated events do not constitute a hypothesis. Rational people do not form conclusions then scrabble around for evidence. Ouch, damn it!' She'd stepped in a rut, saving herself with an ungainly lurch. At least, hearing her cry out, Laurent slowed Héron to a jog. Seeing a chance of catching up, Shauna ran faster. 'You are theorising that the past has returned to haunt us and that I'm some kind of conduit. A channel for extinct people and events' – she gasped for breath – 'for which the technical term is "bollocks".'

Shauna trod on the toe of her left wellington boot and upended herself. Flat on her stomach, she stared up as Laurent pulled Héron to a stop and wheeled him around. Alarming – the horse looked huge from this perspective. Héron came alongside her with a decent margin of safety. Laurent looked very severe, the beret accentuating the hollows of his face. He'd obviously skipped his morning shave and a night's hair growth showed her what he'd look like if he ever decided to grow a moustache.

When he leaned down to offer his hand, she took it, heaving herself upright. Instinctively knowing a horse that could be trusted, she leaned against Héron's sturdy shoulder. She took the same risk with Laurent, placing a hand on his knee. 'Running away solves nothing, you know.'

'Shauna, why won't you admit that something strange is happening? To both of us.'

She laid her cheek on his thigh and felt the involuntary flex of his muscle. Of course, there might be a simple way to shift his mind from this obsession. She slid her hand higher, to his belt buckle, and heard his soft, surprised gasp. See? Easy to change the subject. She crooked her fingers over the rim of his belt, finding a gap between his shirt buttons, skimming his belly. His hand came down hard on hers. 'Look at me.'

Her eyes jumped to his. 'Laurent?' His voice had gained a rasp, as it had in the tower room when he stopped her returning to the violet dress. It wasn't Laurent looking down at her. It was a man like Laurent, but older. Same deep eyes, but the irises were flattened with anguish. A trick of shadow, or did he sport a thin moustache on his upper lip?

'Why did you do it, Yvonne?'

'I don't know! It was so beautiful.' The words jerked from Shauna's mouth, all crisp consonants and rounded vowels. 'I didn't mean any harm. Forgive me.' Shauna jumped away, making the horse start with surprise. She put her hands to her head. 'What's happening? What's the matter with us?'

Laurent's voice reached her, urgent, commanding. 'Say what's in your mind, right now. Just speak whatever comes.'

In that out-dated BBC voice, she answered, 'Your friend Monty needs to get his chisel out again. There weren't just two British SOE agents, there were three. Why is it that the girls always get forgotten?'

Part Three

September

Chapter Thirteen

The children went home to Paris – back to school, back to family life – and the atmosphere at Isabelle's changed. Rooms felt bigger with an echo to them, as if the château walls had expressed a breath. Normality returned, though, when Louette swept back like a bracing sea wind. With no freelance work currently, and the children in her husband's care, Isabelle's daughter threw her energy into a programme of cleaning and cupboard-emptying. Distressed, Isabelle confided to Shauna, 'I hoped she'd stay in Paris. Isn't that awful, to wish my daughter were not here? Why has she come back?'

Shauna answered with what she believed was the truth. 'She's concerned about you and this is her way of showing it.'

'But I have you, and Audrey, too. I don't need a bossy daughter to organise me! I keep catching Louette taking precious things to the dustbin. She calls them "rubbish" because she likes everything to be chi-chi and clean. "Is this what *my* fate will be in a few years' time?" I ask her. She's getting rid of my stuff because she's certain I'll die soon.'

'I'm sure she isn't.' But Isabelle wasn't convinced, and for the next couple of days, Shauna kept discreet tabs on Louette Barends. She was soon satisfied that Louette's purpose in returning to Chemignac was an innocent one. Beneath the bossy exterior lay a childlike craving to be useful and to be rewarded with praise. It pained Shauna to see how Louette would draw her mother's attention to some busy re-organising she'd done, only to be told that she needn't have bothered. That 'As soon as she'd gone back to Paris', Isabelle would 'put it all back in its place again.'

Within three days, things reached a head. The catalyst was Isabelle's fine, antique dining table. Louette had it carried out to a barn, suitably wrapped in dust sheets, and Isabelle's bed brought downstairs to take its place. Blocking her mother's protest with a raised hand, Louette said, 'I've seen you hauling yourself upstairs at night, *maman*, hanging on to the handrail. Why shouldn't you sleep in the dining room for the few weeks you'll be here? You always eat in the kitchen, after all.' Ignoring Isabelle's reply that this was *her* home and she'd choose where to eat, Louette gave way to frustration.

'I'm doing my best, can't you see? Don't become one of those elderly people who refuse every practical offer of help.' She turned to Shauna, seeking back-up, but Shauna had no intention of being sucked in. Laurent, super-sensitive to the currents within his family, had already warned her, 'Don't become the thing that gets squashed between a rock and a hard place. Those two have to sort out their relationship. They've been battling for years.'

Shauna's au pair duties had ended with the children's departure, but Louette once again urged her to stay. 'This isn't working. *Maman* needs help, but I only seem to make angry and while I'm here, I'm neglecting Hubert and the children. I hate leaving my husband in sole charge. He forgets to pick them up from school, and they end up going places with the wrong books or the wrong kit. One day, Olive will find herself playing tennis with her violin.' Louette laughed, but Shauna heard tears in her voice.

Having already agreed to remain until harvest, Shauna now committed herself to staying into October. It didn't take much arm-twisting, to be fair. She wanted to be where Laurent was. Isabelle beamed when she was given the news. 'Laurent will be happy, so I am happy. Something tells me this year will be memorable for Chemignac.'

Late morning, Saturday, September 6th, Shauna and Laurent were huddled over the lab bench, shoulders fused, hair touching. They'd gathered sample grapes from every *parcelle* and had spent the last two hours analysing them for sugar content and acid levels. They were now comparing their findings against the previous year's results. Laurent had been taught a rule of thumb while learning his trade in California. 'If weight decreases sharply while sugar-volume increases, dehydration has started. Get picking.' They read the figures out to each other, and Shauna scribbled sums on paper. The grapes had ripened fast thanks to the searing July and August heat, and were bursting with sugar . . . and lots of sunshine-induced sugar often translated into an exceptional vintage. 'Isabelle predicts a good year,' she said.

'If the air stays dry, it might be my best yet,' Laurent agreed. 'I think we'll be picking the Sauvignon Blanc in five or six days . . .' adding, 'unless it rains, or there's a cold snap.'

'Or your pickers fail to turn up.'

'They'll come.' Laurent slung his arm around her waist. 'And if they don't, you and I will pick together, with extra hands from the village. Perhaps now you feel Chemignac has a claim on you?'

'No – but its owner has.' She turned to him, drawing him into a kiss that ended only when they heard a grumbling cough on the other side of the door, a warning that someone was about to join them.

A moment later, the door was rammed open and Albert hobbled over the threshold. Seeing Shauna, his mouth sunk, his moustache folding in the middle like a wishbone.

Shauna was proud of her cheerful, 'Good

afternoon, Monsieur de Chemignac!'

Albert's gaze fell on the beakers and phials on the bench. 'Bah! Why do you spend so much time here when it is the vines that need your attention?'

Brushing away the reproach, Laurent explained the various pieces of equipment. 'We're recording mallic and tartaric levels versus sugar, versus weight. To gauge the perfect moment to begin harvesting.'

'Pfah!' Albert put a black grape into his mouth. His moustache wiggled as he chewed. 'Five days to go for this one.'

'That's what we thought.' Laurent's gesture included Shauna.

Albert's scowl deepened. He put out his tongue and tapped it. 'This is what tells you when a grape is ready, boy. It comes free and it lasts a lifetime.' He limped to the door, giving the impression that he'd have flounced away, had his hip joints allowed it. But he paused, saying to Laurent, 'I told Louette not to go into the tower. Yet as I came past, I saw her shaking a feather duster out of the window. Why must she?'

Laurent shrugged. 'It's her last chance to assault the cobwebs. She's leaving in a day or two.'

Albert caught Shauna's eye for the first time since their encounter, ten weeks ago, at his front door. 'Louette Barends has no business poking around in affairs that ended before she was born. Make her see it.'

Astonished at being appealed to, Shauna stammered, 'It's not my business, Monsieur.'

'Try. It upsets Isabelle.'

And you even more. Shauna nodded. 'I'll do my best.'

Albert's reply was a grunt and a slammed door.

Laurent groaned. 'I tried to work with him after my father died, making him a director, but he used his role to block every tiny change and improvement, until I was ready to sell Chemignac to strangers just to get away. He behaves as if everything here is his personal property, yet thanks to him, we nearly lost everything.'

'He has a point, though.'

Laurent looked at her sharply.

She put out her tongue. 'Free and lasts a lifetime.'

He shook his head, then indicated the charts on the bench. 'Maybe Albert's right. Science is vanity, and what I'm lacking is experience. After all, he's been producing wine for sixty years.'

'Hit-and-miss table wine that was fine in the 1970s when France had virtually no competitors. But the market's moved on.'

He nodded. 'The future is quality.'

So . . .' she pinned the graph showing the upward curve in sugar levels of red Cabernet Sauvignon grapes alongside the preceding week's graphs. 'Instead of spending sixty years amassing the know-how, you'll get there in ten because you can match your instincts against hard data.'

He gave her a hooded look. 'You know, when you talk sexy like that, all I want to do is drag you to my bed.'

The thought of him doing that, all the way up the track under the astonished eyes of the workers and Albert, made her laugh. He joined in and then they were setting each other off until they were sharing hiccups. They did not notice the door open. Nor did they see Rachel Moorcroft framed there, observing them with resentful bewilderment before quietly closing the door again.

When they finally recovered, Laurent said, 'Would you come into Garzenac with me later? I'm meeting a supplier at the station.'

She jumped at the chance. Anything to distract Laurent from his anxieties. Responsibility to the people he employed weighed heavy on him, as did maintaining a family wine-growing tradition going back for over a century. Would the 2003 vintage have the wine critics raving? Or would Laurent end up with thousands of litres of unremarkable plonk to sell next year? 'Always one eye on the grapes, the other on the weather; it's enough to make a man cross-eyed,' was how Isabelle phrased it. Enough to make a man nervy and over-imaginative. Shauna intended to help Laurent in every practical way, including steering him away from the unsolvable mystery of Yvonne and her fellow Resistance fighters. Capable and loving as he was, Laurent had a vulnerable side. He needed protection – though from what, she wasn't entirely sure.

They took the 2CV for the drive into town, putting the roof down. Laurent always met delivery trucks, either collecting packages from them or escorting them back to Chemignac. Otherwise, their drivers got lost in the unmarked lanes around the winery. More than one lorry had trundled into the village's medieval hub only to get wedged between the church wall and the war memorial. One driver had made it to Chemignac, only to get his rig jammed under the gatehouse, and because that section of the château was a scheduled monument, they'd had to dismantle the trailer from the inside, using chainsaws. It was less stressful to simply meet deliveries in town.

They were meeting todays' consignment at four, but it was a few minutes short of two in the afternoon when Laurent parked a few metres down the hill from the internet café. Time for lunch, he said, and for some research. They were going to Monty's to run a search on Yvonne. No interruptions and no vineyard tasks hanging over their heads.

'I like the sound of lunch. Not sure about the

rest,' Shauna grumbled. So much for steering him away from his fixation.

He didn't answer, just held out his hand to her. A moment later, he was striding up the hill to the café, his long legs forcing her to run.

Monty's place was fuller than she'd ever seen it before. A group of young men had pulled tables together, creating a noisy island in the middle of the floor. They were barracking one of their number as he tapped away at a laptop. Shauna couldn't quite work out what language they were speaking until one of them recognised Laurent and called out 'Olá!' Spanish, she presumed.

Laurent stopped, and enthusiastic hand-shaking and shoulder slapping followed.

'They're here for the harvest,' he said, after they'd secured themselves a laptop and found a quiet table outside, beneath the courtyard pergola.

'The same families come year on year and you get to know them. We get a real international brigade. Australians, New Zealanders, Moroccans and some Spaniards.'

'I thought *they* were Spanish.'

'Portuguese. The man I was speaking to, Adão, has come to Chemignac every September since I took over. He wanted to know if Rachel was working for me still.'

'Hm. I thought I heard her name mentioned.' Shauna disguised her distrust by picking up the menu, burying her face in it. 'Shall I ask for the house special?'

'Yes, you choose.'

She went back inside to order two salads with warm Cabécou goat's cheese and a savoury walnut tart, bringing back bottled water and a half carafe of wine. She found Laurent clicking his knuckles impatiently while the laptop's modem buzzed and whistled. She pulled a chair up next to him. 'I love that noise. It makes me feel a computer is really making an effort for me! I was sad when my university went wireless last year.'

Once he was online, Laurent typed the words 'Yvonne, SOE, France, 1943' into a search engine. He scrolled down a long list of articles until he found a piece about a British agent called Yvonne Rudellat. A closer reading revealed this Yvonne to be a much older agent, captured in northern France, who died in Bergen-Belsen concentration camp in 1944. Typing in 'Yvonne, Chemignac, Sturridge, Barnsley' brought up an article by Monty Watson, which attempted to shed light on the Chemignac forest execution. 'Five men, pierced by German bullets, their bodies strewn about a peaceful clearing,' read the introduction. Other sites mentioned the same names, but as Laurent read them out, it became clear that they were simply parroting Monty's research. Nowhere was there a mention of a female SOE agent in connection with

Chemignac.

'If Monty couldn't find Yvonne, what makes you think we can?' Shauna poured water and a glass of wine each. 'Chances are she got killed too, or was caught and deported. I mean, next to being a fighter pilot, being an SOE agent in occupied territory was about the shortest-lived wartime occupation going. Or perhaps there wasn't an Yvonne at all.'

'There was,' Laurent said with absolute assurance. 'My father spoke of her – from hearsay only, as he was a child of three in '43 – but Isabelle told him a little about her. "A flame-haired English girl whom father hid from the Germans, in the tower."'

'Romantic. Very.' Shauna's tone was flat. Sorrow haunted the tower room. Like a glance into your own grave, it spoke of unavoidable doom.

'And there's another proof – Albert.'

'You said he denied knowing anything about Yvonne.'

'Exactly. My uncle proves her existence by refuting it. I mean, if somebody doesn't exist, why insist upon it? He shouts, "There was no Yvonne" until he's had a bottle of wine. Then he rants, "That Englishwoman. That *rouquine*."'

'"*Rouquine*?"' she prompted.

Laurent ruffled her hair. 'Like you.'

'Ah. The curse of the red. Maybe the next time he's halfway into a bottle, I'll dress up in 1940s clothes and scare the truth out of him. Or perhaps we should just ask Isabelle. She knows far more than she's told us.' Shauna wasn't sure what prompted her to say that. It just felt true.

Monty arrived with their food. In his late forties, hair tied back in a scrappy ponytail and a faded t-shirt advertising the tour dates of a 1970s heavy metal band, he projected the image of a retired rocker who had somehow ended up running an internet café. Which, by his own admission, summed him up. Pulling up a chair, he began chatting in English, asking Laurent about the prospects for this year's harvest, and Shauna about her job-hunting.

'Still sore about losing out to that posh totty?'

It took a moment for her to get his meaning. 'You mean Allegra Boncasson? Er, no, not really.' It all seemed like ancient history, her bitterness at being replaced at Cademus by a leggier science grad. Laurent looked up from the laptop.

'What's this? Who is Cademus?'

'They're a European pharma company, trail-blazing new cancer treatments,' she told him. 'I was going to be on a project isolating antioxidants in berries - including grape skins, ironically.'

'And Chemignac is keeping you from this?' Laurent looked wounded.

'I didn't get the job and actually . . .' she gave her feelings a quick temperature check, 'I'm not that bothered.' *How not bothered, exactly?* she wondered. She was in love, but off the career ladder. Was that OK?

Monty changed the subject by asking Shauna about her home town. Originally from Kent, he'd knocked around Sheffield for a couple of years, he told her, at drama school. Only, he'd dropped out before his third year.

'To be an actor or not to be an actor, that was the question,' he said in a plummy, stage voice. He rolled a cigarette but didn't light it, having established at their first meeting that Shauna detested smoking. ''Fraid the family acting dynasty ended with me. From somewhere I inherited stage fright.' His eyes crinkled at some unpleasant memory. 'Dropped out and became a roadie with a rock band. I spent the next twenty years becoming intimate with the A1, the M1 and all major roads in between.'

Out of nowhere, Shauna said, 'Monty's not your real name.'

'Right. It's Maurice. Try having that in the early '60s. I'd tell the other kids at school it was "Morris" to rhyme with "Horace", and they'd still call me "*Maureece*".'

'Because you're part French.'

'Well spotted. Half French, half English.'

'You're the SOE agent Maurice Barnsley's . . . ?'

'Nephew. He was my darling mum's older brother. So, Miss Marple, tell me why I washed up in this place?'

'Closure. You came to investigate Barnsley's death.'

Monty shrugged. 'My mum needed to know what happened. She and her brother were born in Calais, but they moved to the port of Dover when their mother got married for a second time to an English sailor. When war started, my uncle Maurice was recruited by the SOE because he'd kept up his French. Not because he was a trained soldier or a seasoned spy, but because he could pass for French in France. They dropped him out of a bloody plane into God knows what. Twenty-one years old, beaten with the butt-end of a gun and shot to—' he stopped. Whether to spare Shauna or himself, she couldn't tell. 'I wanted to find out more. But, hey, I liked this place so much, I stayed.'

Laurent, who had followed the exchange in silence, said, 'You have put down roots here, but you still don't really know *why* Maurice Barnsley died. Only how.'

'True enough. I'm hanging on for the last piece of the jigsaw. Too late for my old mum, she passed away last year.' Monty reached for the empty wine carafe. 'I still need to know how he and the others ended up in Chemignac forest, surrounded by Gestapo.' He pushed back his chair as Laurent powered down the laptop and closed its lid.

Laurent said, 'They were betrayed, twice. On arrival, by an informant, possibly one within the

Resistance circuit. They got away that time and were spirited into hiding by my grandfather. They hardly had time to get their bearings before they were sold out to the Gestapo. Same informant, or a different one? Answer that and you have the missing piece of your jigsaw.'

'One of them, at any rate.' Monty tucked the laptop under his arm. 'I'll leave you to finish your lunch. Give me a shout if you need a refill.' He stopped, a foot each side of the threshold. 'When I interviewed Monsieur Albert de Chemignac, he told me to get lost. *Casse-toi!* But as I was leaving, he shouted after me that "It was a girl that did it". A redheaded female who couldn't keep her hands off—'

'My grandfather?' Laurent supplied.

'Off the "Gown of Thorns". Those were his words. A girl did it. *Cherchez la femme.*' Monty gave Shauna a wink.

She took Monty's chair so she could face

Laurent. For a moment, she struggled with the desire to up-end their table and send their lunch crashing on to the paving slabs. Laurent saw it coming and grabbed the table's rim firmly. His cough of warning brought her back to herself, though her voice throbbed as she cried, 'It damn well wasn't Yvonne. I'll prove it!'

'Good luck.' Monty Watson had not moved from the doorway. 'But you won't find Yvonne online, or in any archive. I've been searching for five years, right? I found documents in London listing her as one of three agents dropped into Chemignac on July eleventh, 1943. But after that – alakazam!' Monty flourished an imaginary wand. 'Vanished.'

And who could blame her, Shauna thought as Monty sloped off. *I'd vanish if the world blamed me for sending five men to a horrible death.* Sighing, she dropped her forehead onto her hands.

'Shauna?'

'Monty can't find Yvonne because he's looking in the wrong place.'

'And where is the right place?'

Shauna raised her head and looked around to check that Monty really had gone. 'Chemignac, of course.'

'Go on.' But Laurent's mobile phone rang and he answered it, his voice changing from mildly impatient to anxious. 'All right, tante Isabelle. Yes, yes. She'll come home right away. Yes – I mean it. She's on her way.'

'What's the matter?'

'You must drive home. I'll get a lift back with the delivery van.' Louette's cleaning spree had reached the wardrobe in the tower room, he explained. 'She's brought all the dresses down, accusing her mother of storing them badly. The only way to preserve them, Louette says, is to donate them to a museum. She knows the curator of a costume gallery – well, she knows everybody!

Albert is backing Louette because he wants the dresses gone. Isabelle is distraught. Please go and help.'

'I'm not family! It's not for me to decide.'

He looked at her, hurt, then took her hands in a grip too tight for comfort. 'What are you saying, "not family"? Shauna, if you want to leave Chemignac and me, then say. I would never hold you back from your career – I hate men who do that! What you were saying to Monty about medical research, well, that's more important than anything I can offer. Just know that you are everything to me. But if your future is not here, if you're looking elsewhere,' he gave a lost shrug, 'please say so.'

Emotion sped through her, but she chose not to deepen the conversation right now. Let them return to it later, in the moonlight, in private. Then she'd let him know exactly how she wanted her future to look. Reaching for her bag, she said briskly, 'If Louette intends to have her own way, she's unlikely to listen to me.'

Laurent shook his head. 'You don't understand – I want Louette to take those dresses, the Gown of Thorns most of all. I'm on her side and – for once – Albert's. You knew in the tower room that something about that dress horrifies me. It infects our family. It rips us apart. Isabelle won't let it go, but she might if you add your voice.'

Shauna spread her hands hopelessly. 'It's a purple frock. Gorgeous and no doubt valuable. But only a dress.'

'Not "only".' Laurent briefly closed his eyes, then opened them again with all uncertainty erased. 'You are either our salvation or our nemesis, Shauna Vincent. You are the only person in three generations to wear the Gown of Thorns and come to no harm from it. I am putting my money on salvation. Please – go to Chemignac.'

Chapter Fourteen

As Shauna drove out of Garzenac, stalling several times as she gained familiarity with the 2CV's dashboard gear stick, Louette Barends regarded herself in her full-length bedroom mirror. She skimmed her figure in self-loathing. The spreading waistline and heavy breasts she disguised with well-cut jackets and tunics were mercilessly revealed by the Gown of Thorns. It hugged her without compassion.

Really, it was an insult to wear it. Whatever mystical name they gave it within the family should not obscure the fact that it was a rare, genuine, Delphos gown by Fortuny. It deserved a beautiful form to show it off. Curvy little Shauna would look delightful in it, and the cold-eyed queen bee who tended the horses would be transformed by it. One day, it might even suit Olive . . .

'No. Never,' Louette shouted down at the dress. 'You won't poison another generation.'

Some ten days ago on the night of the August full moon, Louette had crept into the tower bedroom on naked feet. Like an alcoholic breaking a pledge of sobriety, she'd rifled the wardrobe, wrinkling her nose at the grassy-musty scent. Every time she came to Chemignac, she sprayed patchouli vapour over the dresses to keep the moths away. In the darkness, she'd buried her face in silken pleats, reacquainting herself with the coveted, terrifying Gown of Thorns.

This morning, spurred on by her imminent departure, she'd emptied the tower wardrobe of its contents. It had taken three trips up and down to collect them all, and Audrey, who'd come into the kitchen to soak some towels, had caught her at it. Audrey had alerted *maman* who in turn had indulged in histrionics before phoning Laurent and summoning Shauna home to act as intermediary.

Intermediary to what, though? The collection of wondrous garments draped across Louette's bed was not Isabelle's. They were family treasures, and so just as much Louette's as anybody's. Could *maman* even be trusted with them? Isabelle had a poor track record when it came to conserving couture items.

Just as she, Louette, had emptied the wardrobe in the tower, *maman* used to empty her own wardrobes in the Paris house. She'd do it in advance of a soirée or a diplomatic reception, a gown at a time. 'This one? Or this one?' She'd lay them out on her huge, white bed, and stare at them as if they bored and disgusted her. 'Teal or gold? Sage or ivory? Which would you choose, Louette?' That was when Isabelle still had her dresses made for her by the best Paris salons. Louette would try desperately to predict her mother's mood, to make a selection that would earn her a kiss. Gawky even as a child, she'd *so* envied her mother's whip-thin figure, the perfect armature for every style of fashion. It wasn't right, was it, for a little girl to judge herself against her mother?

After papa died, and the parties stopped, *maman*'s dresses had been sold. Louette had been allowed to try them on before they went to the dealer – until she tore a Balenciaga gown, trying to force it to close across her shoulders. She missed the dressing up, the special privilege of being allowed into her mother's dressing room. *'Which would you choose, Louette?'*

'Gold, *maman*?'

'Perfect. Gold it shall be.'

Why had things changed? Deep within Louette's psyche lurked the horrible certainty that it was all her fault that life had altered so radically. Papa dying, maman having to go out to work, she to boarding school, their intimacy fracturing. Her fault.

Aged ten, during a holiday at Chemignac, Louette had discovered the wardrobe in the tower.

Without questioning why, she'd reached for the amethyst gown, dropping it over her head, pirouetting until the pleats belled around her legs. Somehow, she'd known she was doing something forbidden and that it would end badly, and indeed, her mother had come up, looking for her.

'Take it off!' The voice from the doorway had been more a cat's hiss than a woman's. 'That is a family heirloom, and priceless. Get it off, now!'

Louette had quaked in shame as her mother slammed the cupboard door on the dress. Louette had expected to be marched down the steps by the ear, but her mother had fallen silent for a disturbingly long time. At last, she'd turned to Louette. More gently now, 'The Gown of Thorns isn't mine, you see. It was made for my grandmother, but my mother claimed it as her own. Her favourite dress.'

'Why is it called the Gown of Thorns?'

'Never mind that. You must not touch it

because it brings death.'

Louette had burst into tears then, believing she was doomed to die. Well, she hadn't died, but she had developed tonsillitis within days. No ordinary tonsillitis either, but an aggressive form that led to weeks in the local hospital. It had changed her voice, and she'd never caught up with her schoolwork. Held down a year, she'd then developed psoriasis, a painful skin condition which had taken years to overcome. One minute's romantic self-indulgence, and her life had ricocheted in a new direction. A bright, high achiever, she'd become a mediocre student, prone to depression. Look at her now – a jobbing translator when she could have been a diplomat or a politician. *The Gown of Thorns brings death.* So, why this mania to keep putting it on?

Louette stared at herself in the glass, then over her shoulder at the steamer trunk she'd also lugged down from the tower room and which lay open on her bed. In a moment, she'd fill it and snap the clasps shut. Once she was back home, she'd call her friend at the Musée de la Mode and discuss donating the entire haul. Together, those dresses represented a microcosm of French couture between the wars. A squirt of patchouli oil every now and again was insufficient guard against the ravages of moth and damp. It would be a crime not to ensure their preservation.

She stroked the corrugated silk moulded to her belly. This dress had outlived two of its owners. The first, Louette's maternal great-grandmother, had died in the 1920s after giving birth to Albert, her last child. Its second owner, Louette's grandmother Marie-Louise, had died following a trip to Paris with the Gown of Thorns in her luggage. Reason rebelled against the idea of a dress being cursed, and yet, and yet . . . Louette touched her throat, recalling the pain of those childhood quinsies. Or peritonsillar abscesses, to give them their correct medical term.

She might easily have succumbed to sepsis, had it not been for modern antibiotics.

A rapid knock interrupted her thoughts. No time to get the dress off. The door was opening, a girl stepping into the room. Louette shrank into herself.

'You! What do you want?' She uncrossed her arms, which she'd instinctively wrapped about herself. Dignity withered under the girl's mocking smile. *Well, now*, it said, *fancy catching out grand Madame Barends in private vanity.*

'Pardon, Madame, I happened to be passing Laurent's laboratory just now and heard the telephone ringing in his office.'

'Not true,' Louette snapped. 'I know perfectly well that you can't hear the telephone from outside the laboratory, not through stone walls. You were in his office. Why?'

Rachel shrugged. No blush, no denial. 'So I picked up the phone and took a message.' Before

Louette could question her, Rachel tilted her head to examine the Gown of Thorns. 'How old is that dress?'

'It was made in 1914, on the eve of the Great War. By repute, the silk was dyed here at Chemignac.'

'Is it valuable?'

Louette managed a disdainful laugh. 'It's by the Italian designer Mariano Fortuny, who worked in Paris until his death in the 1940s. There are very few left of this age and in this condition.'

'Condition? You mean, stretched out like a net of oranges? It would look fabulous on the right figure.'

It was all Louette could do not to step forward and slap the girl. The dress felt suddenly alive on her, shimmering like a fish dropped into water after a suffocating spell on dry land. 'You brought a message?'

'Oh, yes.' Rachel made a show of recalling

her reason for being there. 'It was your husband.
There's been an accident. I could hear the children
in the background, yelling.'

Panic knifed through Louette. 'What kind of
accident?'

'A burning, apparently.'

'Fire?'

Rachel searched for the right phrase. 'More,
um, a "scorching". Oh good heavens, I don't mean
your house has burned down. Oh, your face,
Madame!' Her expression became, if anything,
more innocent. 'It happened just now – your
husband was trying to cook some kind of pasta dish,
and turned the gas up too high. He forgot it and now
the sauce is black and smoking. They're going out
to eat. For the third time this week. The message is –
hubby wants you home.'

Suddenly indifferent to Rachel's gaze,
Louette hauled off the dress, tossing it into the
steamer trunk. Unceremoniously shoving the other

garments on top, she banged the lid down and leaned on it as if caging a wildcat. Facing Rachel in just her slip and tights, she said, 'I'll tell mother I'm leaving right away. She's next door with Monsieur Albert. Would you take my luggage out to my car?'

'I suppose,' Rachel answered. 'But may I be brutal? You don't look up to a day and night on the road. Shouldn't you take a train instead of driving?'

'I have to get home,' Louette intoned through clenched teeth. Pushing her legs into her slacks, she broke the side zip in her desperation to be dressed and on her way.

Shauna pushed the 2CV's speed whenever she hit a straight stretch of road. She wanted to get this confrontation with Isabelle, Louette and Albert over with. Never a spirit drinker, at this moment she felt she could appreciate a swig of raw gin. She turned into the auburn tunnel that was Chemignac's walnut tree avenue and immediately pulled hard on the wheel and jammed on her brakes. In spite of her quick reactions, she scraped the door moulding of the white Citroën speeding past like a rally car. Recognising Louette, she opened her driver's door and got out, expecting the other woman to stop and do likewise. But Louette didn't and Shauna was in time to see the white car veer out into the lane, stones spitting from its wheels as it screeched away.

Laurent arrived home shortly after four-thirty, riding with the delivery truck driver. He too had seen Louette. Or rather, Louette's car, a smoking, crumpled mess on the main D road into Garzenac. An ambulance had passed him at speed, on its way, he had correctly assumed, to an emergency unit.

Chapter Fifteen

The following morning, after a sparse breakfast of yesterday's bread, toasted, Laurent drove out of Chemignac with his aunt. Their destination was the district hospital where Louette lay in a deep coma. They'd spent most of the previous evening there, until the staff had persuaded them that their presence was of no benefit to Louette.

Halfway along the avenue, they pulled in to allow the haymaker's tractor to pass. 'I'd forgotten he was coming to cut the meadows today,' Laurent muttered to Isabelle. The world had changed overnight. The roads around Chemignac were no longer empty arteries in a tranquil backwater. They were now in the grip of harvest, tractors thundering about, trailers bouncing behind. 'Life goes on, even when you wish it would stop.'

Isabelle turned a blotched face to him. 'It does, and you must pick your grapes in spite of Louette.'

'I will.' Though actually, he'd already telephoned the agent who supplied his pickers to warn him that Chemignac's *vendange* would be delayed. As they approached the hospital, Isabelle began to cry.

Louette had suffered superficial burns along with severe head and chest trauma. For reasons inexplicable to her family, she'd neglected to fasten her seatbelt. Isabelle had said in bewilderment to the surgeon, 'My daughter usually refuses to turn on the ignition until all her passengers have confirmed that they're strapped in. We always tease her about it.'

After escorting Isabelle to Louette's room and getting her a coffee from the machine, Laurent returned to Chemignac where he updated Shauna on Louette's condition. According to the first policeman at the scene, she'd been pulled from her burning car by a group of cyclists, while a passing lorry driver doused the flames with his fire extinguisher. Thankfully, the fuel tank hadn't exploded though everything in the boot and on the car's rear seat was destroyed. An antique steamer trunk full of clothes had been reduced to ashes. 'She overtook a tractor on a blind stretch,' Laurent said, 'and had to pull in to avoid a car coming head on. She hit the verge and rolled. Poor Isabelle thinks it's her fault.'

'Why?'

'They argued over the Gown of Thorns. Isabelle accused Louette of coveting it for herself. And she was right.' Rachel had witnessed Louette packing it, Laurent said. In fact, Rachel herself had loaded the trunk into Louette's car and it had been a deadweight. 'Louette was taking the entire contents of the wardrobe home to Paris with her.'

'As you hoped she would, Laurent. Will you eat?' Shauna had made salad baguettes, rather hurriedly, and the filling was falling out. Lunch reflecting life, she thought.

'I wanted the dress gone, but God knows, not like this.' Laurent gnawed a finger until Shauna stopped him. He'd draw blood. 'I'm wondering if that's why she was driving like a mad woman.'

'The dress infecting her mind? Isn't it more likely she was just anxious to get home to her kids?' Seeing Laurent shake his head, Shauna conceded. 'I admit, that dress has a weird effect when you put it on. I can't explain why, but it does.'

'That tells me you are beginning to understand Chemignac. This land holds its men and imprisons its women – until it kills them.' Laurent sighed. 'Now I'm talking like Albert.' He took a baguette and mayonnaise slopped onto his shoes. He made a rueful face and grabbed a kitchen towel, then kissed Shauna's cheek. 'Thank you for holding the fort. Will you make up some beds? I have to fetch Louette's husband from the airport.'

'Of course. I'll also make more lunch, in case anyone wants it. You'd better get going.' She didn't want him rushing. 'Watch out for those insane tractor drivers.'

At Bordeaux airport, Laurent met Hubert Barends. He'd caught the first available plane, bringing the children with him – they'd refused to be palmed off on friends and were anxious to see their mother. To Shauna's astonishment, the children ran straight to her when they reached the château. She put her arms around them and couldn't help but relive the moment, thirteen years ago, when she'd arrived home from school to find an ambulance outside her house. At her front door, she'd learned from a neighbour that her dad had died. So she knew what Olive and Nico were going through. 'We'll be all right,' she said to the children, forcing conviction into her voice. 'We'll keep busy, ok?'

It took three days for Louette's condition to stabilise. Her medical team then advised moving her to a specialist trauma unit near Paris. Laurent bought a return flight for Hubert, whose indecisiveness and impracticality dominated every interaction, and a ticket for Isabelle too. Lacerated by guilt, Isabelle vowed to keep vigil until her daughter opened her eyes. 'And somebody must keep Hubert company because he falls too easily into despondency,' Isabelle told Shauna. The children chose to stay at Chemignac. They'd been given compassionate leave from school and in a display of maturity that astonished Shauna, declared they would be more use helping with the wine harvest than moping in Paris. The adults agreed.

Against Albert's advice, Laurent delayed the harvest by a further day, letting September eleventh slide by and perhaps sacrificing the moment of perfect ripeness of the Sauvignon Blanc.

However, when they woke in Shauna's bed just before dawn on the twelfth, his first words were, 'Clos de Chemignac has produced wine through two world wars. I will call in the pickers. *Chérie?*' He scooped her into his arms, pulling her on top of him, 'Ready for the hardest physical work of your life?'

'I've had more subtle invitations to a roll in the hay.'

He laughed. 'I meant the *vendange*. I'll phone the agent now. He won't mind.'

'At four-twenty in the morning? Nobody's that good natured. I say this next hour is ours.' She kissed him, dragging her lips across his morning stubble to find the hollow of his throat. He gave in instantly, stretching out in arousal, his neck arching. They had been sharing a bed since Isabelle's departure. The children had wanted Laurent near them, and Isabelle had told him, 'Use my room, though of course, my bed lives in the dining room these days. You'll have to dismantle it and lug it upstairs –' at that point, she'd begun to cry, recalling her irritation at Louette's interference, which now, of course, she would have welcomed.

So, Laurent had shifted his clothes and CD player into Isabelle's room, joining Shauna in hers once the children were asleep. The intimacy of her bed and the bond of responsibility they now shared lent their nights a concentration Shauna had never before experienced. She'd not known that such imaginative, unhurried love existed. Or that her climax could go on for so long or send its echo so deep.

Laurent, too, was enchanted. 'It is different with you,' he told her in the breathless flow that cascaded from him each time he climaxed. 'With you, I feel I am cutting blocks to build a future.'

She wasn't sure the image was wholly flattering, but she took his meaning. This wasn't a holiday affair. She told him she meant to stay and build her future in France, alongside him. And though they both took care that 'the future' did not, for now, involve her getting pregnant, they had begun to casually refer to a time when they were 'a family.' Shauna couldn't shake the idea that they were completing something that had been torn apart in other lifetimes. Along with her career plans, she was jettisoning her scientist's scepticism, willing to challenge the tradition that all de Chemignac women had unhappy lives.

As Laurent drifted back into sleep, his arm across her, another realisation landed like a drop of iced water between her eyes. The Gown of Thorns had been burned to a frazzle in Louette's car, almost taking Louette with it. Whatever bitterness and sorrow lived in its fibres must have gone too. Sliding into sleep herself, she was jolted awake by a chippy voice in her ear: '*It isn't over yet. Keep your promise. I won't rest until I get justice.*'

Shauna closed her eyes tight, while her mind soared to the memorial stone in the glade. The stress of the last days had wiped Yvonne's name from her mind, but Yvonne was not going to go quietly, it seemed.

In a hospital ward across the channel Miss Thorne stared, dry-eyed, at the vinyl ceiling tiles. *Who drew up the cleaning rota at Dakenfield General*? Who thought it a good idea to switch on vacuum cleaners at first light? And would that person enjoy a similar wake-up call each morning?

One small blessing, the tea trolley would be along soon. With luck, it would be the friendly tea-lady doing the rounds today, the one who helped her sit up and turned her tray towards her. Miss Thorne had been dreaming about the Gown of Thorns. Its cold kiss had woken her. Even after all these years, its power was undiminished. Like the sloe berries from which its colour had been derived, it was a thing of beauty with a bitter heart. If only Henri had destroyed it before they met. Before she'd seen it, and reached for it.

A Delphos gown by Fortuny, fashioned to cling like cobweb. What warm-blooded woman could have resisted? And what man would resist the woman wearing it? Henri's eyes as she walked into his arms wearing it . . . if obsidian could catch fire . . .

Darling Henri had paid dearly for her vanity. But *only that*. Whatever else they said of her in France was unjust and she couldn't bear the thought of her life ending without vindication. Without redress. When the tea arrived, she frightened the woman pushing the trolley by screeching, 'Tell them I cannot die until my name is carved on that stone.'

While Shauna made coffee and scrambled eggs, Laurent telephoned the agent who supplied temporary labour. After that, he called his neighbours. By mid-morning, camper vans belonging to itinerant New Zealanders and Australians were parked on the newly-shorn hay meadow. Vehicles with Portuguese and Spanish plates soon drew up alongside. Local pickers arrived on foot, middle-aged women mostly, who had worked on neighbours' vineyards all the last week. Shauna joined Laurent in the *chai* and watched him and Raymond sterilising the press with carbon dioxide gas, ready for the first trailer-load of grapes. The other full-time worker, Armand, was giving the tractor a final check over.

She'd have loved to have had a go at spraying the snowy gas into the press, but she had her hands full. Many of the jobs that would have fallen to Isabelle were now hers, and she had to keep an eye on the children too. Reluctantly, and with Rachel's grudging help, she made her way to the vineyard and set up trestle tables which she laid with drinking water and plastic cups, sunblock, insect repellent and bite-relieving cream. Armand brought along a box of small, sharp scissors for clipping the grapes. There were dozens of plastic buckets and alongside them, a stack of *huttes* – conical baskets that three or four of the stronger workers would wear on their backs. Pickers emptied their buckets into the *huttes*, which in turn would be tipped into half-barrels on the back of the trailer.

By midday, Shauna and Olive were busy preparing lunch for the *vendangeurs*. Over the sizzle of mushroom and red pepper omelettes came the rev and throb of the tractor engine. Armand was giving it a run up the sloping Sauvignon Blanc *parcelle*, their target for this afternoon. The casual workers were milling about in the courtyard or sitting on straw bales, waiting to be fed. Afterwards, work would begin.

Shauna and Laurent were drinking a last cup of coffee and conferring over the afternoon's schedule when Rachel sauntered up to them.

'Pardon me for butting in.' Raising her brows at the coffee pot on the kitchen table, she added, 'You two need to cut down on the caffeine. You're staring at each other like a pair of lizards.'

'How can I help you, Rachel?' Laurent asked.

'More, how can I help *you*? With Isabelle out of the picture, there must be jobs to do.'

Laurent looked momentarily stunned. 'Well, we always need extra help among the vines.'

'Sorry.' Rachel held up her hands, implying 'No go.' 'I'm allergic to whatever it is you spray on the leaves.'

'They haven't been sprayed for nearly two weeks.'

'Even so . . . I was thinking of taking over the kitchen. You'll need somebody to do the honours at the *fête de vendange*, won't you?'

'Audrey is doing that, and Shauna will help.

With Isabelle's blessing.'

Rachel raised her eyebrows even higher, then smiled, accepting the rebuff with apparent good grace. 'Who's going to bring the last trailer-load in and be queen of the harvest?'

Laurent gave that a bare moment's consideration. 'This year - nobody. Out of respect for my cousin, who's still in a coma.'

Rachel headed for the door. 'Perhaps I can saunter along the rows every now and again, and keep up morale.'

'Workers only among the vines. But look,' Laurent's voice turned serious, 'it would really help if you could just look after the stables and the customers and if any pickers need accommodation, help them out. You know who offers rooms in the village.'

'Sure. I'll call on all the village witches, see if they prefer Spanish or Portuguese guests.'

Laurent sucked in a sound of irritation. 'I

appreciate it.'

'Well, you always used to, Laurent. See you later.' Rachel kissed her fingers at them both and went away with a sway of the hips that must, Shauna couldn't help thinking, really get in the way of her stable chores. 'That girl hasn't given up on you.'   'Oh, come on, Shauna. I told you it was a short-lived thing and a mistake.'   'Does she know that? I mean, the way she brushes her upper lip with her tongue when she says your name . . . *Laurent*.' Shauna demonstrated in a smoky voice.

Laurent shook his head. 'What happens in the past should stay in the past. No? Or would you like to tell me about the men you slept with at university?'

She blushed, her pale skin betraying her once again. 'Point taken. It's good of her to offer to help.'

'I hope she means it. Rachel's very good at offering her services, only to make herself absent when you most need her.'

That, considering the conversation they'd just had, wasn't reassuring.

'You do want to help with the feast?' he asked. 'It's our way of thanking the workers, and ensuring they come back next year. So if you think you'd rather not—'

'My cooking's not that bad! I've been talking it over with Audrey. She's got everything planned as far as traditional fare goes and I suggested doing a barbecue as well, and she quite liked the idea. My devilled drumsticks are to die for. Stop!' Laurent had begun to argue that nobody ever cooked a barbecue at a *fête de vendange*. 'Life moves on. Embrace change, or you'll end up like Albert.' *Back me on this, or we'll have Rachel barging in*, she added silently. *Though not if I have anything to do with it.* Petty, but then jealousy always was.

'Petty? More than that.' Clear as flute music,

Yvonne's opinion piped through her head.

'*Sometimes, jealousy kills.*'

Chapter Sixteen

Laurent had described grape picking as 'the hardest physical work of your life' and he hadn't been joking. He'd handed Shauna scissors and a bucket and, along with the other *vendangeurs* who were new to the work, a swift lesson in technique. He spoke clearly and slowly. 'Only pick the healthy grapes. Rotten ones can change the character of a whole vat of wine. You work in pairs, one each side of the vine. Don't swap rows and don't leave the vine until it is picked clean. On no account do you ever put your scissors in a bucket. If they fall in among the grapes, they can wreck the press. Cut the grapes so that they fall into your bucket, not to the ground. If you need water, shout for these two' – he indicated Olive and Nico. 'Any questions? No? *On y va!* We stop for a break in two hours.' He touched

Shauna's arm, his good humour mended. 'I'll be your tutor. Come on.'

Workers fanned out among the rows. Some bent to their toil, others kneeled to work. The *hutte* carriers walked up and down, calling '*Panier, panier!*' meaning 'baskets to fill!' Nico and Olive ran about tirelessly, emptying for the pickers, replacing their buckets and offering water like stewards at a road marathon. They appeared unaffected by the intensifying heat. Shauna took a moment to wipe her scissors, already sticky from grape sugar, and watched one of the *hutte* men emptying his load into the trailer. He was shirtless, his mahogany torso testimony to a season of vineyard labour.

'That was my job from age thirteen to twenty-one,' Laurent told her.

Why he too had such broad, well-developed shoulders, she supposed. She and Laurent worked side by side until the first water break, by which time she'd got the hang of sheering clusters in one decisive clip, shifting her bucket along as she reached for the next bunch.

Watching her for a minute or two, Laurent nodded approval. 'You seem pretty competent already, so this is *au-revoir.*' He patted Shauna's cheek, leaving it sticky. Which, he told her when she complained, augured well for the quality of the wine. 'I have to go and feed the press now, check that everything is going right in the *chai*. Feeling OK?'

'Fine,' she muttered, though actually, her knees and calves ached viciously. The vineyard was on a steep slope and the slow crab-walk she'd adopted was working muscles she'd never been aware of having. She'd been bitten too, by midges and heaven knew what else. She'd chosen a long cotton dress today and leggings, thinking the outfit would keep off the sun and the biters. Even doused in repellent, something had found its way in. She had an ankle chain of bites. As for her dress, it was too long and she kept stepping on it. Twice she'd sprawled on top of her grape bucket. A blister was forming on the inside of her finger where her scissors chafed. *Two more two-hour stints to go*, she reminded herself. And tomorrow, picking would begin at 8 a.m. Thinking of Laurent, in the *chai* with Raymond, piling grapes into the press, she muttered, 'Lucky so-and-so.' Then, 'I'm a scientist. Get me out of here!'

But despite it all, she was enjoying herself. The atmosphere was convivial. Australians and New Zealanders traded banter as they picked, as did the Spaniards and Portuguese. The older women sang songs that had probably been heard among the vines for generations. The air became a minestrone of languages. As the local women talked in their own dialect, suddenly Shauna realised she could understand them. *I've got the language,* she thought with pleasure. *Soon I'll be dreaming in French.*

She had a new picking partner now, too. Before abandoning her, Laurent had introduced her to Madame Guilhem who lived in a cottage in Chemignac. 'She'll keep an eye on you. She knows these vines backwards.'

Shaking the frail hand and looking into a face as wrinkled as a walnut shell, Shauna had thought, *At least I'll be faster than her.* Two minutes proved the danger of snap judgments – she'd been left standing with ten vines already between them.

Resting to let her catch up, Madame Guilhem grinned. 'Except for when I had my children, I've done every Chemignac harvest since I was eight years old.'

Eight? 'So your first time was . . . ?'

'1925, working for the old Comte de Chemignac.'

'Henri, Laurent's grandfather?'

'No, no,' the old woman shook her head at Shauna's ignorance. '*His* father, Gaston. Henri, we called "the young comte" because he was, for a while.' She laughed, displaying stubby teeth. 'Like the thorn tree that guards the *chai*, I have been here throughout the ages. I have seen everybody and everything, and outlived most of it. I turn eighty-six at Christmas.'

It made Shauna ashamed of her shuddering muscles and blisters. At eighty-six, she rather fancied being a retired Dame, ennobled for her contribution to biosciences, giving the occasional university lecture, but mostly listening to music from a recliner chair. They picked in silence until Madame Guilhem whistled through her teeth. 'Look at her. At the end of harvest, we should put her on the cart, like the *Gerbeboade*.'

That was a new word. 'I don't know what you mean, Madame.'

'The wine-maiden. The dolly. I should think that young lady will ensure fertility for the rest of the year.'

'That young lady' was Rachel, who had joined the pickers at some point. Clearly her allergy had been overcome. She was gliding past with a bucket of opalescent grapes held away from her body. In an off-the-shoulder tunic and long, white shorts she looked like a temple maiden taking a sacrifice to the altar. The 'altar' being the wiry Portuguese man, Adão, whose *hutte* clearly had room for one more offering.

'If he falls over backwards,' Madame Guilhem huffed, 'poor lad will never get up again.'

Shauna giggled and Rachel threw her a pitying stare. 'You've just put a mouldy grape in your bucket. We'll know who to blame if the Sauvignon Blanc gets declassified to table wine.'

She was right, blast her. Shauna fished out the bad cluster and threw it under a vine. Rachel turned back to Adão, squeezing his shoulder, jokingly testing his muscles.

'Harvest is the most amorous time,' Madame

Guilhem chuckled. Shauna grunted, and concentrated on keeping up. As an amateur *vendangeur*, she couldn't chat and pick. Not safely, anyway.

'It was a time of love for your mother, no?'

Shauna looked up, amazed. 'You knew my mother?'

'I know that colour.' Madame Guilhem nodded towards Shauna's hair, a few spikes of which poked from beneath her hat. '*Blond Vénitien*. Her name . . . let me remember . . . Elisabeth. She fell in love with an *Irlandais*.'

'An Irishman. Yes, she did.'

'With green eyes.'

Shauna knew she ought to keep picking, not least because stopping would make her seize up, but she was paralysed by the idea that this old woman had stooped among the same vines as her parents. Had seen their love blossom. A wasp, attracted by the sugary glaze on her skin, got between her and the grapes. By the time she'd waved it away, Madame Guilhem was way ahead. Shauna picked as fast as she could to catch up. 'They got engaged here, so Madame Duval said.'

'So they did. They made a cut in each other's arms. Mixed their lifeblood together under the thorn tree. I told them off, not only because the thorn is bad luck, but because the *épine noire* makes the blood septic. But I suppose they were happy even so?'

'For eighteen years. Then dad died.'

'I am sorry. How?'

'His heart. His doctors blamed cigarettes.'

'*Bien sûr*, though my husband smoked from the age of twelve, and he died only last winter.' Madame Guilhem peered at Shauna through a chink in the foliage. 'I wish you better luck. You are in love, of course, and he is a fine specimen, ha?'

'No, I mean, yes . . .' She was blushing again and said, because she had to offer something, '"Now you see why I can't be perfectly happy. No one could, who has red hair."'

'Eh? Has the sun got to you?'

'I'm quoting *Anne of Green Gables*.'

'I don't know her.'

'It was a book I loved as a child. What I mean is, we redheads blush. Our blushes are gathered up by God to colour the sunset. That's the sort of thing *Anne of Green Gables* would have said.'

Madame Guilhem looked unimpressed, then shrugged. 'Huh. And your tears are the rain, I suppose.'

'I suppose. Which means they're scheduled for the end of next week, according to Laurent.' Shauna angled her scissors and another fat bunch fell into her basket. She snipped again and this time, cut a sliver of her own flesh. She squealed in pain and rammed her finger in her mouth. Madame Guilhem tutted and passed her a clean tissue, which turned swiftly scarlet against the wound. At that moment Shauna's tongue seemed to lose its inhibition. 'You've been here all your life, Madame. So you must have known Yvonne. An English girl, here during the war.'

'*La rouquine*. A relation, that is why you ask?'

'No relation.' The blood was still welling and Shauna accepted another tissue. 'Yvonne. That's all I know, and that was probably a code name.'

'Your mother is Elisabeth Thorne?'

'Before she married. She became . . .' Shauna uttered an 'Oh' of dawning comprehension. Here, at Chemignac. Elisabeth and Tim had mixed their blood. Afterwards, Tim Vincent had imprinted Elisabeth's name, Thorne, on his flesh in the form of a tattoo. The couple had pledged themselves to each other and, at the same time, declared an indelible link to Chemignac. Henri had chosen *Écharde* as his secret name. In Shauna's dream, Yvonne had been amused by the coincidence of him as a 'splinter' and she as 'thorn'. Had Yvonne been, literally, a 'Thorne'?

'Do you think we could be related, myself and Yvonne?' Shauna desperately wanted to ask more, but Madame Guilhem's recollection had moved on.

The old woman said, 'I was working here when Yvonne arrived. It was a time when we all thought the war would go on for ever. I came here every day to clean a part of the château that had been seized by a German businessman. I'd sweep and mop, then cook breakfast for the two layabouts who were paid to tend the garden and look after the German's dogs. I'd keep my head down, then go home on my bicycle. So I didn't see much, but I knew she was there and that she was part of the Résistance. Very brave. She fell in love with our Comte Henri.'

'Was that a bad thing?'

'Not bad, no. Henri de Chemignac was a widower with two little children. It was right that he should look to marry again. But love and marriage are not the same thing. And at a time when our country was not our own and anybody – neighbour or friend – might be an informer, it was not wise to love too deeply. Yvonne stayed such a short time and Henri risked everything to save her.' Madame Guilhem pushed tendrils of vine aside, the better to see Shauna. 'It was not only Henri who loved Yvonne. His younger brother loved her too.'

'Albert? No. He hated her. He still does. You should hear him – it's like it was yesterday.'

'The past *is* yesterday. You learn that as you get to my age. You learn too that jealousy is a terrible thing.' Madame Guilhem let the leaves fall back, ending the chat. 'We're falling behind. My husband used to tell me I know too much and forget too little. A fault of character.'

But Shauna had absorbed enough to evolve

her understanding of Yvonne. Recruited by SOE, Yvonne had come here to do a dangerous job. Falling in love must have been well and truly off the script. Yet deeply human. Perhaps that was the fatal flaw - everybody at Chemignac was too human. Shauna massaged her calves, wincing. She'd picked a full row without stopping once other than when she'd snipped her finger – she'd snatch five minutes' rest here. Ah, there was Albert, leaning on his stick, overseeing a group of Spaniards. One of them had missed a cluster and he was pointing it out. Aggressively.

'Why be pleasant when you can shout instead?' she muttered. 'You don't imagine that anybody else has feelings.' She remembered Albert leaning against the kitchen sink the night Isabelle fell, staring down at the unconscious woman. What kind of man was Albert de Chemignac, at heart? What lived beneath that querulous, fault-finding exterior? Shauna wanted to stride over and ask him.

But her picking partner tugged at her dress, telling her, 'Only one more row, then we stop for a break.'

The moment was lost. Albert de Chemignac was stumping towards a different part of the vineyard, doubtless to carp at another group of pickers.

A long stone's throw from where Shauna knelt among the vines, the Gown of Thorns hung in an unfamiliar wardrobe. It was back where it belonged, at Chemignac. It had survived two wars; miraculously, it had evaded a car wreck. Soon, it would enjoy its first public appearance in over sixty years. It would absorb the warmth of its rescuer's body and be transformed. It would regain its power.

In his office at Lancashire John Kay University, Professor Mike Ladriss pressed 'save' then closed the computer document he'd been working on for three days. Coursework for next year's fresh intake. Not usually his job, but he'd been let down by a tutor who had handed in her notice. Without, in fact, any notice.

Reading the woman's written resignation, Mike had instantly thought of Shauna Vincent as the perfect solution to this crisis. She'd have relished the challenge he'd have given her: 'I need two first-year modules sketched out fast. Be fresh, be exciting and be challenging. I can always curb your enthusiasm later.' But, no Shauna. One conciliatory text from France, implying that she was still keen for any work he might send her way, then nothing. His subsequent messages had gone unanswered, including the one he'd dashed off after he'd learned that the Cademus posting had fallen vacant. He'd faxed it to the number Shauna had provided, the one with a French dialling code.

Expecting her to ring back, breathless with excitement, he'd been perplexed by her silence. A silence which robbed him of the opportunity to set things right. Shauna had been passed over for that job in favour of a far less capable candidate and Mike knew now that a donation offered to Cademus by the successful candidate's father had swung the decision. *You say donation, I say bribe.* His beloved LJKU had emitted not a squeak of protest, in a stroke devaluing its reputation as a fair and equal institution. What next? London bankers and foreign oligarchs buying first-class honours for their children? He'd since wondered if he shouldn't have taken more of a stand over it.

His desk phone rang. He stared at it, trying to guess who was on the other end. Term had not yet started and the campus was populated by admin staff and lonely, divorced academics like himself. 'Ladriss,' he answered, prepared to find the caller had pressed the wrong extension number.

Five minutes later, Mike Ladriss replaced the receiver. He was in shock.

Five minutes after that, security men were in his office, duct-taping the drawers of his desk, removing his computer. Deaf to his pleas to give him a chance to retrieve his work-in-progress, they escorted him into the carpark. There, the Pro Vice-chancellor, the man in charge of everything involving salaries and career prospects, informed Mike that he was on paid leave till further notice. He must not set foot on university soil until given written permission to do so. The allegation was that he had brought the university into disrepute and violated data protection law. He had libelled a prominent individual and the university was taking every measure to avoid prosecution.

That fax to Shauna, Mike thought. *Knew I shouldn't have sent it.*

He would be fired, the Pro Vice-chancellor implied. It was simply a matter of time. His accuser?

A man Mike Ladriss had never heard of and whose name made him wonder if he'd been time-flipped into a glossy, early eighties soap opera. His nemesis was Comte Laurent de Chemignac, owner of a wine estate in the French Dordogne.

'But I've never heard of him,' Mike protested. 'I don't know anybody French, let alone a "comte".'

'Then I suggest you ring your lawyer,' returned the Pro Vice-chancellor.

Mike didn't have a lawyer. His divorce had left him with a distaste of all things judicial. 'I'll find out for myself. If need be, I'll go to France and scour the Dordogne for this joker. "Comte", I ask you.'

Chapter Seventeen

This first day of harvest seemed endless. Shauna
took a shower at five that evening while her fellow
labourers took a two-hour break. After supper,
picking would start again. With clear skies expected,
the moon two days past full, it would be light
enough until nine or even ten o'clock. She wasn't
sure her body could take another stint, but she'd
give it her best shot. To be valued as a worker and
honorary local had become a driving need. She'd
filled bucket after bucket with grapes. Nobody could
accuse her of playing at it.

Dropping her sticky, bloodstained clothes
into the laundry bin, Shauna wound a clean bandage
round her cut. It hurt still, but there was no sign of
infection. Wrapped in a towel, she went into
Isabelle's room. Time to rethink her picker's

uniform. Isabelle owned a pair of *bleus de travail*, from the time when she'd still been fit enough to help with the harvest.

She went into Isabelle's bedroom to find them. Laurent's things were scattered about and she took a moment to tidy up, folding his clothes on to a chair, picking up coins and receipts that had fallen out of his pockets. It was interesting, discovering a person layer by layer. Methodical in his *chai* and lab, at home he was quite untidy. She rather liked that. In the same way that he listened to loud rock music to block the circular thoughts that pursued him when he was stressed, his domestic clutter marked the boundary between home and work life. She had different flaws, which he would no doubt discover. Namely, a tendency to index everything from music CDs to the contents of her spice rack, combined with deep insecurity. Talking of which . . .

She pictured Rachel swanning about in

Vestal white, showing off her mile-long legs while squeezing the *hutte*-carrier's bicep. 'Ooh, Adão, you're all beefcake. Let me cut myself a nice, hearty - ' Shauna's mouth dropped as she opened Isabelle's wardrobe to look for the overalls. 'You! I thought you were incinerated!'

The Gown of Thorns hung at one end of the rail, while some shirts and tops that Laurent had hung up were shoved along to the far side as if they were shying away from contact. Shauna reached for the dress, then withdrew her hand. What the hell? How could it be hanging here, glossy as a gemstone? *Ah.* Rachel had watched Louette put the gown into a steamer trunk. Rachel had then, very obligingly, taken the trunk to Louette's car. She'd clearly had a little delve through the contents while she was doing it. The simple explanation was that the Gown of Thorns had never left Chemignac at all.

Finding Isabelle's blue overalls in a corner of the wardrobe, Shauna left the bedroom. In her own room, she belted the garment around her waist with a silk scarf. The legs were way too long, so she fastened them up with safety pins from the first aid box. She did it all on automatic, her mind constantly returning to the stow-away hanging in the wardrobe. Should she tell Laurent that his 'hellish rag' was back?

No. Laurent had enough on his plate. With a lingering sense of crossing a line, she went back to Isabelle's room. 'You are coming with me,' she told the Gown of Thorns, and folded it with all the care and respect given to a silk flag to be laid on a military coffin. Covering it with one of Laurent's discarded sweatshirts, she walked through the kitchen, greeting Audrey, who was making lettuce soup and some kind of hearty rice dish for the children's dinner. Pulling up a chair to stand on, Shauna felt along the ceiling beam for a crack in the wood.

Audrey broke off from stirring her soup to

enquire if she was dusting or doing her exercises. Shauna jumped down, showing Audrey a pair of keys. 'Just taking something upstairs.'

'Up the tower?' Audrey looked at the keys, then at Shauna. 'I went up once. Never again.'

'All right, you two?' Shauna glanced at the children who were at the kitchen table playing *Morpion,* which she called 'noughts and crosses' and which Laurent, with his part-American education, called 'Tic-tac-toe'. They looked depleted and must be ravenous, as was she. 'Have you had plenty of water today? I don't want you dehydrating.'

'About forty litres,' Nico said, his eyes on the game. He was working out his next move. Olive looked up and laughed. 'Those overalls belong to my grandmother.'

'Think she'll mind?'

Olive gave her a critical once-over. 'You look like a girl mechanic. She'd say, "*Avance*, and pick more grapes!" Why are you going into the tower? What are you carrying?'

It was tempting to lie, but Olive couldn't be fobbed off, she was too fly. 'I found the Gown of Thorns in your grandmother's room and I'm hanging it back where it belongs.'

'OK.' Olive inscribed a cross on the grid, winning the game. Nico immediately accused her of cheating, to which Olive replied, 'You can't cheat at *Morpion*, idiot.'

'You just did.'

'For goodness' sake, you two, nobody would think you're descended from diplomats!' Shauna unlocked the tower door and escaped upstairs. The tower bedroom felt peaceful, the only disturbance a fly buzzing at the window. Shauna let it out then did what she'd come to do. 'And not another peep out of you,' she told the dress. Giving the wardrobe doors a solid shove, checking they were firmly shut, she reflected – *Olive's absolutely right. 'OK' sums this room up. There's nothing unnatural here. It's our imaginations fleshing out primal superstition, and we need to stop doing it.* Halfway down the stairs, she remembered she hadn't re-locked the tower room door. She reluctantly went back up. As she turned the key in the bedroom door, she heard a discordant whine from inside the room. She knew it was the wardrobe door falling open. The frame was warped, she told herself. The door catch needed replacing. But damned if she was going inside to check!

She headed down the tower, forcing herself to tread carefully, wishing she'd never gone back upstairs and heard the noise. Its timing felt premeditated, as if some intelligence wanted to show her that it could undermine her logic any time it wanted to.

Shauna helped herself to a bowl of Audrey's soup. How could something made from lettuce be so delicious? Mopping the last of it up with a chunk of bread, she thought, I could happily flop into bed now. But, mindful that the men in the *chai* had been working almost without break for eight hours, she laid a tray for three. She'd take them some supper, then join the other workers for one, last shift in the vines. Audrey filled thermos flasks with the remaining soup, and a basket with bread, goat's cheese and a jar of Isabelle's onion confit. Shauna added a flask of black coffee and they walked together down the Cypress avenue.

She craved being with Laurent. Not to talk – if he felt as she did, anything more than vague grunts would be beyond him now. Just to see him and share a hug would be enough. This had been a life-changing day because for the first time, she'd felt she truly belonged here. Grapes that she'd picked, along – regrettably – with drops of blood from her finger, had gone into the press and were now indivisibly part of Chemignac's 2003 vintage. She wanted to sit beside him, and – all right – display her bandaged finger and be commended for her stoicism. Her blisters were pretty impressive, too. Badges of honour.

She'd poked her head into the *chai* earlier, but the grinding of the press had deterred her from going further. Laurent had seen her and waved, and she'd waved back. He'd been manhandling a length of blue pipe, gesticulating at Raymond to turn something on, or off, and she hadn't wanted to intrude. This basket of food was her excuse, and all sounded quiet now. The teenage boy who'd been helping Armand drive the tractor between the vines and this yard all day was sweeping a glutinous mix of water, vine leaves and grape stalks out of the *chai*. A cloud of vinegar flies hung over the pile he was making in the yard.

'*Salut*, Mesdames.' Noticing their baskets,

confusion touched his expression.

Following Audrey inside, Shauna was struck first by the coolness. The *chai's* stone walls protected it from extremes of heat, but there must be air conditioning going on too. She knew the juice in the vats had to be kept between five and ten degrees Celsius, or there was a danger of rogue fermentation. The air smelled of honey and fruit and something more pungent . . . she sniffed. Sulphur dioxide. Laurent would have added that to kill the wild yeasts that came in on the grape skins.

Audrey greeted her husband, then said, 'Oh. I see.' Though from the tone of her voice, she did not like what she saw.

Laurent, Raymond and Armand, their work clothes a testament to the day's pressing frenzy, sat around a table laid with a cloth, white crockery, glasses and silver cutlery. Shaving slices of dry-cured ham was Rachel, wearing a short, pink dress that looked remarkably inappropriate in this masculine environment. A barbecue apron tied tight around her waist lent her an hourglass shape. She flashed Audrey and Shauna an unapologetic smile.

'You left your men hungry. Put the baskets down if you like, though I doubt they'll have room for any leftovers.' She shared the slices of ham around three plates, spooning on rice salad mixed with glazed root vegetables and red pepper. As a final touch, she added slivers of black truffle, using a little hand grater. Shauna watched, feeling powerless and foolish. Even given the fact that they were in the heart of truffle country, how much had that little black nugget cost Rachel? And *why*? 'Showing off' might have been Isabelle Duval's opinion, had she been here to ask. It was clear Audrey wasn't impressed either, and her husband Raymond was picking up on it. Looking sheepish, he waved away the plate Rachel tried to hand him.

'Merci, merci. I prefer a bowl of soup.'

Armand, who had no wife to placate, happily

took what Rachel offered. Shauna waited to see what Laurent would do. She wished she had the knack for raising a single eyebrow, a restrained and dignified response to an excruciating moment, but she probably only managed to look hurt and cross.

'Laurent?' Rachel invited. Laurent took the plate, looking straight at Shauna.

She flinched. Such pain in his eyes, and anger – of the implacable kind. Where had her teasing lover gone? Shauna grabbed her basket, clenching her teeth when its handle tore the film of new skin off her blisters, and walked out. Tears started halfway along the Cypress walk. For the second time in a few months, she'd lost something precious, robbed by another woman. She'd not realised until too late that Allegra Boncasson was after her job. She hadn't appreciated how expertly Rachel Moorcroft would slide between her and Laurent. Was this her fate, to bumble through life losing everything that mattered?

Her picking partner for the night shift was an Australian in his early sixties, who claimed to have picked grapes in every European country except Albania. Good humoured, full of stories, he hauled Shauna along in the slipstream of his enthusiasm, even when her muscles were screaming and her blisters bled. Laurent was driving the tractor this time. A monochrome shape in the moonlight, if he looked her way, she didn't notice. At ten, he called a halt. Too dark now to work safely. She returned her scissors to the table, added her bucket to the pile and went straight to the château. Albert was meant to be keeping the children company, but she found them watching TV alone. 'Bed time,' she said, in English, because their fluency had slipped without their regular sessions. 'Another day lashed to the galley tomorrow.'

'Pardon?' Nico demanded.

'What's wrong?' Olive asked in French.

'I'm exhausted.'

'That's all?' The girl's face was stern with anxiety. An expression startlingly similar to Laurent's.

'Yes, that's all, I promise.' Shauna hustled them to bed, then washed, brushed her teeth and crawled under her own covers where sleep wrapped her in a fist. She woke, the moon stark through undrawn curtains. It didn't take an extended hand to tell her that she was alone. She cried like a child until, disgusted with herself, she threw back the covers and put on the cotton print maxi-dress she'd thrown off earlier that day.

She'd let Justin, her first love, move on without a fight. Robbed of her job, she'd wallowed in bitterness when in fact, she should have staged a one-woman picket outside the University Chancellor's office. She'd run away, to a place with no phone signal and its own strife. Here, like the lotus flower blossoming in still waters, she'd become somebody else and found somebody new. Someone she dearly loved. Now *that* seemed to be over. Reasoned thinking and civilised manners were no damn use. The time had come for passion, for unreason.

The night would be chilly, so she grabbed one of Laurent's hoodies from the end of her bed. At the kitchen door, she jammed on Olive's sunflower-print wellies. Letting herself out quietly, she stood in the courtyard and gave herself a pep talk. 'Nothing to lose, all or nothing, go down fighting. Laurent de Chemignac is going to look you in the eye and explain what has happened to change his feelings. He'll do it tonight, even if you have to drag him out of Rachel's bed.'

Chapter Eighteen

She knew where Rachel's quarters were. Following an unproven hunch that nobody locked their doors around here, Shauna tried the one next to the stable office. Hunch correct. It opened with a turn of the handle and she climbed the stairs. At the top, the murmur of voices and the soft insult of two-tone laughter dulled any qualms she might have had about invading Rachel's privacy. The bedroom door banged open at her push. A scream greeted her entry, then angry swearing. A man and a woman lay together, a bedside lamp gilding his almond brown skin and dark hair, turning the girl's body bronze.

'What the fuck?' Rachel Moorcroft demanded. She displayed no physical embarrassment. In fact, she wore her nudity like a medal. Her fury was at the timing. Her partner was not so relaxed. He grabbed a sheet, covering himself up frantically.

Rosy relief melted Shauna's tension and her laughter filled the room, curdling with the outrage emanating from the bed. 'I'm sorry, Adão,' she said to the man wrapped in the sheet. 'Rachel and I need to talk.'

'It can't wait till morning?' Rachel demanded.

'No.' Shauna switched to English, wanting to keep the next words private from Rachel's bed partner. 'I want to know what you're up to with Laurent. Serving him food like a handmaiden . . . truffles, for God's sake!'

'The black gold – it's the way to a Frenchman's heart. I've done quite a lot of freelance cookery in my time. Watch out on the night of the *fête*, I might just stage a competing event.' Rachel chuckled, ignoring Adão's demand to be told what was going on. Her tawny hair fanned out as she lay back against the pillows. 'What am I up to? Well, you know how Laurent puts aside a few hundred bottles of wine each year to mature? That's what I'm doing. My good friend here' – she patted Adão's muscular forearm – 'is for drinking now. Laurent, I'm laying down for later.'

'Does he know that?'

'At some level. A base level, I grant you.'

'Don't you care about anybody?'

'Yes. Me. Oh . . . did you think you were going to find him here?' Rachel sat up. 'How cute, you're wearing Laurent's top. Over your nightie?'

'It's a dress.'

'Really? It looks like something my granny would order from a catalogue. And rubber boots, so I suppose your next port-of-call is the vineyard or the *chai*.'

Shauna had moved to the door, but she made a last salvo. 'You took the Gown of Thorns out of Louette's trunk, didn't you?'

'I . . . what?' The infinitesimal pause suggested Rachel was caught off guard.

'Isabelle's dress, the Fortuny gown. You watched Louette pack, then filched it before she set off in the car.'

'What would I want a stinky old dress for?'

'Did you try it on?'

'I just said, I don't know what you're talking about.' Rachel's eyes held Shauna's too fixedly. Lying eyes.

Closing the bedroom door behind her, Shauna noticed a key in the lock. She turned it and called through the crack between door and frame, 'The day you locked me in the tower room, I warned you I'd repay the compliment. Goodnight!'

Rachel swore furiously, then called, 'Oh, do as you please. Go and find Laurent, make the most of him. He knows you won't stay. Women never stick around here long. Either they hightail it to the big city or they die. Unless they're Louette Barends, and have a go at doing both at once.'

Shauna searched the vineyards that were due for picking the next day, in case Laurent was making a late-night inspection. Calling his name was out of the question – too intrusive, too desperate. The owls were vocal as ever, as shrill as school recorder music, and she saw their swooping silhouettes above the vines. Not wanting to wander alone in the dark any longer, she tried his apartment, but it was empty, all lights off. He could be in her bed by now, of course. But after the way he'd looked at her earlier, she doubted it.

And indeed, her bed was just as she'd left it. She was tempted to crawl back under the covers, but something told her that if she did, her next move would be a taxi-ride to Garzenac station. Whatever energy had brought them together was in flux. Grasp it, or lose it. She had a precious interval in which to reach Laurent. Where the hell was he?

In the courtyard, she stumbled upon the answer. Albert's downstairs lights were on, his shutters wide open. When she peered through the glass, she saw deep into his lair. Saw Albert, gesticulating, his body slanted forward as he made some vital point to somebody. To Laurent? So here we are, she thought, right back where we began. Taking a deep breath, she pulled hard on the bell beside Albert's door.

Chapter Nineteen

Albert didn't so much invite her in as retreat into his apartment, allowing her to follow. Shauna entered rooms of low beams, heavy furniture and lighting as dim and yellow as a Dickensian Christmas. In a rear sitting room was Laurent, uncomfortable on a lumpy sofa, contemplating the messy surface of a coffee table. He'd changed out of his work clothes and showered, she noticed. His hair still held a moist gleam. His white hoodie with its surfing brand logo looked as if it had shrunk in the wash. Or maybe he'd expanded since he last took to a surfboard. He looked up.

'Where were you?' They both said it at the same time.

He answered first, 'Walking the vines. You weren't in your room. I thought you might be here.'

She said, 'Likewise, pretty much. What's all this?' The coffee table was spread with black and white photographs. She glanced at Albert who, in a zip-up cardigan and the suit trousers he wore on Sundays for mass, looked simply like a little old man, and less the perennial woman-hater he normally was. It gave her the confidence to add, 'My legs have had it,' and to plump down next to Laurent.

The photos had an old-fashioned matt finish and white borders. They looked sharply professional, though they smelled of dust and long-term storage. One showed a young man who could be Albert, posing with a young lad of around twelve or thirteen. They were in courtyard outside; *that* hadn't changed at all. There was portrait of a young woman wearing a headscarf and a tired-looking dress, her youth and sweetness a reproach to her threadbare clothing. She held the hand of a very little boy. In other pictures, a young girl was performing ballet steps in the sunshine.

'Isabelle,' Shauna said. 'She had the perfect build to be a dancer.' Nobody contradicted her.

Laurent laid four pictures out in front of Shauna, silently inviting her inspection. Two were of the same woman. She was seated on a dining chair in the courtyard. Slim, with runner's legs, she was reading a book, or trying to. Geese were clustered around her, whether greeting her or pecking her, it wasn't clear. The third picture was of a good-looking man casually posing in front of the door that now belonged to Albert. Shauna recognised the brass bell. The last photo captured the same man and woman together. Something about their expressions, the shape of their mouths, told her they'd either just been kissing or were wishing the cameraman would go away so they could start.

'I don't understand.' But she was beginning to comprehend that her 'understanding' – her consent – was not required. Change the hairstyle and the clothes, add a few years, and the woman surrounded by geese, could be her. And the man in the photo – he was the spitting image of Laurent.

Yvonne

The boys she'd met on the espionage training courses had all said that the danger 'was like a drug'. Yvonne had always refrained from commenting – the nearest she'd ever been to drug-taking was a strong cup of tea and an aspirin. Danger, to her mind, was a most unpleasant stimulant, of which the sole benefit was a radical sharpening of focus. After her parachute drop, Écharde had bundled her away from the moonlit fields into the woods where they rested a moment.

The intervals between bursts of crossfire were growing shorter, suggesting the battle was reaching its peak.

'What about your friends?' she panted. 'And can I stop calling you *Écharde*? Seems idiotic, as I know you're Henri de Chemignac.'

'Call me "Monsieur" and I will call you "Madame". My friends are trained soldiers, prepared to die – but always hopeful of escape. Our tactic is to keep firing volleys from the front rank while the men at the back slip away one by one. The last remaining choose their moment to retreat, then split up. Nobody wants to get caught. Your colleagues are in safe hands. Ready?'

The next hour consisted of hacking through woodland, field and scrub, sprinting in short bursts with rests between. Absolute murder in bandaged-up shoes, with so many bulky layers under her flying suit. She fell more than once. Just as she glimpsed ahead the comforting bulk of walls and a square tower, Henri informed her they were doubling back into the woods. 'In case we are followed.'

So, instead of the fireside and tot of cognac she'd been promised, she got to stumble along yet more deer paths, followed by a brief sit down in a cave-mouth. Though this was no mere cave, it transpired. Following her guide into its womb-like recess, she discovered a gap between the rocks. They were to squeeze through it, apparently. It was narrow enough to bruise her ribs and she was finally glad of her padding.

'Our tunnel,' Henri whispered, 'leading straight under the meadows to the château tower. I hope you are impressed.'

'Do the others know about this?'

'One or two. Your friends will be brought this way, if it's safe. Ready? Once in the tunnel-proper, bend low or you'll strike your head on the roof. I will let you see where you are, but then we must go in darkness. We can't afford to consume too much oxygen.'

In the flare of his cigarette lighter, she saw that it really *was* a tunnel, like a mine-shaft with props and chisel marks in the stone. Like something out of a Boy's Own comic. Her flying helmet was a life-saver as she misjudged the height and tried to stand upright. 'Take care and follow me closely.' Henri dropped the flint of his lighter and absolute dark engulfed them. 'Let's go.'

The air was thin. Soon, her lungs and her back muscles were aching. As they rested part-way along, Henri explained that the tunnel had been excavated in the twelfth century by the castle's chatelaine, a native Gascon, as a guard against siege by the French king. 'My ancestor was an ally of the English, who were sovereign in this part of France at that time. I cannot applaud him for his choice of allies, but his burrowing was exemplary. If you are trapped in your castle by a hostile army, it is helpful to have a way out into the woods.' The passage had fallen into ruin over the centuries, Henri went on to say, but had been hastily re-dug and shored up at the outbreak of the Terror, in 1793. A much later ancestor, he told her proudly, had led his family to safety when a revolutionary mob surrounded Chemignac. 'And ever since, we have kept it in good repair. One never knows when a new enemy might come. A good tunnel, *hein*?'

'Every home should have one,' Yvonne quipped. Even that sapped her breath.

It *was* good as tunnels went, but her back was ready to break by the time Henri whispered, 'We are here.' After a silence, during which no sounds of impending ambush reached them, he used a wooden staff to push open a trapdoor. Hauling himself out, he reached down to help her, then flicked his lighter to show her the interior of a circular tower, stone steps rising steeply, a studded oak door to one side.

He unlocked that door, and led her through a room of heavy, farmhouse beams. She reeled at the ammonia smell of animal dung. From behind a wall came the noise of disturbed creatures.

'Geese,' Henri told her as he led her out into a courtyard. 'Every night, we shut our flock up in that part of the château.'

'Into your home?'

'I don't use that section, and it's the lesser of two evils. Their presence discourages the Germans from requisitioning any more of my home, you see?'

'Not really.'

'Our enemy likes to goose step, but he does not like to step in goose droppings.' Henri chuckled at his own joke.

'You'll need a big clean-out one day.'

'One day. One glorious day.' A few steps to another door, then Henri gave a brass bell a single clang, damping the sound instantly. The door was opened by a man.

'Go inside, Madame, and welcome to my home.'

At last, Yvonne got to crouch in front of a glowing stove while Henri introduced her to the young man who'd let them in. 'My brother, Albert.'

She'd assumed the spotty, lanky boy must be his son.

'I can tell what you're thinking. He really is my brother, and yes, there are many years between us.' Henri ruffled the younger man's hair. 'He was my parents' wild card.'

Young Albert de Chemignac stared fascinated at Yvonne's leather helmet and grass-streaked parachute suit. Uncomfortably, she felt that he was trying to see through it to her body beneath. Perhaps thinking the same, Henri sent him to make coffee. 'First, though, bring some cognac. The best. You will take a glass, Madame? There is also a small spread here of bread and cheese, a bowl of soup. Will you partake?'

'I will, thank you,' she said, gratefully taking the platter he offered and setting it on the floor by the fire. 'But must we keep up the "Madame, Monsieur" thing? Call me Yvonne, please. Excuse me one moment –' At last, she could take off her flying helmet, though she waited till Albert was out of the room. 'You don't know how long I've been waiting to do this.' Tipping her head forward, she pulled the pins out of her bun and raked the itches from her hair, forgetting that Titian gold melts to amber near flames. It was only when she raised her head that she saw she was being devoured. By two men, though not in the same way. Albert stood some way behind his brother, riveted. Henri was pouring brandy, his eyes also on her.

His gaze was warm. Arousal was there, with an undercoat of surprise, as if he was only just seeing the woman beneath the packaging. His voice remained urbane, however. 'It seems we are guarding a lioness. *Salut*, Madame. Ah, *votre pardon. Yvonne.*' He passed her a glass of tawny liquid, and the momentary fusion of their fingers brought a smile to his lips. Which, with that film star moustache, made him look wicked and unutterably sexy.

'*Salut*, Henri-Écharde,' she answered. It wouldn't do to show too much. Frenchmen, in her experience, expected admiration. It made them untrustworthy. As she piled cheese on to her bread before dunking it inelegantly into the soup, she asked, 'Why that code name, by the way?'

'Écharde fits my family history, being a splinter in the side of whoever threatens us. A dangerous habit, but incurable.' His eyes never left her. They'd never really left her since the moment they met. Even when his back was to her, he'd become *her* eyes as if they were welded together. She liked him. Loved him, for being there. For being part of the terrain that had absorbed her and would hide her until it was safe for her to leave. She smiled.

A muted clang at the door signalled the arrival of the others. It was the veteran agent, Jean-Claude, who limped in first, clamping his obvious pain behind gritted teeth. His knees and shins were filthy, indicating he'd crawled through the tunnel. Behind him came wounded, whimpering Cyprien who had been half-carried, half-dragged by two of Henri's Resistance colleagues. These men were introduced simply as Luc and Michel. They shook hands with her and with Henri, crowing with the exuberance of successful warriors. Albert hung back, Yvonne noticed. Not a man's man, she judged.

Luc and Michel stayed long enough to warm themselves with a glass of cognac – and offer an admiring toast to Yvonne – before returning to the tunnel. Henri invited her to help see them off, and as she helped him secure the hatch behind them, Yvonne asked, 'Will they return to their homes?'

'Not for a while.' He headed toward some wooden wine barrels alongside the tower steps, that Yvonne had noticed on her arrival. She realised the barrels' purpose as the brothers tilted them on their edges and 'walked' them to the trap door, squaring them right over the top to conceal it. The casks must be at least half full, if the heaving and grunting sounds that accompanied the job were anything to go by.

Henri blew out a breath and continued where he'd left off. 'My friends will take paths through the woods that only the hunters know, and find their way into Périgord Noir – Black Perigord – and lose themselves for a while in the oak forests. We'll see them again, eventually.'

'If they don't get caught,' Albert proffered.

'Go to bed,' Henri told him.

Yvonne waited until Albert had slammed a couple of doors behind him before asking, 'Will *you* be safe?' As Comte de Chemignac, Henri was a sitting duck. Forget code names and secret tunnels. He must be one of the best-known men in the district, as much trapped by his fortress as protected by it. 'Doesn't everyone know where to find you?'

'Naturally. But I keep in with the Germans and with all the local *Milice* commanders,' he assured her. 'I supply them their wine. They consider me to be a good, collaborating fellow and I do nothing to disabuse them.'

'They won't guess you're Écharde?'

'Never! Écharde is a rough fellow, a bumpkin who wouldn't know good wine from pigswill.' Laughing, he kissed her hand and she flinched pleasurably. She'd never before been kissed by a man with a moustache, on any part of her. The touch of hair was as disturbing as it was thrilling, a preview of the naked, male body as yet unexplored.

'This is where I'm to sleep?' Yvonne had followed Henri up curving tower steps to a room which he assured her was quite habitable. Their light was a stub of candle no bigger than Henri's thumb. Yvonne's eyes strained to translate the shadows. A bed. A real bed, and large. The room seemed ancient though, reminiscent of the Tower of London. 'Or is this where you confine errant wives?'

'Not personally, no.' He set the candle down on the floor, where it guttered, throwing chrysanthemum shapes on the ceiling. 'This and the gatehouse are what remain of our ancient stronghold, and this was where the guard was billeted in olden days. The last modern occupant was my mother's favourite maid. She slept here and did her sewing, and took care of the clothes. My mother's evening gowns are still here.' He opened the wardrobe door, releasing a whiff of preserving oils that made Yvonne sneeze. 'My late wife would come up here sometimes, to be alone.' He ended on a note that discouraged the obvious question. *Why did your wife feel the need to be alone?*

She said, 'Not much fun up here by oneself, with nothing to do.'

'I will bring you some books.'

'Am I allowed to put on the light?'

'Never.' He pointed to the shuttered window which, he told her, looked out on to the courtyard. 'The apartment opposite is where my parents lived until their deaths. Last year, it was commandeered for the use of a German industrialist who oversees the supply of timber to the Atlantic ports. Fortunately for us, he is rarely here, but he has two French lads who supposedly keep the place aired and exercise his gun dogs. We don't trust any of them, not even the dogs, so you must take great care.'

She peered through window glass and shutter slats. 'It all looks pretty deserted to me.'

'They've boarded up the rear windows to block out the noise of the geese, but even so. I have two children, Isabelle who is eight and Pierre-Gaston who is three. They live with their nursemaid and her family on one of my farms, and visit every day. Their nurse, is a decent girl, as is her young friend, Raymond, whom you will soon meet. But it is too much to expect children to remain silent if they see strangers. Particularly –' his gaze touched Yvonne's hair – 'a stranger with hair of Venetian gold. So you must not be seen by them.' He became brisk. 'Do not leave this building without my permission, nor open the courtyard window. As for that window - ' he indicated the opposite wall,'you can sit by that one during the day. It faces west.'

She saw no window, only an oil painting that appeared to be some kind of landscape, its detail obscured by the flickering light. Perhaps he was teasing her . . . why was he blowing out the candle?

She discovered why as he lifted the heavy frame from its hook. As her eyes adjusted, she made out a six-paned window, matt black against the night. Henri replaced the picture. 'During the day, you may take the picture down. No-one will see you if you sit to the side. But don't stare out, or open the casement. People walk across the château meadows all the time. My workers, their families, Germans sometimes, to call on me. Huntsmen stalk the woods at night. So replace the picture at dusk, and always if you have a candle lit.'

She understood. A light burning after dark might be visible two miles off.

He took her hands. 'You must be exhausted. You have eaten enough?'

'Quite enough.' She didn't want this moment to end, but somebody was stumping up the stairs and Yvonne felt a flutter of panic that she accepted as the SOE agent's lot. *The stairs were the only way down from here.* Unless she fancied a plunge from a window – which she supposed would be an escape of sorts – she'd be trapped if those steps belonged to an enemy.

The heavy tread was Albert's. He brought hot washing water, a towel and a shard of soap.

'Splendid, well done,' Yvonne said in her jolliest, games-mistress manner. Albert's lurking stare that began at her pelvis and crept upward, gave her the shivers. If any voice could scrub a dirty-minded boy's mouth out, it would be the one she'd developed to summon lazy schoolgirls out to the hockey pitch on winter mornings. 'Put the hot water on the side-table. That's the ticket. I'll say goodnight now.'

'We'll all say goodnight, though the night is almost over.' Henri nodded and motioned Albert out of the room.

By the close of her first day at Chemignac, Yvonne had thoroughly disobeyed Henri's orders by taking a chair out into the courtyard. The sun had the radiance of an electric fire, but she could sit in the shade of the château walls, reading the novel by Dumas she'd found in her bedroom. The German industrialist's apartment still showed no sign of life and she'd be perfectly safe, surrounded by geese who would surely honk up a storm at the mere suggestion of visitors. She was just getting into her novel when Jean-Claude hobbled out of his ground-floor room and asked if he could take her picture.

'You remind me of Britannia, dear girl, afloat in a sea of white wings.'

'It's absolutely forbidden for us to take snapshots of each other, you know that.'

'Scout's honour, if the Germans come within fifty yards of me, I'll swallow the film. I'll go potty if I don't do something other than lie around. Our host has billeted me in with our feathered friends. They generate a lot of heat and that is all the good I can say of them.'

'Oh, go on, then.' Yvonne kept her eyes lowered, feeling reassured by the bland disguise of her brown-and-beige outfit and the mousiness of her hair in photos. 'Shall I smile and say "Cheese"?'

'Try "Camembert", it's more dignified. Ready?'

Henri came into the courtyard as Jean-Claude clicked his shutter for the third time and his face turned to granite. Without a word, he hustled Yvonne inside, grabbing her chair and slinging it against one of the interior walls. He waited for Jean-Claude to join them and rounded on him. 'Take out the film,' he ordered. 'Expose it, now!'

Jean-Claude remained imperturbable. He never boiled up or grew flustered. It was probably why he'd passed all his agent training in spite of his age. 'Tell you what, old chap, I'll take some shots while I'm here, then hand the film over to you. You hide it away, in the dungeon or wherever, because we really do need a record of these times. This war won't last forever, and without pictures, who will prove who was where? Who will prove who was on whose side? One day, Monsieur, you might be called upon to explain why you supplied so much wine to the enemy.'

The sense of that reached Henri who answered with a curt nod. 'But I will keep your camera, and hide it until you leave here.' He held out his hand. With a pained sigh, Jean-Claude gave up his precious Kodak.

When it was just the two of them, Henri snarled, 'Are you insane, after what I said?'

Yvonne patted her hair defensively. Henri's handling had destabilised the hairpins. Her bun was slipping down her neck.

'I told you about that German and his staff, no? Pox-ridden informants, the both of them, and no more than fifty feet away.'

'Albert told me they spend most of their time in Garzenac, drinking.'

'Albert does not make the rules here or give the orders.'

'No. Clearly not. Oh, don't look at me like that.' His scathing fury was making her curl up inside. But he wasn't ready to relent.

'I thought the British SOE trained their people. Look what they send us! Old men, schoolboys and female amateurs. We deserve better.'

'How dare you?' Her anger was forced, disguising her shame. He had a valid point. Cyprien and Jean-Claude were useless until their injuries mended. Worse than useless. Liabilities. As for her, she wasn't sure why she'd disobeyed orders to keep indoors. Perhaps she just didn't *like* taking orders.

An apology was in order, but somehow, she couldn't get it out. 'Cyprien wouldn't have got shot in the first place if your people hadn't made a hash-up. How did the *Milice* know the time and place of our drop, unless your network has an informant?'

Henri rubbed his chin uncomfortably. 'It does – clearly it does – and most networks do. We recruit only those we know we trust, but men and women break. I lost four friends yesterday, Yvonne. Three men, one woman, *résistants* whose families will now pay a heavy price. For their sakes, we have to make this work. Stay indoors for now, please.'

She bowed her head. 'I just hate being up in that room. It makes me uneasy and . . .' she groped for something that didn't sound silly or far-fetched. She'd kept waking in that big bed, feeling she wasn't alone. Once she'd even hissed, 'Albert? Is that you, you wretch?' Except it couldn't have been Albert. It couldn't have been anyone, because she'd locked her door from the inside. Waking at daybreak, the light through shutters making a pattern of piano keys across her bedspread, she'd thought she heard gunshots and heavy boots. A minute of heart-arrest, listening with one foot on the floor, had reassured her that it was only the morning congregation of geese. She'd lain under her covers, thinking she ought to get up, when the wardrobe door had whined open, bathing her in its strange, spicy breath. A dress had slipped off its hanger in a plop of violet silk. Utter despair had stolen over her.

The recollection of it made her temper surge. 'You spend your days striding among the vines! You think I should sit day and night in a dark room, counting the cobwebs? I'm trapped up there and bloody miserable.'

He said stiffly, 'If you would prefer to sleep down here, we will bring a mattress into this room.'

She looked around. Where they stood must once have been the household's laundry. A tarnished copper boiler dominated one wall, while a line of stone sinks spanned another. It had been some years since any washing had been done here, she reckoned. The window glass was grey and though she could apply elbow grease and shine it up, that wasn't what she wanted. 'Stay with me in the tower.' There. She'd said it. 'I don't want to be alone up there.'

'Yvonne.' The two syllables communicated reproach, desire, exasperation. 'You are my guest.'

'I'm asking. Giving you permission. Why not? You're not married.' He'd referred to 'his late wife', after all. 'And neither am I.'

'I have my children to think of.'

'All night? Surely, once they're tucked up in bed in their nursemaid's home, whatever we get up to can't affect them.'

He groaned, gazing down at her, and then their mouths met, neither of them aware who moved first, who closed the gap faster. Yvonne closed her eyes. When she heard the scrape of boots in the courtyard, she knew that somebody was peering in at them through the dirty window. *So be it.* She disliked being spied on, but danger was a drug, after all. So was the taste of Henri's mouth and the restless exploration of his hands.

Shauna pulled out of her trance and took Laurent's hand, pulling him out of Albert's apartment, bidding its owner a hasty 'Goodnight!' Out in the courtyard, she squealed in astonishment as Laurent blocked her progress and locked her against the house wall. 'Who is he?' he demanded. The animosity he'd displayed in Rachel's presence was back.

'Who is who? Laurent, don't cram me in. It's not like you and I don't like it.'

'No? What do you like, this?' His lips were against hers then, marauding, demanding. She struggled but there was so much strength in him, she couldn't escape or even bend away. All she could do was reach up and grab the drawstring neck of his hoodie and pull until he had to break off for air. Then she slapped him, just hard enough to bring him back to his senses.

'Shauna?'

'That was like being mugged in a back alley. Oh, wait a minute . . . you've been with Albert. Has he been filling your mind with his brand of progressive feminism?'

Laurent was breathing hard. Shauna remained ready to fight, until the pattern of his breath changed and she knew the person she loved was back with her.

He said, 'It's not Albert –' He broke off to touch her face. 'Did I hurt you?'

'You haven't shaved, so you sandpapered me.'

'I'm sorry. I won't ever do that again.'

'Well, that would be a shame.' She drew him to her and kissed him, murmuring, 'Uh-uh' when he tried to take over. 'I don't mind implacable passion, so long as I know who the man is behind it.' Her tongue found the sensitive places behind his lips, the roof of his mouth. He writhed, straining against her, but she still wouldn't let him take over. Her lips moved around his lips, his throat and cheekbones, the prickly sideburn hair, the lobe of an ear until he was lost, pushing her back against the wall, unable to stop himself. Responding to his arousal, her loins ached and nothing would have stopped the primal act taking place there and then – until Shauna happened to glance up at the tower.

'My God, there, see that?'

Most unwillingly, Laurent followed her gaze. The light at the top of the tower was flickering on and off.

'I told you about that, didn't I?' she said. 'Your wiring's faulty.'

'I have it checked every year, for the insurance. Shauna, don't leave me in pain, please.' He raked her thigh, his hand beneath her dress, urgent, tantalising, but she pushed him away, aware all of a sudden that they were in the courtyard, where anyone might see them.

Laurent said heavily, 'Rachel tells me you're leaving, that there's someone else. An older man. Your professor, she said.'

So that's what had triggered the storm!

'Why didn't you tell me, Shauna?'

'Because it isn't the case. Rachel's lying.'

'Earlier today, she took a phone call from the north of England. The caller had tried many times to reach you.'

'Kind of her to mention it. Who wanted me?'

'As I said, your professor.'

Shauna put her arm around Laurent, to steer him towards Isabelle's door and, ultimately, to bed. But whatever tormented him made him resistant. 'I am not leaving Chemignac,' she said, each word emphatic. 'Not unless you tell me to. Rachel is dishonest, as you well know, and at this moment she's locked in her bedroom with Adão, not a stitch between them. I am not involved with anybody else.'

She felt him shudder, waiting for his answer. That *frisson* had felt to her like jealousy. Good, because it proved his feelings.

He said slowly, 'You must not leave, Shauna. And we have to learn the end of Henri and Yvonne's story.'

'And then?'

'I can't see past them. Everything emotion I feel is magnified. I have no control and I can't go through this alone. In Albert's room, I *was* Henri. What did you feel in there? What did you make of the photos?'

She admitted, 'I was in Yvonne's head. I came here and I took a lover. Henri. I was a fast mover!'

'And I wanted you from the moment I saw you in your goggles and overalls. As Henri, I couldn't get enough of you and now, it feels like I'm making up for lost years.' His smile, absent for so much of the day, lit up. She reached up to stroke his mouth and felt his teeth close lightly on her finger.

'It's our story too, isn't it?' She'd denied the idea for so long, as being outside rational possibility. But consciousness of an alternative reality had been growing for a while. Indelibly, like the shadow on an x-ray plate. To negate it in the face of so much proof would be illogical. Lights still flickered on and off at the top of the tower. She took a deep breath and told Laurent that the Gown of Thorns was back in its wardrobe.

'How?'

She explained about finding it in Isabelle's wardrobe. 'Rachel, yet again! I decided it ought to go back to its lair. I'm sorry.'

'No – you did right. I wouldn't want it anywhere near the children. That dress betrayed Yvonne and Henri.'

A shred of rationalism held. 'I don't buy that a dress can be imbued with evil. It's cloth,' she repeated, mostly for her own sake – having worn the thing, she was already half convinced of the contrary. 'Treachery is a *human* vice.'

'The dress corrupted Yvonne. Albert swears it was a woman who brought the Germans to Chemignac. He accuses Yvonne.'

'Well, he would, wouldn't he? Yvonne would never betray Henri, not willingly.' Shauna grasped Laurent's hands, squeezing them in time to her words. 'He was her soulmate. She'd never have used that word, but that's what they were. Soulmates. She'd never sacrifice him unless she was under such duress, she couldn't hold out.' *Men and women break*. Henri had said it to her, through Yvonne. *I don't want to know if Yvonne broke*, she thought. *But I'm going to know*. The room was signalling. On-off. On-off. 'Laurent, do you have what it takes to find out what happened to Henri and Yvonne?'

Laurent folded his hands over hers like pigeon wings. Whose touch was the colder? 'I don't think we have any choice, do you?'

In Dakenfield, Miss Thorne lay in her curtained niche, staring at a fog of sleepless dots. Strip lighting through pimpled glass panels meant that the ward was never properly dark. One more reason she couldn't sleep.

There'd been talk of sending her to a rehabilitation unit, and then – just perhaps – home. Did she have family, they'd asked? There had to be somebody to check on her at least twice a day in case she fell again.

She had no family, she told them, though that wasn't entirely true. She had a half-brother, Paul, who had done his all to keep the ties between them alive, but even he had given up when she sent a

Christmas card back to him 'Return to Sender'. After the war, she'd wanted desperately to vanish, and that's what she'd done.

Any children? A male nurse had asked her that. Thirty-five years a schoolteacher, she could still slap down impudence. 'Young man, I am *Miss* Antonia Thorne. I don't know what values you hold to, but in my day, respectable women did not breed out of wedlock.' To herself, she acknowledged, *No children. How could there be, after Henri died?*

What a series of blunders her life had been. What a failure of an existence. *Not long now*, she thought. She felt such a strong connection to Henri – to Chemignac – she was more often there in her mind than here these days. She didn't even have to wait for dreams. She just closed her eyes . . . soon, soon, she would melt away and be with Henri for always.

Chapter Twenty

The sputtering lights had died during their ascent to the tower bedroom. Dark serenity greeted them.

'Let's get into the bed,' Shauna murmured. Under the satin coverlet, they could share body heat and besides, she always felt threatened and unhappy in this room. Standing about, she'd feel she was waiting for something awful to happen. Stripping off her dress, she climbed into bed in her bra and pants. The mattress creaked as Laurent got in beside her and for a while, they competed in shivering. As warmth finally stole over them, Shauna directed Laurent's hand so it lay over her tattoo. She slid her hand inside his sleeve and grasped his forearm, and the image of the thorn. A circle, thorn on thorn.

'What are we trying to do?' he murmured.

'I'm emptying my mind to start the film again. I'll tell you if I see anything.' She tried to clear random thoughts, but the proximity of the Gown of Thorns acted as a disturber. Like having the TV on when trying to meditate. Her eyelids grew leaden and she thought, *I give in. I'm going to sleep*, when Laurent murmured, 'It was an error to let the children visit.'

'They need to be here,' Shauna answered. 'Can you imagine the atmosphere in the Paris apartment, their father veering between despair and depression, and their grandmother constantly blaming herself for what's happened to Louette? They're much better off with us.'

'Not those children. Isabelle and my father. Their nanny brought them here while the British agents were in hiding.'

'Did they see anything they shouldn't?' she prompted

'My father was at the toddler-talking stage, babbling his own language a lot of the time, so it didn't matter what he saw. But Isabelle was eight.

Bright and opinionated, much like Olive and deeply
. . .' he tailed off.

'Deeply what?'

'Attached to me.'

'I know that. After Nico, you're her favourite
male.'

'Who is Nico? Attached to me, their father.'
Laurent sounded as though he was speaking through
a layer of wool. His breathing was too shallow for
him to be falling asleep, though. Shauna waited.
Was Laurent to be the channel this time?

'Isabelle is attached to me and it is why I've
sent her away, and the boy.'

I have sent . . . Laurent's voice, always deep,
had grown huskier. 'Am I speaking to Henri?'

'That's who I am.'

'You sent your children away because it was
– I mean, *is* – safer?'

'Naturally. They have no mother and at the
Valles' farm, they are well cared for. The Valles are

trustworthy and Audrey makes a good nursemaid for all she is young.'

'Audrey as in 'Raymond and Audrey'?' Whoa, where was this going?

'The Valles are my tenants and Audrey is their daughter. She loves Isabelle and Pierre-Gaston, and plays with them like an older sister. A good solution for motherless children, don't you think?'

'I hadn't thought about it.' Shauna put her lips to Laurent's knuckles, testing his reactions. He didn't respond. 'Did they – I mean, *do* the Valles know what you do at Chemignac?'

'Other than make wine?' Laugher made his ribs bounce. 'They know about the "guests" I take care of, but they don't speak of it any more than they would of a neighbour's ailments or infidelities.'

She had to ask again, 'Am I speaking to Henri de Chemignac?'

His arms tightened around her and his answer came in the form of a kiss, deep and demanding and her breathing grew shallow too, a yielding moisture between her thighs, her nipples responding as Laurent – was it still Laurent? – cupped her breasts, chafing their peaks. She remained aware of herself as Shauna, in the tower room with a man who wanted to make love. She unhooked her bra and his lips instantly sought her exposed flesh. When his fingers invaded her, she succumbed quickly to waves of pleasure that went on and on until she thought she would lose her senses. Her mind seemed to dilate, her inner vision traveling super-fast through darkness. Like a camera bedded in a bullet passing through the barrel of a gun, her inner eye kept pace until, like a lucid dreamer, she touched down in a different reality. She was Yvonne, but also Shauna. The man with her, whose clothes she was helping to remove, was Laurent *and* Henri.

Yvonne stretched her arms behind her, linen bed sheets falling away like a spillage of cream. It was early afternoon, July heat at its zenith. Henri had opened both windows, west and east. The room would have been unbearable otherwise. If anybody saw him up here, he'd explain that he was airing the place. She must stay on the bed, and not risk a limb or a bright curl coming into view.

They had dined on bread, the local goat's cheese called Cabécou and preserved walnuts. Henri had uncorked a bottle of Cabernet Franc that complemented the simplest, and one of the best, meals she'd ever tasted. Afterwards, they had made love. Her limbs soft and sated, Yvonne thought dimly of the job she'd come to do. In three or four days, somebody would collect her and hustle her on to another location. After that, she'd be conducted to Bordeaux and an anonymous, town centre apartment where she'd get on with the job she'd been dropped for – running messages between Resistance personnel and SOE wireless operators – one of whom was probably jumping up and down for those replacement radio crystals right now. Her life would be clandestine meetings and messages relayed back to London. Whenever she ventured out of the flat, she'd walk on metaphorical eggshells, eyes staring out of the back of her head. If she had any sense, she'd put Henri de Chemignac out of her mind.

She heard Henri swear, saw him put a finger in his mouth. He was repairing the oil painting's hanging wire, having noticed it was fraying. It looked like he'd driven the end of it into his finger.

'It's a hideous picture,' she said.

'That's why it's up here. My wife had it removed from the drawing room after we married. She hated it too, and before you say anything else rude about it, the painter was English.'

'Of course. Only English water meadows could be so dank-looking on what must be a summer's day. One could catch fever of the lungs staring at it too long.' Then, because she felt she'd known Henri far longer than two days, and because they had so little time left together, she asked to know more about his wife.

For a while, he said nothing and she supposed she'd offended etiquette. But it seemed he was concentrating on twisting the ends of the picture wire. 'Marie-Louise died in June, 1940. She'd been in Paris when the Nazis invaded and was trying to get home. She was with her maid, and both women were killed. Murdered, I should say. The last trains had already left Paris, but they got a lift in a van as far as Orléans. From there I believe they went on foot, heading for Chateauroux where the maid had family. As far as I know, they were shot by German pilots, who strafed refugees on the road at low altitude.'

'The shits. No wonder you're so angry, Henri. No wonder you do what you do. Did you . . .' *love her?* She cleared her throat. 'Were you a happy couple?'

He tested the wire to ensure it could still take the painting's weight. Then, leaning the frame against the wall, he poured out the last of the wine. Balancing two glasses, he eased himself down on the bed next to her. 'We married when I was twenty-nine and she thirty-two. I know. A bit late. I didn't want to marry, but my family expected it.' He handed her a glass. 'I was born in 1902, making me a year young ever to fight in the Great War. My elder brother was killed within weeks of it starting, and an uncle a few months later. I joined the army the year after the war ended, feeling I should do something for my country. Back then, I didn't want to grow grapes. But when my father died, I had little choice; I had to return. My mother had been dead several years, but my grandmother was still alive and she arranged a marriage for me, with a friend's daughter – Marie-Louise de Sainte-Vierge.'

Yvonne hazarded a guess. 'She'd lost her

fiancé during the war.'

He drained his wine. 'Correct. So she made do with me. I had land and a title, she had family money. A sensible arrangement, as we like to do in France. People of my class rarely expect happiness, but we do expect the appearance of fidelity. What I did not know at the time of my engagement was that Marie-Louise had a career in Paris, as a writer and painter. She was, I later learned, in a relationship with a fellow artist. Our temperaments were unsuited, and we were too set in our ways to change. But, we muddled through and had children, which was the point of it all.'

'Most people muddle through.' Yvonne put their empty glasses down on the floor. 'Artistic temperament is grossly overrated, in my opinion, whereas "muddling" is the mature realisation of one's own limitations. It is the great, unsung human virtue.'

'She hated this place, and at every

opportunity went to Paris. She liked clothes, so we pretended it was to view the collections. In May 1940, when Isabelle was five and Pierre-Gaston just a baby, I wrote to her at the hotel where she was staying, warning her that I feared an invasion was imminent, and that Paris might be bombed. She must come home, her children were asking every day for her. She wrote back saying that she had gowns being made, and one being altered, and would leave as soon as they were finished.' He pulled Yvonne to him, blowing a strand of her hair away from his nose. 'I should have fetched her. Whenever I hear my children crying for *maman*— Who is that?'

Henri went still. Somebody was calling from the courtyard below. A child's voice. He waited until he heard the clear call of 'Papa!' before getting out of bed and wrapping a sheet around himself. 'Don't move,' he told Yvonne.

He went to the window and she saw him give

a slight wave. He pushed the window wider and shouted, 'Stay there with Audrey, *ma fille*. I'll be down in a moment. I said wait!' He swore through his teeth, turning to Yvonne. 'Quick, get dressed. My daughter Isabelle is coming up. I had hoped to keep the children from seeing you, but I suppose there's no avoiding it now.'

'Shall I hide in the wardrobe?' She wasn't entirely joking. Henri looked strained. Not ashamed or shifty, for which she was glad, but like a man who knows the next few minutes are going to be unpleasant.

He was throwing on his clothes. 'No, no point. She'll fling open the wardrobe door anyway, to see the Gown of Thorns.'

'Gown of what?' Yvonne was out of bed, hauling on her knickers, her blouse – no time to put on her brassiere, which she shoved under a pillow as Henri roughly remade the bed. Just time to button her waistband and smooth down her skirt before a black-haired child rushed in.

'Papa!' The little girl threw herself at Henri, who absorbed the impact and picked her up.

Isabelle de Chemignac was a long-limbed child with an elfin face and pointed chin. Truffle-dark eyes regarded Yvonne warily over her father's shoulder.

'Who is she?' she demanded.

Henri put his daughter down. 'That is rude, Isabelle. We do not say, "she". This lady is Yvonne, and she is my guest. Come and shake her hand.'

'Why is she up here?'

'We're tidying,' Yvonne improvised, when Henri failed to come up with an answer. *Oh dear.* Daddy's little girl looked distinctly put out. Charm and appeasement was called for. 'He was telling me about the Gown of Thorns, is that its name? I'm intrigued. Will you show it to me?'

She knew instantly that she'd made an unimaginable gaff. Henri shook his head warningly, while Isabelle let out a shriek, flew to the wardrobe and spread-eagled herself against the doors, a human barricade.

'Nobody must touch the dress. It killed *maman*! It killed *maman*!'

Even when her father pulled her away, and removed her from the room like a cumbersome parcel, Isabelle de Chemignac kept up the harrowed chant – 'It killed *maman*!'

Yvonne sat down heavily on the bed. 'Goodness. Poor little mite. Missing her mother, naturally.' The 'killer dress' was, presumably, one of those that had kept Madame de Chemignac in Paris, resulting in her being caught up in the chaos of invasion.

And yet, Yvonne was curious. Creeping like a cat – Henri's instruction to stay hidden had been well and truly rammed home – she crept to the wardrobe. She crouched in front of the doors and opened them from the base, squinting up at a hoard of sumptuous skirts. 'Goodness,' she repeated, drawn irresistibly to her feet. Hidden within the wardrobe's embrace, she rifled through the folds until her fingers stopped at a gown of violet, lavender and silver-grey pleats. So delicate, she was reminded of the gills under the cap of a mushroom. Quite forgetting Henri's injunction to keep below window level, she lifted it off its hanger and turned towards the mirror.

'Put it back, Yvonne.'

She jumped like a thief. 'Only looking.' She held the dress against herself. 'Sorry. But it's lovely. It's my colour.' Her voice rang hollow as she justified herself. 'We auburns and Titians can't wear red or pink or orange, so we go nuts for violet and green. Admit it's my colour.'

'It *is* your colour, but it is not your dress.' Henri took it from her and hung it back on the rail. He closed the cupboard, then the window shutters. He then drew her to sit next to him on the bed. 'It was made for my mother, from silk dyed with berries picked on the estate.'

'Which berries?'

'Of the *épine noir*.'

Blackthorn, whose berries were called sloes. Whose thorns were the Devil's fangs – if you harvested them without wearing stout gloves. Every winter, after the first frost, she and her mother used to raid the hedgerows in Derbyshire's Hope Valley where she'd grown up, where she'd lived until moving north to Sheffield to train as a teacher. Sloe gin had been their kitchen-cupboard standby, the winter cordial to fend off throat infections and sniffles. 'Aren't we a pair of witches?' her mother would say as they set off with their baskets. Happy companion-witches, until her mother's death.

'I don't believe it,' Yvonne said brusquely.

'What do you not believe?'

'The colour. Mother dyed her own wool, you see. She kept a few sheep and spun their fleeces.

She'd use ground up barks, lichens and berries to create colours. Sloes look dark when you mash them, but the fibres come out a slubby grey. They're never this bright. It's a myth, your Gown of Thorns.'

'The dye was intensified by adding red grape skins from the last vines picked in 1914. That year's harvest was brought in by the women, the children and the old men. I told you my brother died almost as soon as he entered the war? He was blown to pieces in the first battle of the Marne, the day we began to pick the Cabernet Franc. We hadn't known the war was serious, and suddenly, Pierre was dead. When my uncle died a few months after, this dress gained its reputation for being unlucky.'

'I can see that. But that's what people do, focus their anger and sorrow on something closer to home. Easier than blaming the politicians and the generals.'

She had to lean close to hear his answer. 'My

mother felt the same way and wore the dress exactly ten years later, at our 1924 *fête de vendange*. She was five months pregnant with my brother Albert. Only just showing – she was a slight woman. To wear the clinging Gown of Thorns was an act of defiance.'

'Against superstition?'

'And against the gossip that we were an unlucky family. She adored the Delphos gown. Do you know, the designer Fortuny and his wife kept their method of pleating secret? However they were created, the pleats always keep their shape. A Delphos gown can be rolled and put in a suitcase, or knotted over the shoulder.'

'The perfect dress for an SOE agent, I'd say.'

He shook his head, looking at the wardrobe. 'Don't be tempted. Three months after wearing the dress at the *fête*, my mother died giving birth prematurely, after a labour that lasted the better part of three nights. After that, the old women in the village said the dress was cursed because it was made from the fruits of an ancient thorn tree and grapes tainted by war.'

'But you don't believe such hocus-pocus.'

'Oh, I do.' Henri spoke fervently. 'Perhaps not then, but later. My wife coveted the Gown of Thorns, though she was too tall for it. I eventually allowed her to wear it for a Christmas dinner, and shortly after, we lost our firstborn son to measles. As soon as the roads were free of snow, I took the damn garment to Bordeaux, to a used clothes shop. I didn't want money for it. Sell it privately, I said. Under no circumstances show it in the window.'

'Why not just burn it?'

'Would you burn your mother's favourite gown?'

Of course she wouldn't. Her mother's things were still hanging up in the Derbyshire house. If – when – the war ended, she must clear the house, and sell it. Perhaps she would come to live in France? 'I take it the dress returned, like the proverbial bad penny?'

'My wife's maid was in Bordeaux buying linen and happened to pass the shop. The shopkeeper had disobeyed my instruction not to put the dress in the window.' Henri's mouth creased at the memory. 'It wreaks havoc on every generation.'

'Every family has its share of pain, Henri. My father left my mother after I was born. Started again with somebody else, the rotter. I have a half-brother, Paul. He likes me, the poor, misguided little sod, and I can't stand him because of what he represents.' She sighed. 'People behave badly.'

Henri didn't respond, his memory lodged in the past. 'My wife was furious that I'd tried to get rid of the dress, and to spite me, she took it with her to Paris. It needed to be re-pleated, she said, because the woman in the shop had tried to iron it . . . a few weeks after Marie-Louise was killed, the dress arrived back here. She'd taken it to the House of

Fortuny, hoping they could lengthen it for her. How they'd do that, I can't imagine! It was returned with a note explaining that, because Paris was now under German occupation, they no longer had the resources to remake the dress.' Henri got up. 'I have to go; I promised to saddle up a pair of ponies and take my children for a ride through the vines. Pierre-Gaston is mad about horses, though he has to ride with me because his little legs are not strong yet.'

A ride through summer greenery, what heaven . . . oh, this bloody war! 'You won't forget about your poor, incarcerated princess in the tower?'

'Of course not. We will all dine together tonight. Isabelle has met you, after all, and now Audrey knows about you.'

'The children's nanny? Lord, we're making a poor show of being secretive!'

He returned a shrug. 'By now, my boy will be agog to know about the flame-haired lady in the tower. You and your colleague Jean-Claude might as well dine with us as family. We'll keep Cyprien in his room, though. Explaining away a man with a bullet hole in his shoulder would tax my powers of invention.' His humour died as fast as it flared. 'May I have your promise that you'll keep your hands off the wardrobe?'

'You have it.'

He kissed her, and left.

'Cursed are you?' she directed at the cupboard. She wouldn't go back on a promise. Honour bright, and all that. But as she put her foot to the floor, a floorboard sank an inch or so. The wardrobe rocked and its doors slowly opened. Yvonne spied violet and silver among the other colours and said, 'Well, hello again.'

Her skin still felt peppery from Henri's caresses and it came to her that nothing would sooth it as well as a silken Delphos gown.

Chapter Twenty-One

Dawn sky the colour of pink grapefruit filled the window. Returning to consciousness, Shauna stared at the strands of cloud, slowly recollecting where she was. Laurent's head was butted against her breast. They must look like a pair of gingerbread men baked together, limbs conjoined. She tried to stretch. Her legs felt stiff as concrete. Her arm muscles ached as well. Heaven help her, yet another day of bending and picking ahead!

Laurent muttered, 'I need to know what happened next to Henri and Yvonne. That dinner he planned was their last together.'

He sat up, looking hungover, though that couldn't be as they hadn't drunk last night.

'A meal to remember,' she said, 'but not in a good way. Jealousy was top of the menu. Albert had

seen them kissing. We'll have to ask him . . . Oh!'
She remembered then that Rachel and Adão were
still locked in the stable-yard flat. She reminded
Laurent, who only laughed.

'I should let them out before one of them
tries to jump out the window,' said Shauna.

'They're tall and fit. Let them,' was
Laurent's opinion, but Shauna pushed back the bed
covers. 'Adão won't be much use to you with a
broken ankle. Which *parcelles* are we doing today?'

'The Semillon, those I'm harvesting for dry
white. I leave half the Semillon and all the
Muscadelle in the hope of a noble rot pick later in
the month. For sweet wine . . . if we get the correct
conditions.'

'If, if and if. Come on.' She held out her
hand. 'Let's get a shower running. Will you make
coffee while I rescue the lovers?'

'You make coffee. I want to check the horses
anyway. I don't like Rachel bringing them in when

she's in a bad mood.'

'OK, if you're sure.' *How would he react to finding Rachel with another man?* She believed Laurent cared for her, and not at all for Rachel, but insecurity had put deep roots in her.

As they put on last night's clothes, Shauna kept her back to the wardrobe. Entering Henri and Yvonne's minds last night had arguably been a sustained joint hallucination. And although she was grateful to whatever force haunted Chemignac for bringing her and Laurent to such closeness, she couldn't face another trance just yet. They should keep out of this room, she suggested, until after the harvest. 'I can't wrestle with vines all day and embrace quantum reality at night.'

He smiled. 'So that's what it is. Yes, I agree.' He locked the tower room door and in the kitchen, poked the keys deep into their hiding place.

While the kettle boiled, they showered together. Over the hiss of the water, Laurent asked her, 'Did you smell smoke in Rachel's flat?'

'From a stove?'

'Tobacco. Adão smokes roll-ups when he's not working, and Rachel smokes weed. It's forbidden anywhere near the barns. I don't care what the two of them do together, so long as it doesn't involve matches and glowing cigarette ends.'

She didn't remember smelling anything, and said so. But she did remember Rachel's heartless observations about Louette's crash and as she towelled herself dry, she pondered the ill fortunes of the sons and daughters of Chemignac. Death in war, death in childbirth. Even Isabelle – two falls in the space of three months, following a car accident that broke her femur. But these things happened in every family, didn't they? Look at hers. Her father, gone in early middle age. Dig back and no doubt she'd find plenty of stillbirths and war-deaths among her own tribe.

Dakenfield

The nurses were busy around the bed next to Miss Thorne's. Curtains were drawn. A poor old thing with dementia had been brought in the previous afternoon. She'd spent the following hours crying out to invisible family members, and faded into silence at around six that morning. 'Passed away', a nurse told Miss Thorne, who replied, 'Damn. She took my slot.'

The nurse was too busy to unpick the meaning of this, saying only, 'Try not to mind too much.'

As Miss Thorne slowly ate her breakfast, a trainee nurse brought a large bunch of white roses to her bed. 'You've got an admirer, Antonia.'

'Miss Thorne, please. And take it from me, nobody with any sense could admire me.'

'They're definitely for you. Shall I read the message?' The nurse extracted the card tucked in with the flowers, and opened her mouth to read the greeting. 'Oh. It's in French. I can't make it out.'

Miss Thorne couldn't either. Her eyes were too weak. She had to wait until Joelle, the friendly tea-lady, came by on her afternoon rounds. Joelle spoke French, she'd been born in Cameroon.

'"We think of you often, and wish you well. *Never forget*. From Raymond and Audrey at Chemignac." Shall I pour your tea, honey?'

No answer. Miss Thorne was writhing under an onslaught of memories. Audrey and Raymond were the only people alive who knew that she had once, briefly, been Yvonne Rosel. They were the only French people she'd kept in touch with, and only because Audrey had sought her out and kept a correspondence going. *How had they traced her here?*

They'd been so young when she met them in 1943. Shy sweethearts, hiding their devotion because Audrey came from respectable farming stock while the Chaumiers, Raymond's folk, were labourers. The two of them had been children really, thrust by war and the realities of rural life into premature adulthood. Audrey Valle, her black curls flattened under a headscarf, playmate and surrogate mother to Henri's children. Raymond, just thirteen, doing a man's work in the vineyard and around the stables. Rounding up those bloody geese every night, before settling down in his nook among the birds. A boy of varied talents, he'd cooked dinner for them all on that last night, rustling up rabbit in red wine.

How frustrated with life she'd been that day! Confined to her room, fed up with reading. Unable even to get up and exercise unless she covered the windows. Envying Henri and his children riding in the sunshine.

The appearance of Albert at her door that afternoon had hardly improved her spirits. She'd rather have had a visit from one of the ganders. He'd brought a note from Henri, formally inviting her to dine, though not until nine o'clock. By nine, the sun would be setting and it would be safe then for her and Jean-Claude to slip between the buildings. When she realised that Albert had also brought a wind-up gramophone, her spirits leapt. Finally, she could expel the deadly silence. 'Modern or classical?' she asked as he placed a pile of records on the wash stand. Without answering, he came further into the room. From inside a jacket made from some kind of rough sailcloth, he produced a posy of summer blooms. 'For you.'

'How kind.' She put them to her nose. 'Are these Bourbon roses? Aren't they exquisite? An old-fashioned rose shows all nature's imperfections, yet keeps its beauty.' A pretentious comment that was lost on Albert. His face fell.

'I knocked off all the bugs.'

'Good for you. I'll wear this one in my button hole tonight.' She selected a rose whose white petals were streaked with dark pink. 'Thank your brother for the gramophone. Music in the afternoon, what a treat.' She meant – *please go now*. Albert's expression, poised somewhere between lustful intensity and hang-dog reproach, made her queasy. He didn't scare her. She was trained to defend herself. 'I'm sure you have a busy afternoon . . .'

He seemed to be staring at the bed. He pointed. 'What's that?'

Before she could react, he'd swooped on an object on the floor. A moment later, he was thrusting one of Henri's cufflinks towards her. 'What's this doing here?' he demanded.

'Clearly, not its designated job of holding shirt cuffs together. Give it to your brother, won't you? He's likely missing it.'

'You fornicate with my brother. I know what you are. I've *seen you*.'

She flushed. 'Because you pry at windows! Has nobody told you, nothing is as detestable as a voyeur.'

'I know what you are.' His voice was nasal. Insistence or obsession? 'You fornicate.'

'Say that again, and— ' she broke off as he lunged for her. 'How dare you!' No ambiguity about which part of her anatomy he was aiming for. A moment later, he was face down on the floorboards, one arm twisted behind his back, Yvonne's knee on his lumbar.

'Bitch!' he shrieked.

'Get up and get out. From now on, don't even look at me.'

'I could have you arrested!'

'That would make you a traitor, a coward and a collaborator.'

At the door, bravado deserted him and he dipped his head sideways. 'Will you tell Henri?'

She weighed up her choices. Albert was now a threat and really, she should break his neck. Had he not been Henri's brother, she'd have done it. But her sense of fair play argued that he was just a boy, his mental age closer to fifteen than the eighteen that he apparently was. All that sneering was surely just self-loathing, a groping for love. A literal groping, in this case. Henri had told her that Albert had been rejected for war service and passed over for forced labour. Some would call that a stroke of luck, but it was hardly an endorsement to raise a boy's confidence. Pity propelled her answer, 'I won't tell him this time.'

Raymond's rabbit casserole was superb, thick with swede, garlic and herbs, with chunks of unbleached bread to soak up the sauce. As promised, Audrey brought the children to the table. They'd slept through the early part of the evening and were now wide awake, the little boy Pierre-Gaston chuckling and singing delightfully. Isabelle, who slithered onto the seat next to her father, greeted Yvonne politely, though she spent most of the meal gazing at her papa. Henri conversed with Jean-Claude.

Yvonne directed her attention towards Audrey Valle, ignoring Albert and tossing only a few polite comments in Henri's direction. They'd be together later and it was rather fun, pretending to be mere acquaintances. In fact, the whole evening was jolly. Jean-Claude regaled them with stories about his work for a leading British newspaper in Paris. He'd been a news photographer for Calford Press, he told them, and his impressions of the choleric, violently unreasonable Lord Calford had them in stitches. Yvonne was even able to forget that this was not her home, that she was a fugitive. A stranger with a short life-expectancy.

At the end of the meal, Henri raised his wine glass to Raymond, saying, 'Thank you to the excellent chef.'

Albert joined the toast, adding snidely, 'You'll make someone a damn good wife one day, Raymond.'

'Mockery is the resort of the stupid,' Henri snapped at his brother. 'If you cannot be generous, at least fight clean.'

Oh, the venom in Albert's eyes! It crystalised around them like spun sugar in ice-cold air. 'I am not allowed to fight, as you well know,' Albert snarled. 'Medically unfit.'

'There is another fight and you are free to be part of it.'

'The Resistance?' Albert turned up his lip. 'A bunch of big-heads who can't keep their gobs shut. Obviously, or *she* wouldn't be here.' Albert jabbed a finger across the table at Yvonne.

Raising his glass, swallowing wine without

showing the emotion Yvonne knew was rippling through him, Henri replied, 'I sometimes wonder, Albert, if you will ever grow into a man.'

'Oh? You think you are the lord and master here, brother, but even you have your weaknesses. You will fail in the end.'

'Albert was a nasty little shit,' Miss Thorne said loudly, using up her strength so she had none with which to sit up for her tea. 'A groping little shit.'

Joelle, stirring sugar into a mug, replied calmly, 'I've met a few of those in my time.'

'No doubt you have,' Miss Thorne agreed. But she hadn't been referring to your average bloke with wandering hands. She'd been speaking of a little shit who had betrayed his brother and got away with it for sixty years.

Chapter Twenty-Two

Amber beads sprayed with atomised honey. That's how Shauna described the luscious bloom on the Semillon grapes. They were reaching the end of the second day's picking, and that would complete the main white grape harvest. A half-hectare would be left to succumb to 'noble rot', a strain of botrytis mould essential to the production of sweet Montbazillac wine. What was needed, according to Laurent, was a humid spell followed by drying winds. Without the dryness, they'd get rotten grapes, good for nobody.

True to their agreement, they'd not spoken of Yvonne or Henri since their night in the tower room. Laurent needed every grain of energy for the *chai*. Loaded trailers left the vineyards in relay, the crushers and presses roaring and grinding the day long. The vats were filling.

'You've missed a cluster.'

Shauna tensed. Even if she hadn't recognised the round-toed boots planted on the ground beside her, she'd have known that critical tone. Without looking up from the vine she was denuding, she said, 'I've seen it, Monsieur. Thank you.'

'You missed another one further back.'

'Because some of the grapes looked bad. But feel free to check.' The boots did not move.

'I know what you are,' Albert de Chemignac said, not seeming to care who heard.

Madame Guilhem, who'd specially requested another stint as Shauna's picking partner, paused, scissors aloft. 'Don't fight with him,' she advised in a low voice.

But Shauna had waited a long time for this moment. She got to her feet. 'Did you know, Monsieur Albert, there are as many red-headed people in my home county of Yorkshire as there are in Ireland? We have a reputation for being fiery tempered, but it's not strictly true.' She breathed down her rising emotion, reminding herself that whatever else he was, Albert was an old man. He was looking all at once wary, or perhaps he was trying to follow what she was saying. So she explained. 'You say you know what I am. But what is that, exactly? It's convenient to stereotype people, particularly if you're out for a scapegoat – "Oh, it was that *rouquine*, the red-headed one. The foreigner. Put the blame on her, since she's not around to argue back." But I've discovered something extraordinary, Monsieur.' Shauna lifted her hair at the roots and let it fall. It had grown out of its bob in the weeks she'd been here and the highlights were fading to reveal her natural colour. 'She *is* here. Yvonne is here, looking out through my eyes. When the harvest is done, you, me, Laurent and Yvonne are going to talk. Maybe even Henri, too. We're going to reminisce about old times. Talk about the war years. What do you think of that?'

Albert did not reply, but made his escape as fast as his painful joints allowed him.

Pipes everywhere, the elephant-roar of the crusher . . . the *chai* was still going full blast when Shauna joined Laurent there, bringing another of Audrey's packed suppers with her. No competition from Rachel this time. Shauna had come from the kitchen by way of the stable yard, and had seen her rival leading horses out to the fields, Adão alongside. *You fry your fish, I'll fry mine.*

Armand, who had just delivered a final tractor-load, gave her the thumbs-up and nodded appreciatively at her overalls. Taking the basket, he said loudly, 'You are the cavalry! Raymond's back has gone again,' he nodded towards his colleague, who looked to be in some considerable pain.

'Laurent wants him to go home, but he won't. Now we can say you're here to relieve him.'

Laurent turned off the crusher and silence rocked the air. 'This lot into the press, then we'll put that lot – ' he indicated a trailer that had been backed into the *chai*, the half-barrels on its back overflowing with white grapes – 'into the crusher. Then the Semillon is finished!' He was shouting, but everyone did that here until they adjusted to the machines being off. A few minutes later, the place was shuddering again as the press got to work on the de-stalked grapes, sending juice up through a pipe into a stainless steel vat. Laurent climbed a step-ladder at its side.

'He's ensuring the pipe is securely connected,' Armand roared at her. Shauna was helping him decant the grapes from the crusher into the press. 'If it comes away, a geyser of grape juice paints the ceiling. It happened to him in his first season here, when Albert was watching. Ha! You can imagine.'

As Shauna emptied the last bucket into the press, Laurent raised his hand. 'Ok, we're full, switch off.' He asked for a jug, which he dunked into the vat. Armand brought four glasses.

They let Laurent taste first. 'Mmm-hmm.'

Raymond and Armand echoed his opinion, though Armand added, 'Oui, très jolie.' *Lovely.*

Shauna gulped the cool, smooth liquid, hit first by its sweetness, then its complex fruitiness.

'What do you taste?' Raymond asked her.

'Honey . . .' put on the spot for a second time in this place, she didn't want to come across as pretentious or ignorant. Her appreciation of a good wine had developed apace since her first days here, but these men had spent their adult lives tasting. 'And grape, of course.'

'What does your palate tell you?' Laurent had his nose over the rim of his glass. Unlike her, he had savoured only a sip or two.

This time, she let the liquid stay in her mouth for a few seconds. 'Citrus. Lime, I think. Yes, lime, not lemon. Passionfruit sorbet. And . . .' she might as well give them a laugh, 'buttered toast and the leaves of *Ribes*, a garden shrub we call "Flowering Currant" in England. I suppose that comes from the volatile compounds—'

Armand waved away the science, saying to Laurent, 'She has a good palate, this one. You should send her to Bordeaux to a wine master's course.'

'What I wouldn't give for an excuse to keep her here.' Laurent downed his juice and started shovelling grapes from the trailer into the crusher.

Two hours later, the last batch had been de-stalked, pressed, and the juice pumped into yet another of the steel vats. Supper sat in its basket, forgotten.

Laurent said to Shauna, 'Now we're going to

rack off yesterday's pressing into the *cuve*. The concrete tank,' he explained. 'Fancy spraying it with CO_2 while we eat? Unless you want to join us.'

She'd been fantasising about slipping into a hot bubble bath, but this was too good an opportunity to miss. 'Audrey's already fed me. Hand me the gun.'

Spraying CO_2 foam into every corner of a concrete *cuve* was the ultimate de-stresser, Shauna reckoned. It satisfied the child within, letting loose with a water-gun. It also appealed to the obsessive, adult steriliser bent on annihilating rogue bacteria. Standing right inside the huge vat, she reflected that with the door shut, it made the perfect place for a tone-deaf person to sing without shame . . . she launched into a power ballad, camping it up until Laurent's laughter reverberated over the snort of the CO_2 gun.

'Has the gas tipped you over the edge, *chérie*? Come and see what you've done.'

She wriggled out to find that Armand and Raymond had left and she and Laurent were alone in the *chai*. 'Oh no. Not my singing?'

'We enjoyed it.' Armand hadn't needed much persuasion to go home, he told her, as his eldest daughter was about to go away to university and they were having a family dinner. 'And poor Raymond has been chewing pain killers all day. I said that if he didn't rest, he'd not be fit to help with the red grapes. He's not missed a harvest here in over thirty years.'

'Who brought in the 1943 harvest, after your grandfather was—'

'Albert and the village women.' Laurent laid a finger against her lips. 'Not them, not now.' He chivvied her back to the present. 'You and I are going to spend the next few hours playing musical vats. Never say I don't show you a good time.'

'Musical vats' turned out to be separating yesterday's white juice from its sediment and pumping it into the freshly fumigated concrete *cuve*. Laurent tested the juice's temperature as it flowed. It was edging towards six degrees Celsius. Too warm, he said, but the concrete would cool it. 'Some of my neighbours got rid of concrete in favour of stainless steel but I prefer the old way. It cools the wine without electricity.' While the vats drained, they sluiced out the crusher and the press, using hose pipes and brushes. Soon, they were both soaked, spattered with grape residue. Declaring a moment's recess, Laurent took a bottle of four year old dry Semillon from the fridge in the corner and poured them a glass. He showed her the label with its 'Clos de Chemignac' coat of arms. 'This one ages well and I love it, though most growers blend Semillon with other whites these days.'

'But you do things differently.' They clinked glasses. She took a sip. 'Mmm, I like it. It's . . . grown up.'

He laughed in pleasure. 'I'll write that on the back of the bottle: "A grown-up wine, ideal for drinking with seafood and salted meats."'

After that, a dozen other things had to be hosed down and re-sterilised. The sun was sinking as they closed the *chai* behind them. They stood, hand in hand, not speaking. Shauna thought – *he does this every day, for weeks.*

The air was warm and an efficient breeze took some of the moisture out of their overalls. Tomorrow, they'd be picking the Cabernet Sauvignon vines, two days' labour topped off by the *fête de vendange*. Audrey had promised that it would be a feast to remember, telling her, 'The women in the village consider it an act of friendship to help this year, for Isabelle's sake and for yours, because now, you are one of us. You have proved yourself. *Voilà!*' Stepping back, Audrey had cupped Shauna's face and stroked her red hair, as if she didn't quite believe the colour. Tears welled in her eyes. 'You and Yvonne must have been kin,' she murmured.

'Audrey, what do you know of her?'

But Audrey turned away and Shauna had to be satisfied with the very real compliment that had been paid her. Being accepted by Chemignac's wives and mothers was the finest accolade she could ever hope for.

Now, she bent to rub her aching knees. 'I can see why a lifetime here leaves you all limping and crippled,' she remarked to Laurent.

'Let's walk it off.'

They crossed the meadows towards the woods. Evening mist rose from the shorn grass, icy on the toes. The air's perfume was of resin and roses. 'I love this place,' she said. 'I don't ever want to leave.'

'What Armand said about you doing a wine master's course . . . you could study viticulture and oenology, all the wine sciences. My own *oenologue*. My own genius. There'd be no stopping us, though all the other growers would want to kidnap you!'

'Lock me up in the turret then!' she joked, unsure if he was proposing or offering a job. 'But surely you'd let me out every September?'

'September and October.'

They stopped and turned back to look at the château. The tower loomed milky-grey and Laurent stifled a shudder. He said, 'Soon, we'll take a few days to ourselves. Go away maybe? I want to ask you . . .' He broke off. A window shone bright at the top of the tower. A window where there ought to be solid stone – stones they'd both seen and touched. They stared at unmistakeable panes of glass throwing back the sunset. A figure stood behind the glass. Female, undoubtedly.

'That's what I saw!' Shauna gripped

Laurent's hand. 'I didn't want to believe it.'

He squeezed her hand in return and she felt his rising excitement, and his fear too. He said, 'I saw the window and the girl years ago, when I was just a bit older than Nico. It scared the hell out of me and everybody I spoke to about it shook their heads and turned away. When you related the same experience, I couldn't quite cope with it. Who is she? *What* is she?'

'If we close our eyes and count to ten, she'll be gone.'

They did, and she was, and so was the window.

'It could be Yvonne,' Shauna said. 'Asking for justice. Albert framed her for a war crime and she wants her name cleared.'

'You have it in for Albert.'

'You bet I do!' Shauna hooked her arm around Laurent's waist, sensing his desire to stride away. '*I* have no family allegiance getting in my way. What we experienced last night was no hallucination, right?'

'Right.'

'Albert as good as threatened to betray Yvonne and Henri. He had the opportunity and the motive.'

'Fraternal jealousy . . . is that motive enough? We're talking of the most vicious of crimes.'

'My God, Laurent, you've clearly never been passed over in favour of someone else! Sex, money and revenge top the charts of motives for murder. Albert had them all. He was lustful and humiliated, out to get even, and his brother's death – your grandfather's death – handed him control of Chemignac. How many years was it until your father took over the reins?'

'About twenty-five.'

'So – Albert de Chemignac got control of the family farm for a quarter of a century while all the blame, all the mud-slinging and howls of "treachery," landed squarely on Yvonne.'

'Motive and opportunity doesn't make a person guilty.'

'Won't you give Yvonne the same benefit of the doubt?'

Laurent pointed out that he had never accused Yvonne of anything, but Shauna was walking towards the woods by then. She knew Yvonne was innocent and Laurent knew it, too, she told herself. Or he would do, by the time she had finished with him.

He caught up with her. 'You have a destination in mind?'

'That cave,' she answered, 'then the memorial stone. I want to see how far apart they are.'

'We don't know where the cave is, remember. We couldn't find it even in broad daylight.'

'So.' She gave him a meaningful push. 'That

proves my point.'

A silence. 'Which is?'

'That somebody close to your grandfather betrayed the existence of the tunnel to the Germans. You said it yourself at Monty's, your phrase was "sold out to the Gestapo".' She walked on, her mind spewing pictures. 'I'm guessing that something forced Henri and the English agents to flee from Chemignac. They emerged from the tunnel straight into the arms of the enemy. Imagine a bitter, desperate struggle –' actually, Shauna didn't have to imagine it. She'd felt it, sharing the men's panic at the mouth of the cave. That desperate struggle to get away, and the feeling of splitting apart, of the mind flying outwards . . . that was death by machine gun fire. 'None of them had a chance. Cyprien useless from his wound, Jean-Claude not much better.' Henri, trying desperately to protect his guests and save himself, until a hail of bullets felled him . . . she deliberately shook the images away. 'My guess is that the Germans meant to take them alive, so they could shoot them in the square at Garzenac as a warning to others. But the men wouldn't surrender and after a bloody massacre, they had bodies on their hands. They dragged them to a nearby clearing because they wanted to keep the existence of the tunnel a secret. It might be hiding an arms cache, or other supplies. Resistance fighters might be tempted to use it again, and be captured in their turn.' Hearing Laurent's troubled sigh, she re-issued her point. 'We couldn't find the cave. So how did the Germans? Why were they waiting for the fugitives, weapons cocked? Who showed them where the tunnel came out?'

'You're going to say "Albert".'

'Exactly. He was a German stooge. He tipped them off whenever the tunnel was to be used.'

'Albert would not be so craven.'

'Then why did it take our friend Monty ten years to get recognition for the Frenchmen's deaths, and even longer for Sturridge and Barnsley? Why does everybody hush it up? Even Madame Guilhem urges me to leave well alone. They are protecting somebody.'

'None of this makes Albert—'

'Guilty as hell? Yes it does. Who else knew of the tunnel?'

'Quite a few.'

'So let's count them. Henri, the male British agents, the other Resistance men, Michel and Luc – all killed. The traitor has to have been somebody who survived and was party to family secrets. It has to be someone with a motive for treachery.'

'Yvonne. She knew where the cave was! My grandfather led her home through the tunnel. Albert always insisted the woman knew too much.'

'What did she know, though, really? Henri took her to the cave, sure, but only after he'd hustled her for hours along a maze of paths, through acres of woods, *in the dark*. You admitted yourself, even you wouldn't have a hope of finding that cave at night. And you *know* these woods.' Shauna looped her arms around his neck, kneading his muscles until he relaxed and their lips met. 'Besides, you're being too logical, Laurent. Think with your heart, your body. That's how Yvonne was thinking that night.'

'Of Henri, you mean?'

'And of the night they were about to share. She wanted to make love, not betray her lover.'

'I've grown up with Albert's version. He said the traitor was a woman. I *have* to believe it.'

'And I believe that ghosts come from a whisky bottle and that psychic communication is a form of temporal lobe sensitivity. And yet I know what I've seen and I know what I've heard since I came here. We've both seen and heard the same things. Take me to the clearing where the stone is, Laurent. Somebody is waiting.'

The temperature had dropped, the mist thickening. Their clothes felt damp again and they'd probably end up catching colds. But now was not the moment to leave the woods. A channel was opening in Shauna's mind, and she felt superlatively receptive. Maybe being chilled helped. When Laurent placed his hand over hers on the memorial stone, she instantly heard Yvonne's crisp voice: *I don't mind being the last name on there. I mind not being there . . .*

'That last night, the household went to bed,' Shauna murmured. 'Henri left a decent interval before climbing to the tower room. He set his candle down outside the door and knocked. Yvonne said, "Come in". He expected to find her in bed, but she was waiting in the dark, fully dressed. The next moment, gramophone music filled the air. A sad ballad, "*Vous, qui passez sans me voir*". The singer's voice, toffee melting over flame. Yvonne said—'

'Dance with me.'

Henri took her in his arms, but immediately stepped back. 'What are you wearing?' It was an accusation – he already knew the answer.

'Don't be angry. What harm, borrowing something that's been shut away in a cupboard for years? It's just cloth, Henri, and I want to feel something good against my skin. I'll be wearing Government Issue for heaven knows how long. This dress—'

'Yvonne, I told you – you may not wear it. Take it off.'

Had he used a softer tone, she might have complied, but the autocratic note echoed the one he'd used with Albert earlier.

'I will take it off, when we've danced. Bring in your candle so we can see each other.' He made no move so she fetched it herself, saying, 'I've hung a blanket across the window. See? Not even an arc light would show in the courtyard. And look, I've hung that dismal oil painting across the other window. We are quite invisible, except to ourselves.'

The candle had burned halfway down and she placed its holder on the post at the foot of the bed to make the most of the flame. She stood in front of Henri and indicated she would like to dance.

As the singer crooned his sorrows, Henri measured her in long sweeps of the eye. She held herself still, willing him to see through the artifice of dye and pleats to the yearning body beneath. She knew she was different from all the women he'd known. She was no high-born lady, no poised clothes-horse, nor a compliant peasant girl. Just a schoolteacher from England, lately re-baptised as an intrepid agent, in sore need of courage and hope. Of a loving touch. 'Don't be afraid,' she whispered.

'I *am*, Yvonne. Every woman who has worn

the Gown of Thorns has wanted something we men of Chemignac cannot give. Oh, we provide what is needed, but never what is wanted. That is our curse, the thorn in our sides.'

She pinched him. 'I want you, *Écharde*, splinter and thorn. What a prickly couple we make! If you won't dance with me, I suppose I'll take the dress off.' It would have to be pulled over the head, which would put her in an undignified posture. 'Here's a deal,' she coaxed. 'Let's dance until the candle burns down, then I'll undress. Let's prove this thing has no power to hurt us.'

With a sigh, he put his arms around her and they swayed in their restricted space as another song began, this time by Lucienne Boyer. They didn't hear the intruder's advance until the door thumped open and a shrill voice cried, 'I knew you'd be here! I knew I would catch you! I hope that dress kills her, too!'

Chapter Twenty-Three

Henri made a barrier of his arms to stop his daughter leaping with teeth and fingernails at Yvonne. Once again, he lifted Isabelle off the floor but this time she fought back, kicking and screaming, arms flailing. She whacked the candle into the middle of the bed.

Yvonne hastily retrieved it, and retreated to the side of the room, her back to the landscape painting. In the candlelight, Henri's face was a mask of shock and distress. Yvonne felt more detached. In her professional life, she'd met many unhappy young girls. She'd dealt with hysteria. Girls weren't all the good little mice they were supposed to be.

Isabelle certainly was not. That was a full-blooded, adult cyclone ripping through her vocal chords. 'You send me away so you can be with *her*!

That's wicked, wicked, wicked!' A child's unexamined morality. Surely Henri would see the misery at its heart?

But he did not – or perhaps he was simply afraid that the tower was insufficiently soundproof and someone might hear. 'I am going to send you back to the Valles',' he told the thrashing child, 'and you will not come back here until you have learned to control yourself. I will tell Audrey I don't want to see you if you do not behave!'

'Henri, don't. That's not going to help.' Yvonne's intervention was smothered by Isabelle's answering shriek and the hiss of the gramophone. It needed re-winding. The singer's voice had sunk to gruff maunderings, like a corpse communicating from beyond the grave. And then the song exploded in a scratch as Isabelle's kicking feet flipped the gramophone upside down. The shock of it sent the child limp, and Henri seized his opportunity, heaving Isabelle over his shoulder, clamping her legs against his ribs.

'I'll take her down,' he said, turning for the door.

'Be careful—' a second crash cut short Yvonne's warning. In a bid to stay in the room, Isabelle had grasped the oil painting and its new wire snapped. Yvonne was suddenly in front of a naked window, holding a candle, wearing the Gown of Thorns. The moonlit sky was the washed out blue of a prayer book.

'Come away,' Henri warned.

She froze, something seizing her attention. That was a flare of light in the fringes of the wood, wasn't it? For a while, Yvonne hoped it was a reflection of the moon, but when it came again she knew it for a torch. The beam was aiming directly at the château. On, off, on, off, in short, irregular bursts. It wasn't Morse code, which she knew, so it must be a private signal. 'Henri, come and look!'

He put Isabelle on her feet, and joined

Yvonne. Frustratingly, the bursts stopped for maybe half a minute, but just as Henri was turning away, they returned in quick-fire sequence. 'See it?' she hissed. 'It's a torch conversation.' Which meant that somebody was responding from the château. 'Henri, is anyone else here a member of your Resistance circuit? Could it be one of your colleagues sending a message?'

'No.' He bit the word off. 'No to both questions. We pass on messages in person, in verbal code. God help us, Yvonne, we are betrayed.'

It was like trying to outrun an avalanche. Yvonne blew out the candle as Henri said, 'Get dressed, then go and rouse Jean-Claude. Get him to the trapdoor – in his underwear if necessary. I'll bring Cyprien. Fast. We may only have minutes. Isabelle, find Audrey and *stay with her*.'

Yvonne dragged on her day clothes,

screaming curses as buttons and clasps evaded her shaking fingers. She shoved her feet into her shoes, her socks inside-out. No time to tie laces. Her last act was to grab a wad of emergency currency, her papers and her pocket knife with its folding blades. Down the tower steps at breakneck speed, pushing her arms into her jacket sleeves. At ground level, she spared a glance for the oak barrels standing four-square over the trapdoor. She couldn't shift them alone, and who would replace them after they'd all made their escape? Raymond? Albert? Logical deduction said that one or both of them was likely the traitor.

She ran to rouse Jean-Claude. Stepping between huddles of geese, unpleasantly aware of what she might be treading in, she felt her way to his billet. She crouched beside his pallet and prodded his solid shape. He sat up immediately. 'Problem?'

During their training, they'd often been

hauled out of bed in the small hours, a non-commissioned officer bawling in their ears to acclimatise them to emergencies like this. She said, 'We have to get out.'

Jean-Claude shoved his blankets aside without protest. 'Ready and able,' he said, before yelping in pain, having forgotten his swollen ankle. As he struggled into his trousers and shirt, Yvonne collected up everything she could see, stuffing his knapsack.

'Where did our host hide my camera?'

She had no idea. 'You'll have to leave it. With luck, this is a false alarm.' But she didn't really believe that. As she helped Jean-Claude through the old laundry room, she saw the dark shape of a man in the courtyard, and smaller silhouettes. It was Henri, instructing the nursemaid to remove the children. Audrey must go straight to her parent's farm by way of the vineyards. 'Go now and don't look back.'

Isabelle was crying, 'Papa, don't send me away. I didn't mean to break the picture or the gramophone. I'll be good for ever, I promise.'

Yvonne hissed at Jean-Claude, 'Go and start shifting those barrels off the trapdoor, do your best.' She stepped outside, sick with premonition. Grinning like a clown in her effort to sound cheerful, she said, 'Henri, I'm sure you want to tell Isabelle you forgive her, that you don't think she's at all naughty.'

Henri nodded and said to his daughter, 'I love you, *chérie*. Now be a good girl and help Audrey with Pierre-Gaston.' He unlatched his daughter's arms and pushed her gently but firmly away. 'I will see you tomorrow.'

'Where's Cyprien?' Yvonne asked when the young ones were gone.

'Raymond's getting him dressed. It'll be a swine, dragging him along the tunnel.'

'It was done before.'

'But my good friends were not too bothered if Cyprien lived or died. Me, I'm tender-hearted. Where's Jean-Claude?'

'Rolling barrels, or trying to. More to the point, where's Albert? Where is your brother?'

'Not in his bed. I checked.'

'Where's Albert?'

This time, it was Jean-Claude asking. He'd failed utterly to shift any of the barrels off the trapdoor.

Henri muttered, 'Hunting rabbits.'

'Then I hope he comes back soon,' Jean-Claude responded. 'The lad won't stand a chance of pushing these bloody things back once we're in the tunnel and there's only Albert to help him.' By 'lad', he meant Raymond who, having dressed Cyprien and brought the wounded man to the tower, was waiting quietly for his next instructions.

'Raymond isn't going to hang around after we've left,' Henri replied tersely. 'He needs to run as well.' He said to the boy, 'Ready, *gamin*?' He and Raymond shifted three of the barrels aside, rested for a few seconds, then tackled the last one. Somebody had topped up the liquid in that one, Henri muttered. It was far heavier than it had been the day before, he could swear it.

As Jean-Claude struck matches to give them light, Yvonne checked on Cyprien. The young agent sat against the wall, his pallor worryingly similar to the stones behind him. *Would he survive a rough transit to the woods?*

Henri and Raymond put everything they had into shifting that last barrel and at last, the trapdoor was exposed. Yvonne crouched and levered it open with her penknife, wrinkling her nose at the rush of dank air. She wasn't relishing a second trip down that rat-run. 'Jean-Claude should lead,' she suggested to Henri. 'You and I will carry Cyprien.'

Henri disagreed. 'Jean-Claude last, because if he falls over, he will block our way—' he stopped, listening.

They all listened. Deep in their sanctum, the geese were honking in rising discord.

'They hear something.' Henri jumped down into the tunnel, telling Yvonne and Jean-Claude to lower Cyprien down to him. 'Raymond, go to the front of the house, see what's coming.'

Because something *was* coming. By the time Raymond returned, he had to shout over the geese's cackling.

'Germans, from the direction of Garzenac!' They couldn't see the boy's expression but his voice warned that he was not talking about one or two soldiers. 'A stream of cars and trucks.'

'How do you know they're Germans?' Henri demanded.

'Because they're all together. The *Milice* never set off all at once, and where would they get so many vehicles?'

Henri ordered Yvonne to join them in the tunnel, adding, 'Raymond, close us in then run! Don't wait!' He clapped his hands furiously when Yvonne hesitated. 'Come on, woman!'

'It won't work!' she shouted back, marvelling that her mind could still rationalise. 'Unless the barrels can be put back, the Germans will see immediately how we've escaped. We'll never outrun them in the tunnel with Jean-Claude and Cyprien.'

'All right. You take my place.' Henri braced his arms to heave himself back up through the hatch. 'The boy and I will deal with the barrels and meet up with you later. Head west, towards the river. Can you find your way by the moon?' He didn't wait for Yvonne's reply. 'Raymond, did you fasten the gatehouse door? Yes? Good lad! That will give us a few extra minutes. Yvonne?' She hadn't moved. 'Get in the tunnel.'

Her answer was to smack his hands away from the mouth of the hatch. 'Even if I could drag Cyprien half a mile along a shaft,' she yelled, 'I'd be no good once I left it. They need a guide who knows the ways through the woods. I'd probably stumble into whoever was flashing that message. I'll remain here.'

To end up in Albert's clutches? Part of her hoped so. She'd cut the bastard's throat and ask questions afterwards. 'Damn you, go!' She dropped the trapdoor, forcing Henri to whip his fingers back and duck into the darkness. 'I'll find you!' she yelled through the wooden boards. 'I love you.'

They tried to get one of the lighter barrels back in place, but Raymond was spent and her hands were too slender to get a proper grip. She tore her fingertips as the wine sloshed inside the cask, threatening to upturn it. Any moment, they'd surely hear the hideous splintering of wood as the Germans broke through the gatehouse. *Any moment* . . .

Except they didn't hear it. After a while, they crept outside. 'The geese have gone quiet,' Raymond said.

It was true. Unwilling to believe they'd been victims of a false alarm, Yvonne whispered, 'They might be creeping up on foot. I need to get to the woods. Can you lead me by the safest route?'

Raymond took her through the stables into the vineyard, tracking through the rows with the confidence of a fox crossing its territory. It was such a clear night, anybody watching from a vantage point might have seen their flitting forms. But nobody challenged them, and there were no sounds of break-in or pursuit from the château either. Yvonne wondered if Raymond hadn't perhaps mistaken a routine *Milice* night-patrol for a German advance.

They learned more when they reached the

highest ridge and looked over the château roofs towards the forest. Powerful lights that could only belong to military trucks stole the beauty of a near-full moon and exposed whole sections of forest.

Yvonne cried out, 'The convoy was going to the woods, not coming here. Oh, Raymond!' Had the boy lingered outdoors another minute, he'd have seen the column pass by, and Henri would not have entered the tunnel. 'We could have been safe out here, together. Oh, my poor Henri! What's waiting for him?'

He would come out of the tunnel, hampered by his injured fellows, and would be pinned down by lights. Only if he abandoned Jean-Claude and Cyprien, and ran through the undergrowth like a wild boar, had he a chance. Those woods were his back garden . . .

Rattling gun fire from the woods cut hope dead. On and on it went, muffled like firecrackers going off inside their box. 'Albert brought the enemy to us.'

Under the pure moon, Yvonne and Raymond stood hand in hand, helpless witnesses to a brother's treachery.

Shauna spoke in weary continuation of Yvonne's grief. 'Albert signalled with lights. He brought the German Gestapo to Chemignac, then made himself scarce. Five men paid the consequences and he's spent the last sixty years blaming a *woman*.'

Laurent's doubts had vanished too. 'Yvonne melted away into the dark. With her gone, Albert could pervert the story any way he wished.' They were sitting with their backs to the commemoration stone, slumped like two rucksacks left at a bus stop.

'Why didn't Raymond speak out?' Shauna asked. 'He must have guessed that Albert was an informant.' She felt Laurent shrug.

'Raymond was only thirteen, and in a tiny community, silence is sometimes necessary for survival. Raymond would want to protect his family, and Audrey's, and the children, of course. I don't really know how he got through the war, but I know he eventually went to work for the Valles, married Audrey and took over his father-in-law's farm. Only when his eldest son took over in his turn did Raymond ever come back here, to work for my father.'

'Your father, Pierre-Gaston, the toddler Audrey carried away to safety.'

'The same. Have you noticed Raymond never comes near the château? He works only in the *chai*.'

'Yes. Who blocked up the window in the tower?'

'Isabelle. She inherited a share of the château from her father, and chose the part where the geese had been kept. Well, you know she has an eye for design! She saw possibilities nobody else did. While she was having her apartment converted, she got the mason to block up the west-facing tower window. She said she never wanted to look out on to the woods where her father had died.'

'And it was Albert who propagated the myth of an English female betraying the men of Chemignac,' Shauna mused out loud. 'No wonder he was agitated when Monty Watson came asking questions.' She reached above her head, stroking the stone which was slick with dew. '"Casse-toi!"' *Get lost!*

Laurent got stiffly to his feet, pulling Shauna up too. 'There are five names on this stone.'

'I'll have Yvonne's name added if I have to carve it myself. Let's get home and under a hot shower.' Her lungs felt wasted, her heart loaded with grief.

'OK, but something doesn't add up. Why are Michel Paulin and Luc Roland's names there? They weren't at Chemignac on the night of the escape, nor in the tunnel with Henri. They couldn't all have died in the same massacre.'

Shauna tried to answer, but her mind had run out of battery. As they plodded across the meadow and saw the château tower through the encroaching dawn, she muttered, 'If Yvonne hadn't put that dress on, Isabelle wouldn't have flipped and pulled the picture down—'

'And Yvonne wouldn't have glimpsed the lamp in the woods that was returning Albert's signal. They'd have been sleeping when the Germans came for them. Dragged from their beds and hurled into the backs of trucks, taken to interrogation centres, even the children. Raymond and Audrey would have been tortured along with the adults. In Audrey and Yvonne's case, likely raped too. Don't you see, Shauna? That night at least, the Gown of Thorns saved lives. It saved Chemignac.'

After standing under a steaming shower until the tank ran out of hot water, Shauna and Laurent drank coffee and ate their way through a mound of toast. They then parted. He was anxious to get to the *chai* to test the temperatures of yesterday's pressing. Shauna made her way up the tower. In the top room, she took out the Gown of Thorns. Holding it in front of her, she addressed it directly.

'"Never forgive, never forget", right? I don't know if you are a force for evil or for good, or somewhere in between, but we need a resolution. Albert may be nearly eighty, but surely he should answer for what he did. Oh, and I want to marry Laurent, but I don't intend to be another of Chemignac's victims. Got that?'

She laid the dress on the bed. Nodded at it, and went out, deliberately leaving the door open behind her.

The Cabernet Sauvignon vines were picked clean in just under three days. All that was left now was a half-hectare of white Muscadelle and Semillon, hanging in the hope of a *vendange tardive*, a late 'noble rot' harvest. Chemignac's 2003 *vendange* was declared officially over.

The trestles were out in a long line in the meadow. It all looked to Shauna like a scene from a Thomas Hardy novel. Having first phoned Isabelle in Paris to ask permission, she'd raided the cupboards for table linen, choosing the embroidered napkins that Isabelle had been ironing the day she fell and knocked herself out. Each place setting had a spray of wild flowers, two glasses and a violet napkin folded like a yacht sail. The children had blown up pink and purple balloons – not very Hardiesque, admittedly – which bobbed on silver ribbons along the length of the tables. Seating was straw bales and a fire bowl had been lit a safe distance off. Later, there would be dancing. Monty

Watkins had organised a local folk band to come and play.

Audrey and her neighbours had spent the day cooking and the buffet tables creaked under traditional fare. The brazier that had been Shauna's idea spat and sizzled with hamburgers and chicken drumsticks. In a moment, the fly covers would be whipped off and thirty or so workers, neighbours and friends would dig in. All they were waiting for was their host and the *gerbeboade*, the wreath whose appearance marked a successful harvest-home. Laurent had woven it from the last vine of the last row, making a figure-of-eight of leaves and purple grape clusters. Every woman present had kissed him, and the men had slapped him on the back. Set on a pole, this pagan garland would preside over the feast.

Rachel was bringing it in the pony cart and the two oldest harvesters were riding with her – Madame Guilhem and Albert de Chemignac.

Rachel had given up her notions of staging a competing feast after Laurent warned her, 'It'll be like putting on a puppet show with the full Broadway cast of Chicago making a guest appearance in the next field. Of course, you may like eating sausages on your own . . .'

Rachel had laughed and said, 'I was only kidding, anyway. Do I look like a woman who needs to impress people with her cooking?'

Shauna was watching for Laurent, wanting him at her side. She was half-regretting her one-sided conversation with the Gown of Thorns. Of course she didn't believe in curses, or the raising of evil spirits, but she had no doubts now that human existence was more than the linear progression from A to B. It was more like a complex concerto, with many lines of music playing at the same time, all in slightly different time signatures. She and Laurent had discovered how to jump from line to line. They had melded minds with Henri and Yvonne. And if that could happen, then anything could happen.

She was also anxious because with the harvest over, the clock was ticking. Nico and Olive were itching now to get back to Paris and unless she had a meaningful invitation from Laurent to stay, she'd also have to go. No, who was she kidding with 'meaningful invitations'? She wanted red roses and Laurent down on one knee. Either she took his name, the name of this place, and lived out the happiness stolen from Yvonne and Henri, or she quit. And if she quit, the next generation of lovers would have to mend Chemignac's wounds. Last night, she'd dreamed again of Yvonne. Not the fiery beauty who had stolen Henri's heart. A frail, wrinkled Yvonne whose face had swum up to hers and whose lips left these words in her ear: *'Brave, aren't you? A life for a life, that seems to be how it works. Henri gave his for me. What would you do?'*

A cheer went up nearby. Someone shouted, 'They're coming!'

Shauna stood on tiptoe and saw Nico and Olive hurtling towards the *chai*. The cart would come that way and Raymond, who would not trespass on to the meadows, not even for a feast, would hand over a pitcher of fresh-pressed juice. Just as Shauna thought she spied Laurent's muscular outline, a glint of metal between the branches of the walnut avenue stole her attention. She glanced right and saw a silver saloon car gliding up the drive. It looked like a Mercedes. Monty's band, coming in style? Actually, it looked like the station taxi, the one she'd tried to get into the day she arrived.

It progressed slowly up the avenue before disappearing between the walls of the gatehouse. She forgot about it then because here was the cart, pulled by the faithful white pony. Someone had entwined flowers and vine leaves in the creature's mane. Rachel sat on the driver's seat, with Laurent walking alongside carrying the *gerbeboade* on its lance.

Rachel's toffee-coloured arms were elegantly extended, the reins relaxed in her hands. Queen of the harvest, she was wearing the Gown of Thorns. Laurent was staring up her like a man smitten.

Shauna's world tipped upside down. Adão came to stand beside her, and in broken English he said, 'We are the left behind ones. Each season, Laurent takes a new love and Rachel too. I am told that whoever they use in the beginning, they end up together.'

'Who told you so?' she rasped, but Adão's insistent gaze was back on Rachel. The Delphos gown made the perfect foil for her shape, every honed and proud inch of her exaggerated by its pleats. *Is it true?* Shauna wondered. Every year Laurent unceremoniously dumps his 'harvest girl' and returns to Rachel? Maybe this crowd had seen it a dozen times before.

People were gathering around the cart,

helping down its elderly passengers. A throne had been made out of straw bales, decorated with garlands of greenery and purple balloons. The seat of honour was intended for Madame Guilhem, but Albert took it, folding his arms in defiance.

Madame Guilhem protested, 'I'm the eldest. That is my place.'

Audrey added her voice, 'That's right. Monsieur de Chemignac, that seat is reserved for the oldest of the harvesters. That's not you.'

'Not for a few more years,' Madame Guilhem agreed. 'You can have it when I'm gone.'

But Albert stayed put. Shauna glanced at Laurent, who was surely the proper person to mediate. But he was helping Rachel down from the cart seat, and she was sliding into his arms like a knife returning to its sheath. Shauna would have run then, had she not been clasped from behind by somebody who had approached unseen.

'Gotcha!'

She looked down and saw arms clad in a bright cotton print. Instantly, she smelled a scent as familiar as childhood. Soapflakes and wool, talcum powder and cooking spices. Hair soft as angora tickled the nape of her neck and she shouted, 'Mum! What are you doing here?'

'I've come to find out if my runaway child is still alive.' The arms relaxed and Shauna turned round with a cry. Bundled in unmatched layers, white curls piled up any-old-how, Elisabeth Vincent could have been air-dropped from her Sheffield kitchen. Unusually for her, she exuded an energy that seemed to electrify her to the tips of her crystal chip earrings. 'So you're now a *vendangeur*, tried and true. And a little bird has been telling me you've fallen in love. Do I get to meet the poor sap?'

'Oh, Mum.' Shauna dissolved, hiding her sobs in Elisabeth's hand-crocheted waistcoat. It made an effective tissue, but Elisabeth wasn't inclined to indulge her daughter.

She pulled a silk square from a pocket and wiped away Shauna's tears. 'Whatever's gone wrong, you have a few questions to answer and so does he. This is not entirely a friendly visit.'

'Not . . . friendly?'

Was this the Gown of Thorns' doing – the loss of Laurent's love, and her mother's too?

'You've been hiding for too long,' Elisabeth Vincent said. 'Time to face the music. And here it comes.'

Shauna looked in the direction of the château. Progressing across the meadow were two people she could never have imagined together outside a bizarre dream. Isabelle Duval, heavily reliant on her stick, and supporting her stronger side, Professor Mike Ladriss.

Chapter Twenty-Four

Elisabeth put Shauna in the picture. A few days ago, she'd had a desperate phone call from Isabelle in Neuilly-sur-Seine, from the landing outside her daughter and son-in-law's flat. Isabelle had just arrived home by taxi from the hospital where she'd spent hours sitting by Louette's bed. Exhausted, she'd discovered her son-in-law had double-locked the door and she couldn't get in. It was the third time that week it had happened.

With his wife 'stable' but showing no progress, Hubert's visits to the hospital had become fewer. He would drive Isabelle there in the morning, promising to pick her up at lunchtime, only to disappear all day, his phone switched off. 'In the end,' Elisabeth said, 'she got it out of him that he'd gone back to work, but was too guilty about it to tell her. And he expected her to keep house for him too, cook and do the washing. Poor thing was at the end of her rope. She could hardly manage the steps from the apartment lobby to the street.'

Elisabeth had booked a flight to Paris straight away. 'I didn't ask Hubert's permission to move in. I told him so, and I said, "I'm not sure which of you needs the carer the most, you or Isabelle". He didn't put up a fight.'

'But what's Mike doing here?' stuttered Shauna.

'Well, there's another story. I had a couple of missed calls from a Lancashire number, and I supposed somebody was trying to sell me double glazing. Then there was a knock on the door. I thought it was the taxi come early to take me to the airport for my flight to Paris. I was swearing because I couldn't find my reading glasses. I opened the door and there was this big, tall chap scowling like a clap of thunder. "Where is she?" he demanded.'

'He wanted me?' Shauna's heart bumped. Mike Ladriss . . . threatening?

'Really, he wanted your friend Laurent. "Where the bloody hell is the Comte de Chemignac?" he said, and I said, "In the Dordogne, I should think, getting his grapes in". And he said "Give me his address!" And I said, "I won't be shouted at in my own"—'

'Mum, get on with it!'

'I handed him a map of the Dordogne, and drew a cross on it. We met again just now at Garzenac station and shared the taxi. I think he's a nice bloke, underneath.'

'He is. Very.'

'But he's mad as hell. Some trickster . . . no, on second thoughts, I'll let him tell you.'

Isabelle and Mike had joined them by now. People swarmed forward to hug Isabelle and express their astonishment at her arrival. There was a presumption it must mean that Louette was recovered, and Shauna heard Isabelle dashing hopes, insisting sadly that her daughter's condition remained the same. 'She is stable. That's all they say. Stable. Ah, *mes petits sauvages*!' She opened her arms for her grandchildren. Mike, meanwhile, had spotted Shauna.

His long legs covered the ground frighteningly fast. 'Well?' he demanded. Shauna saw what her mother had meant. If a thunderclap could have a persona, Mike Ladriss was it. He'd lost weight, his hair seemed duller. His glasses had broken and were mended with a sticking plaster. 'I've been raising hell, trying to get hold of you, Shauna. That job with Cademus came free.'

'Oh.' She closed her eyes as a wave of pleasure, then disappointment, then confusion, broke over her. 'I didn't get your messages. My phone doesn't work here and I haven't checked my emails for ages.' Actually, she couldn't remember the last time. She was meant to be a career scientist on a trajectory to success, and she hadn't opened her computer since the first day of harvest. Shame burnt her cheeks.

'I sent faxes. You said I could reach you that way. I must have sent twenty before I gave up.'

'I didn't get them!'

He looked mightily unconvinced. Elisabeth appeared equally sceptical, saying, 'You used to check your phone every three minutes at home. I'd hide the blessed thing in a drawer sometimes, just for some peace.'

'Things are different—'

Mike Ladriss wasn't interested. 'This Comte de Chemignac. Is he here?'

Shauna pointed to the pony cart. Laurent and Rachel hadn't moved. Two waxworks, melting into one another.

'Right.' Mike strode towards the cart, then walked right past. Shauna opened her mouth to say something, but in the end, just followed. Her mother came after her. Mike had positioned himself in front of the straw bale throne. He'd obviously misread her pointing finger.

'Um, Mike, that's Albert de Chemignac. He's not the Comte—' but her professor had evidently sealed his ears to her as well.

She heard him say, 'Monsieur, what you did was utterly and absolutely unforgiveable.' Soft-spoken, given to wry observation and quiet irony, Mike Ladriss exercised his anger-muscle only rarely. It was obvious to Shauna that he exercised his French even less. His syntax and grammar were all over the place. But the emotion was real. Shauna caught the giveaway tremor.

'Utterly unforgiveable,' Mike repeated. 'A mean-spirited act that has ruined lives. Destroyed hopes.' He must have worked out his phrases ahead and learned them by heart. *He's about to accuse Albert of treachery and collaboration . . . but how does he know?*

People were shuffling forward, curious. Mike addressed them haltingly. 'I don't suppose any of you imagined I'd come all the way from England, stand in front of you and demand an explanation of cowardly actions. Well I'm here, and my next stop is the newspapers. I've decided to let the press run the story.' From his pocket, Mike pulled a folded sheet of paper which he waved at Albert. 'I have nothing to lose now. Do you have the guts to admit to what you did? To apologise, Monsieur le Comte?'

Albert de Chemignac stared up at Mike Ladriss in absolute horror.

Mike turned to Shauna. 'Why isn't he answering?'

'Because he's not the Comte de Chemignac.' She took the paper and read it through twice. Understanding started to dawn. The dates and telephone numbers running across the top of the page showed it to be a copy of a fax sent by Mike, back in August. Sent here, to her.

On university letterhead, it informed her that the Cademus job was unexpectedly up for grabs, Allegra Boncasson having got a better offer. It urged Shauna to come home. It wasn't one of the guarded, depersonalised missives a man of Mike's status was supposed to send to a student. No, he'd let rip with some fruity comments about Allegra's father and the financial chicanery that had secured Ms Boncasson the job in the first place. Had Shauna received it, she'd have laughed, and then burned it.

'I never saw this.' She spoke English, and kept her voice low.

'No?' Mike answered in English. 'But your Comte de Chemignac did. He saw fit to fax it back. But not to me, oh no – to the legal department of the bank where Sir Christopher Boncasson is chairman and chief shareholder. It turns out they took a dim view of allegations of bribery and swindling. Boncasson's lawyers piled in to the university and this ended up on the Pro Vice-chancellor's desk. My head –' he tapped his skull wearily – 'was invited to submit to the executioner's block. I've been sacked, Shauna. Minus a large chunk of my pension and my reputation. What made him do it?' He spread his arms.

'I don't know.' She glanced helplessly at Laurent, then again at the letter. It ended with some hand-written lines, presumably added by whoever had faxed it to the bank. "To Whom It May Concern, something's gone tits-up between our esteemed universities and those that fund them. The fat cats have taken over the halls of learning. At least, Professor Ladriss clearly thinks so." It was signed "Comte de Chemignac".

'Mike, it's a cheap trick. For a start, Laurent doesn't use phrases like "tits-up". That's colloquial English, and it's sexist. He isn't sexist.' He *was* sexy, but that wasn't for Mike to know. Nor for her now either, it seemed. Laurent and Rachel were still locked as close as lovers in a telephone booth. 'And he wouldn't sign it that way. He doesn't even have "Comte de Chemignac" on his cheque book. Look. *That's* your Comte right there.' She pointed to Laurent, but all Mike saw was an unshaven young man in Bermudas and a t-shirt that could have come from a charity shop's remainder bin.

'Don't try to pull a fast one, Shauna. What the hell have I ever done to make some French stranger want to ruin me? God knows, I've done my single-handed best to keep the French wine industry afloat.' He looked ready to cry.

'I think I know what happened,' Shauna said slowly. Rachel was as slippery as an eel, as opportunist as a jackdaw. Look at her now – she'd decided to crown herself queen of the harvest and put on a dress worthy of the title. 'Somebody *was* in the office when your fax arrived. But not the man you're accusing.' *Not a man at all.* 'They saw it, read it and instead of handing it over to me, withheld it. An act of malice. They then decided to extract a bit more fun—'

'Fun?'

'Oh, this person likes a joke, so long as it's at someone else's expense. They looked up Sir Christopher Boncasson's details. Probably typed his name into an online search engine, found the fax number of the bank and hey-presto – your career is ruined, and someone else is framed for it.' She turned to Albert, repeating in French, 'Someone else is framed for it. A good move, Monsieur?'

Albert de Chemignac twisted his lips. '*Casse-toi, rouquine.*'

Isabelle had joined them, and hearing that remark, she flashed anger at her uncle. 'Don't you dare! This girl has saved our skin this summer. A little more gratitude for the sacrifice of others might have made you a better man, Albert.'

Albert muttered something oblique in reply. Shauna felt certain that he was bitterly regretting stealing Madame Guilhem's throne and would like to make his escape, but hadn't the physical strength.

Audrey was urging everyone to start eating. 'Quick, come along, or the food will spoil.' When she clapped her hands, the crowd responded, people heading to the tables. Not everybody moved. Laurent and Rachel were still lost in their bubble. Impatiently, Audrey chivvied Shauna, Isabelle and Albert. 'We can't start without you all. Monsieur de Chemignac, Madame Duval? To table, please.' She touched Elisabeth's hand. 'Welcome back, Madame.'

'You recognise me?' Elisabeth asked in astonishment.

'The redheaded English girl who found true love at Chemignac? You are a legend. But please, take your friend to the table.'

'We're not really friends,' Elisabeth said, giving Mike Ladriss a long look. 'More "ships in the storm".'

'Ah, *pardon*,' Audrey said. 'But take him to the table anyway.'

Shauna offered Isabelle her arm, though food was the last thing she wanted. Isabelle didn't move, just stared at Albert. And he stared back, his pupils shifting. Mike had frightened him, Shauna realised. Albert had really believed his transgressions were about to be recounted to his family and neighbours, and even shared with the British press. He looked like a man confronted with his direst nightmare.

Laurent and Rachel had at last emerged from their trance. They approached, like dancers, their footfall oddly weightless. Shauna rubbed her eyes. Then went cold as Isabelle uttered a mewling cry. It was not Laurent and Rachel coming towards them. It was Henri and Yvonne.

'It's Papa,' Isabelle grasped Shauna's hand, transferring her disbelief and shock. Shauna put an arm round her, though she felt unsteady herself. She blinked, convinced she'd open her eyes and discover it was a trick of a sun low on the horizon. But she couldn't deny that the womanly shape under the Gown of Thorns was not Rachel's. It was lithe, but not gym-sculpted. The arms and neck were pale, with a redhead's freckling. The lips were smiling, the eyes deep green under a crown of copper hair. As for him – it was Laurent, with a hint of a rakish moustache. Laurent, an older version. He caught her eye, reminding her wordlessly that she'd held both versions her arms.

They stopped in front of Albert. 'Tell her,' Laurent-Henri commanded the old man. 'Tell Isabelle the truth.'

Albert started to cough. Softly, persistently, behind his hand. He flapped feebly at Rachel-Yvonne. 'Why is she wearing that dress? Nobody is allowed to. It's cursed.'

'Tell Isabelle who betrayed the men of

Chemignac and the English agents!'

'She did!' He pointed at his niece. At Isabelle. '*She* revealed the English spy in the window of the tower room. My brother and the English whore were fornicating, but Isabelle de Chemignac gave them away. She pulled the blackout down from the window.'

'I didn't mean to,' Isabelle said in a piteous voice. 'It was a big, old picture. I took hold of it and its wire broke.'

'Ah, but there were Germans in the grounds, watching. Crouched at the edge of the wood. They saw into that room, saw the face of a wanted woman.'

Shauna felt the horror travel down Isabelle's spine.

'It's true,' Isabelle quavered. 'I betrayed my papa because I could see he was falling in love and I wanted her gone. I would have thrown Yvonne out of the window if I could! But never would I have hurt my papa.'

'You did not betray anybody, *chérie*,' Laurent said, though it was decisively Henri who spoke. 'We were already sold to the enemy.'

'Then she did it!' Albert blazed at the figure in the Gown of Thorns. At Yvonne because it was she he was seeing. Even as he accused, he strained away from her, as much as his straw bale throne would allow. When, caught by a little breeze, the Gown of Thorns floated near enough for its pleats to touch him, he writhed as if it burnt him.

'I was not the informant.' Yvonne's voice rippled with long-supressed rage. 'I was a fool, for sure. I fell in love when I should have been doing my job.' She turned to Henri and Shauna saw how their eyes united. 'When I finally got home to London, SOE wiped the floor with me. Thoroughly deserved. But you evaded judgement all your life, Albert, letting poor little Isabelle believe she killed her father. How cruel! And you traduced my name. I

should have come back and got you by the neck . . .'
Her hand flashed out and Albert gave a strangled
shout. 'Now tell the truth. You were betraying us
even before we arrived. You gave the co-ordinates
of the landing field and the parachute drop to the
Milice, didn't you?'

'Why would I?'

Henri took over. 'You'd overheard me
discussing the arrival of foreign agents with Luc.
Always lurking outside windows and doors! You
rode into Garzenac and passed the details on to your
contact at the police prefecture.'

Albert said nothing.

'The *Milice* did badly in that battle, losing
more of their own than they shot of ours. The
Germans liked to let the *Milice* take the casualties
on those occasions. They were in no hurry to arrest
me. Why risk a gun-fight within the château? Had
you not warned them that it was full of dark corners
and ambush points? They waited, like cats at a hole

in the skirting board. You knew they wanted me and you decided to make their job easier.'

Albert shook his head.

'When did you go first to the Gestapo at Bordeaux? Spring of '43, or earlier? Maybe it was when the forced labour laws came in, and you wanted to be sure of being spared the call-up. You were in touch with Nazi informants in Garzenac. You practiced signalling with lights. You showed your contacts where our secret tunnel lay. Do you deny it?'

Albert made no answer.

'You are a murderer, Albert.' Henri put his hand on one of his brother's knees, and its sudden trembling showed how terrified Albert was. 'I wanted my life, brother. I wanted to love and marry a fine woman. I wanted to see my children grow and to harvest my grapes. You stole everything, and you dare to sit enthroned?'

Entranced, Shauna became aware of Yvonne

reaching into the neck of her gown. She was extracting a leather thong, with a cigarette lighter hanging from the end. The one Rachel always wore. Surely she didn't intend to take revenge by fire?

As Yvonne flicked up a flame and held it towards the nearest bale, Shauna surged forward and grasped her arm. Hers and Yvonne's torsos meshed and it was like looking into her own soul. *We're family*. She knew it beyond doubt. *Our irises are the exact same mix of green and hazel*. 'I won't let you. One more atrocity won't change what's happened.'

Yvonne's pupils expanded with the darkest of humour. 'They didn't train us to be nice, you know. He'll tell us the truth when it's him feeling the pain and I don't have much time.'

'The war's over.' Shauna snatched the lighter, breaking the leather cord against Yvonne's neck. 'That dress has corrupted you!' She reached for its neck, wanting to tear it to shreds, until Yvonne's shrill protest broke the spell. The dream-state fled and Shauna was looking at Rachel, who was rubbing her throat and regarding her with furious disdain.

'What the hell did you break my pendant for? That really hurt.'

'You'll live.' Shauna threw the lighter far into the long grass. Albert was slumped forward in shock. Isabelle was leaning heavily on her stick, breathing erratically, but her expression was full of wonderment. Shauna turned to the man she loved. Laurent was back - just.

She said, 'At least Isabelle now knows it wasn't her fault that her father was killed. That's something. Laurent?'

He was staring beyond her, at Rachel, and Shauna vowed, *If he touches her, smiles at her, I will leave and never come back.*

He didn't smile. He was frowning, as if he'd just noticed something out of place. 'Rachel, go and take that dress off. You've no right to wear it.'

Rachel flicked her hair and pushed out her lips. 'Now you tell me? You're going to say it brings bad luck, I suppose. You believe that crap?'

He said slowly, 'This dress is a magnet for powerful emotions, and it's dangerous. Please take it off.'

'Seriously?' Rachel waited for him to add something, and when he didn't, fetched up her mocking smile. 'Fine, if that's what you want.' She untied the waist cord. Ignoring Shauna's gasp, she pulled the Gown of Thorns over her head and dropped it at Laurent's feet. Then walked away.

Later, Rachel Moorcroft was to say, 'I left Chemignac without a backward glance, and every eye in the place on me.'

Shauna reached for Laurent. His hands were marble cold. She shook him, to haul him back from wherever he was drifting. 'Shall I go too?' she demanded harshly. 'Is it over? Was I just a harvest fling? The way you were gazing at Rachel, wrapped in her arms—'

'It wasn't about her.'

'Um, hello?' Shauna mimicked a lovelorn stare.

'I wasn't *seeing* her. I saw the Gown of Thorns and understood. That dress embodies our fears. Our dreams, hopes and our bitter failings. My father, my grandfather, my great-grandfather – they all fell in love with the Gown of Thorns. Each in turn was ripped apart by misfortune, war, bad luck and betrayal. The dress isn't cursed, but the century that made it most certainly was.' He tipped back his head, inviting sunlight to strike his face. 'Chemignac has survived it. And look at those clouds . . . rain tonight and the harvest in. We've been blessed.'

When he stood tall again, he was smiling. 'You,' he said.

'Me?' Shauna yelped as he picked her up in his arms and held her level with him, then kissed her with unself-conscious desire. Clapping showered them as their friends at the table expressed their delight. The diners began banging their cutlery in rhythm, urging Laurent and Shauna to join them for the feast. Laurent put Shauna back on her feet, and moved away, still holding her hand. Stretching their clasp as far as it would go. 'Madame?' he invited. 'Shall we go to our table?'

'Ours?'

'Of course. You are one of us now. You are part of me. I exist in you.'

Before going to join them, Isabelle spared a glance for Albert. Reluctantly, she too held out her hand. 'You are an evil old man, and in time you will go to your judgement. But for the wrong you did me, I forgive you. Come and join your family at the table.'

Chapter Twenty-Five

Shauna had never encountered such a variety or such a quantity of food as that prepared by the women of Chemignac village. Tarts, cold pies, vibrant salads, rice moulds, Spanish paellas, game pâtés, meat, fish and vegetarian terrines. Laurent presided at the table's head, Shauna on his right. Everyone was tucking in - everyone but Laurent and Shauna. Her stomach felt expanded – as if someone had exploded a firework behind her a short while ago and the shockwaves were locked inside. She had to keep checking that Laurent was really Laurent, his soul once more his own.

Actually, he still looked a shade absent. But Audrey did not intend for her culinary efforts to be ignored. 'Both of you, fill your plates,' she chided, 'or everyone will imagine there's something wrong with my cooking! Laurent, how would you like it if nobody drank your wine?'

Laurent jerked out of his dream-state. He nodded and cut himself a large slice of duck and apricot pie. Filling Shauna's glass, leaning forward to top up Isabelle's, Elisabeth's and Mike Ladriss's, he proposed a private toast. 'To family, new friends and enduring friendship.' Turning to Shauna, he raised his glass again. 'To love.'

He spoke louder than he meant and others heard. Quickly, the toast spread down the tables until soon, everybody was noisily raising their glasses to *l'amour*. Shauna caught Mike Ladriss's eye and he returned a half-smile, and later, passed a note to her on paper torn from his pocket diary.

Love, one. Science, zero? he'd written.

Her answer was make an origami lily from the page, place a luscious red grape in its centre and push it across the table to him. She watched him trying to work out the hidden meaning. There was no hidden meaning. She didn't know the answer because actually, the question was wrong. She wanted both her career and Laurent's love and didn't really see why they should be mutually exclusive. Laurent had encouraged her to take a wine master's course and study viticulture, and to help him grow his business. The real question was, did he still want that from her?

Monty Watson's folk band arrived as the fruit tarts, sorbets and éclairs were uncovered. Dessert was eaten to the music of violin, guitar and hurdy-gurdies, stringed instruments shaped like fat banjos, whose plangent tone was accompanied by a drone, as of bagpipes. This style of music must have been heard on farms and in market squares for centuries, Shauna thought. After the empty plates were cleared, everyone formed a circle, and danced in a side-stepping pattern, with raised arms. Then the older French folk danced complex *bourées* while the younger ones, and the guest-workers, partnered up and waltzed or jigged to the best of their ability. Shauna saw Mike Ladriss inviting her mother to waltz.

Blimey, she thought, I've never seen mum dance in a man's arms. Not even in dad's. Her parents used to groove to the likes of T.Rex and Redbone, throwing their hair about, clicking their fingers. Can mum actually waltz? And with somebody so much taller? The question didn't occupy Shauna long, as Laurent took her into his arms.

'I want to ask you something.'

Her heart crashed like a bird against its cage. But frustratingly, Laurent followed up with, 'Do you think it will rain later?'

'I think it could go either way. The clouds are very high.'

He led her away from the dancing, to the straw throne now vacated by Albert. They sat side by side, greenery and balloon strings tickling their necks. Laurent put his arm around her.

'What would you think about developing a new wine, in honour of my grandfather?'

'I'd say do it.' She was glad she could answer robustly. Disappointed, though, by the impersonal nature of the question. 'A deep, strong red, I should think.'

'Mm. Cabernet Sauvignon blended with Cabernet Franc, and Petit Verdot for a manly flavour. Verdot's a tricky grape, it makes you work hard. I'd have to plant at least half a hectare. Really, this area is too cool for it.'

'Cool? Are you joking?' Even though the day was spent, Shauna could still feel the sun's rays through the crown of her hat, her layers of cotton. But this wasn't the conversation she wanted. Stifling irritation, she asked, 'If you plant in spring, how long till you get mature vines?'

'Depends. I could see the first harvest by 2010.'

I not *we*. 'That's a chunk of your future. Do you have the land to cultivate?'

'Not unless I dig up the meadows.'

'You wouldn't!'

'True, I wouldn't. I could never drain them properly. No, I would have to buy a few *parcelles* from a neighbour.'

'Sounds better!'

'Not straight forward, actually. In France, you cannot just buy a person's vineyards. They must be offered publically– '

'Oh, for God's sake! Why are you telling me this?'

'Who else should I tell?' He made to kiss her, but she turned her face away and his upper lip grazed her ear. It was the end of the day, his beard was making itself felt. 'First, I'd have to talk to the bank. I'd have to take somebody on to help with the extra work. Raymond told me this morning that he wants to retire at Christmas.'

'You'll miss him but it can't be hard to recruit vineyard workers around here.'

'I will certainly miss Raymond. He was my rock when I first took over.'

'Isn't this place littered with rocks?' Shauna didn't like the peevish note that had crept into her voice. It had wormed its way in, but really, it was a mask for the sob in her throat. Sometimes Laurent could be so infuriating. 'You're a pretty effective one-man band, you'll manage.'

'The thing is –' his voice, in contrast to hers was patient, warm, as if he hadn't noticed her crossness. Or perhaps he had, and, like all obstacles in his path, he was looking beyond it. 'I don't want to work with anybody I can't wake up beside.'

'Beside . . ?' A moment ago, she'd had a clear image of Raymond's replacement. A typical French labourer in *bleus de travail*, cigarette in mouth, gunning the engine of a tractor. That image slowly faded to be replaced by an *untypical* labourer in a short, flowered dress and jazzy wellington boots. 'In bed, you mean?'

'In bed, or anywhere. Shauna, come with me for a moment.'

Going into the woods was like a dip into fresh water, a rest for the eyes from the glare of the setting sun. The forest floor breathed a white mist and Shauna felt herself sliding back into a dreamlike state.

Hand in hand, they walked towards the memorial stone. Entering the glade, they pulled back in unison. In shock. Laurent muttered, '*Putain!*' An uncharacteristic profanity for him. The stone was shrouded in a golden miasma. Beside it hovered a male figure with untamed hair, visible only from the waist upward. The torso slowly turned and spoke.

'Hey-up you two – didn't hear you coming. I'm communing with my uncle and his chums.'

Shauna began to giggle. Laurent gave an embarrassed cough. Monty Watson's lower half was obscured by the ground mist filtering through the stalks of wild maize. He'd untied his pony-tail and his grizzled hair stuck out like horsehair stuffing from a busted sofa. He must have been raking his hands through it. Walking forward, Shauna's laughter fell silent as she entered the stone's aura. She read again the roster of names, of lives sacrificed in the cause of freedom. 'We must get Yvonne's name added,' she said.

'Yvonne Rosel,' Monty affirmed. 'But under the dignity of her real name.'

'Antonia Thorne.'

'"*L'Épine de Chemignac*."' Laurent's suggestion fell like a breath of mist.

'"The Thorn of Chemignac" . . .' Monty rolled the concept around his mind. 'Thorn and Splinter. They'd have made a great team, if things had been different.'

'If things had been different, they'd never have met.' Laurent spoke flatly. He'd come back to earth.

Shauna read out the names, tracing the chiselled grooves with her finger. 'Luc Roland, Michel Paulin. We haven't thought much about them, have we? We've made this Henri and Yvonne's story, with the two, brave Englishmen as the supporting cast. We've written out the two French Resistance fighters, and that's not fair.'

Laurent nodded. 'They offered up their lives for France and died here.'

'No, not here.' Shauna gave her words authority because the buzz forming inside her head was the music of certainty, of *knowing*. 'They died at the cave. They died running. But not on the same night as Henri and the others.' Laurent and Monty waited for more but she walked out of the clearing, striking left when she reached the main path. Laurent and Monty, after a short hesitation, followed her.

She found the steep spur of a path – no more than an animal track – which she'd scrambled up the day she'd thought she was following Laurent. Still no sign of a cave mouth. She hadn't expected to see it. Its appearance before had been an aberration, a split in cosmic time offered to her alone. But she knew without doubt that it was there, hidden behind the shuttering of green growth so dense only a machete would clear it. She waited for the men to catch up, then sketched a rough line with her finger. 'They all died here on this slope, but Luc and Michel were killed a day ahead of the others. They helped Cyprien and Jean-Claude through the tunnel on the night of the drop, shared a glass of cognac with Henri, raised their glasses to Yvonne. Came back the same way, meaning to slip out into the forest –'

    'Only, the enemy was waiting,' Monty filled in.

    'Right there.' Shauna pointed to a scrape of rubble where, for some reason, saplings and brambles had not taken root. 'They were German Gestapo men in leather coats, ranged in a line in the undergrowth, guns pointing. When Luc and Michel emerged into the moonlight – dudh-dudh-dudh-dudh –' she imitated automatic fire. 'Torn to ribbons, here.' She jabbed a finger at her feet, driving her point in like a nail. 'When your grandfather used the tunnel the next night,' she said softly to Laurent, 'Michel and Luc's bodies had already been dragged to the clearing. Soon, five bodies lay where the stone now stands.'

'Albert's doing,' Laurent whispered. 'God that he'd never been born.'

Monty left them, concerned about abandoning his musician friends. 'I need to pay them,' he muttered. 'They'll think I've forgotten. Can I send you the bill?'

'No problem,' Laurent answered. 'We'll follow you in a while.'

He and Shauna walked back at a leisurely pace. As they crossed the meadow, they could hear the drone of folk tunes, and see the glow of the brazier. Laughter reached them like shreds of paper on the wind.

Such a balmy night, gently moonlit, no sharp corners to it. Laurent stopped halfway across the meadow and kissed her. His weight bore her down. They sank together on to the fragrant grass and made love like drowning people.

'Stay with me, Shauna,' Laurent said afterwards, his voice rousing the surface of her skin like a breeze on ripe wheat. 'Help me make Chemignac a modern, award-winning business. Your mind, your skills, my knowledge – together, we cannot fail. Will you?'

'Stay?' She stared upward, consulting the moon. Unmasked and full, it warned her of the dangers of half-truths. Of leaving things unsaid, questions unasked. 'You want me to stay because I'm a scientist? A useful adjunct to your business?'

Laurent sat up, blocking her view of the heavens. 'I want you to stay because I love you. Do you think we can be apart? I don't think we're meant to be apart and I don't care if that sounds crazy.'

She put her arms around him, pulling him lower until his lips were a hair's breadth above hers. 'It sounds fine. I want to make wine with you, and love to you, and someday, even grow a family. Laurent, I want to stay.'

Five years later, 13 July 2008

Dakenfield, Somerset, western England

The PA system had arrived. Hairy men in baseball caps were laying cables under mats, securing them with tiger-stripe duct tape. A local TV news team would be along in a couple of hours. For the staff and residents of The Beeches care home, it was a gala day. Red, white and blue bunting criss-crossed the dining room and fluttered in the garden. Entwined Union Jacks and Tricolores trumpeted the *entente cordiale*.

At ten-thirty, Mr and Mrs Ladriss arrived on foot from the B&B where they'd stayed the night, and presented themselves to the home's manager as she came out of her office to greet them.

'Is Aunt Antonia ready for all this?' asked Mike.

'One never knows with Miss Thorne,' the manager replied cautiously. 'Shall I tell her you're here, Mrs Ladriss?'

Elisabeth made no reply, then realised that the question was directed at her. She hadn't totally absorbed her new name. 'Vincent' was going to be hard to erase. Marrying Mike had been a wonderfully impulsive decision after a whirlwind romance. They'd begun their relationship in a spirit of mutual distrust, everything about them in opposition. He was over six foot, she was barely over five foot on tiptoe. She collected crystals and planted vegetables by the phases of the moon. Mike forgot to eat, and he took clocks apart for fun. Each came ready-packaged in a protective outer layer, designed to keep love and other such hazards at bay. They couldn't quite say who had thrown off the armour first, but agreed that Chemignac's moon and the fruit of its vines had played a strong part. 'Why don't we go and find her ourselves?' Elisabeth suggested to the manager. 'Best if we play this whole thing very casually. One thing I've learned about Aunt Antonia, she can't bear a fuss.'

The manager nodded. 'She says it's all bunkum, today's celebration. Bad taste.' The woman touched the posy of carnations in her lapel; red, white and white-sprayed-blue. 'But she's decided to humour us and speak on camera. You'll find her in the conservatory, but I should warn you, she told me yesterday that you're not related. She says you're an imposter.'

'I have the family tree in my handbag,' Elisabeth replied. 'She was my father's half-sister, and though it took me fifty years to track her down and get her to admit our connection, I have birth certificates to prove it.'

Mike Ladriss put a protective arm around his wife. 'I'm sure she'll relent when she hears we've brought messages from France, from Elisabeth's daughter and her husband. This is what today's about, isn't it? Her connection to France.'

The manager gave a fraught smile. 'That reminds me, could you drop a word in her ear about not swearing in front of the camera?'

At eleven o'clock, an official car drew up, disgorging the Lord Mayor of Dakenfield and other dignitaries. They were followed by members of the Royal British Legion and a deputation from the town of Garzenac. With them were two guests of honour, Raymond and Audrey Chaumier. A troop of boy scouts and girl guides arrived next with their pack leaders, and finally the film crew – harassed because the carpark was full and they'd had to leave their vans down the street.

At eleven thirty, the ceremony began with a representative of the mayor of Garzenac presenting Miss Antonia Thorne, otherwise known as the SOE agent Yvonne Rosel, with a medal struck in her honour. The cameras homed in for a midday news feature. Sixty-five years ago today, at a place called

Chemignac, members of the local Resistance attempted to escape an ambush. They failed, but one woman made it out . . .

The reporter crouched beside Miss Thorne's wheelchair and even though she'd been briefed not to mention her interviewee's age, began – 'So, Antonia, I believe we have to congratulate you on being ninety-five years old?'

'Miss Thorne, please. And great age is not an achievement. It is a pain in the bum.'

'That's me told! And you were in France in 1943, parachuted into hostile territory to aid the French Resistance. Is it true you were nearly shot before you'd even touched the ground?'

'One is either shot or not shot. There is no such thing as "nearly shot".'

'Right, no, I suppose. I was told you fell in love with the man who rescued you?'

'He didn't rescue me. He was part of the reception committee and I was perfectly capable of defending myself. I'd been taught to kill. They talk about women being allowed to fight on the front line nowadays – let me tell you, we SOE girls were on the front line fighting for our lives in the 1940s.'

'Amazing! It must have been nerve-racking, dropping into enemy terrain—'

'It was terrifying. And it was exhilarating, dangerous and dreadfully, dreadfully sad. It wasn't a game.'

'And afterwards, you came home and told nobody about your exploits, not for years. That's pretty awesome.'

'Official Secrets Act. And there was nothing to tell. I didn't win the war. I didn't defeat the Germans. I was a tiny cog in a huge machine. I got buckled, spat out and that was that.'

'You never wanted to go back?'

'As an agent? Someone had taken photographs of me, so my cover was blown and I couldn't go back. After the war, I didn't want to.'

The reporter flashed a desperate smile at the camera, saying, 'In a minute, we're going over live to Garzenac, in southwest France. But now, let me speak with two of our French guests, Monsieur and Madame Chaumier who met the intrepid Antonia – Yvonne, as she was known - in the dark days of Nazi occupation, and have stayed in touch ever since.'

The reporter pushed a microphone in front of Audrey. 'I believe you tracked down Miss Thorne when she was in hospital, by writing to the Mayor of Dakenfield? You were worried when she stopped answering your letters.'

A translator repeated the question in French.

Audrey gave the matter some thought, nodded and said, '*Oui.*'

'You met "Yvonne" when she was hiding in your village? That must have been pretty amazing.'

Another pause. Then, 'No. It was the worst time. We had to run for our lives and I heard the guns. The shooting went on and on . . . how many bullets does it take to kill cornered men? I am glad our friend is at last being honoured, but I do not like to remember the past.'

With visible relief, the reporter handed over to her colleague in France.

In the square of Garzenac, Laurent and Shauna watched the dedication of the memorial to the town's Resistance fighters, tears in their eyes. Donations from Clos de Chemignac and other local businesses had paid for the stone to be moved from the woods to the town, and the carving of one more name.

'Stand by,' one of the British film crew researchers told them. 'After the mayor has done his speech, we'll be interviewing you, Monsieur le Comte, then you, Madame.'

'Shauna and Laurent, please.'

'Cool. We'll be asking about your family history and what you know about "Yvonne" and her time at Chemignac.'

Shauna and Laurent exchanged glances. They knew too much. Albert's crime had not evaporated, even with his death in 2005. Those few who knew of it held the knowledge close. They always had done. Not to protect Albert . . . to protect Isabelle.

'What can I say?' Shauna muttered when the researcher was out of range. 'That Yvonne came to me in a waking dream, and shared her pain and her love life with me?'

'Just talk about a brave, strong woman,' Laurent advised, 'one you are proud to be related to. People love that story, how you and your mother traced her, proving she was a lost relation. The mayor and Monty have spoken of the other men who died. I will talk about my grandfather.' He gave the smile that always made Shauna want to hug him and sink her teeth lightly into his neck. 'Then, I will tell them about our new wine, and why I named it in his honour.'

The wine, *Écharde de Chemignac*, was being liberally poured out to the gathered company. Establishing itself as their bestselling brand, its label carried the Chemignac coat of arms above a twisted thorn tree. A blend of Cabernet Sauvignon and Cabernet Franc grapes, it had been developed by Laurent and Shauna as a full-bodied, muscular wine that aged well. They were currently working on a blend of whites, to be called *Épine de Chemignac* – 'Thorn of Chemignac'. Crisp, dry with hints of gooseberry and a suggestion of flint, it ought to be a fitting tribute to Shauna's great-aunt.

Splinter and thorn. Harsh fruits of a harsh world, but safe enough if treated with caution and respect. At Chemignac, under a sunshade in the rose garden, Isabelle Duval wriggled her feet. She was winding

crochet cotton and enjoying the summer scents, and
the drone of bees making short-haul flights between
flower heads. She'd cried off the ceremony, citing
her bad legs, knowing it would be too much for her.

Justice had been served. The stone block,
cleaned and polished, sat on a brand new plinth, the
correct names carved on it for all to see. Chemignac,
she imagined, was proud of its achievements, not
the least of which was creating two new pairs of
lovers.

Laurent and Shauna, a matched pair of
science-obsessed wine makers who were taking the
world by storm. And more quietly, Elisabeth and
Mike. That second marriage had 'come out of left
field,' as Nico would say. When she and Elisabeth
had run into Mike Ladriss at the railway station, he
had been an angry, sacked, divorced academic about
to ignite a scandal and launch a lawsuit against his
employers. The perfect partner for Elisabeth, who,
Isabelle had often observed, soothed unhappy

people like cucumber on burned skin. Elisabeth had advised Mike, 'Let it lie'. He had, and remarkably, the scandal had fizzled out and he'd been given his job back.

Then Albert had died, and Louette had woken within days. A life for a life. That's how things worked. Hearing the fluttering of wings under the tower eaves, Isabelle glanced up. Many times in the past, as she drifted off to sleep, she'd feel she was leaving her body and joining the doves in flight. She'd soar up and into the tower room to stare out of the window. A window she herself had blocked, but which melted into glass under the force of her need. She would gaze over the meadows, offering her life for the chance to go back and do things differently. To be a good child and not the jealous hysteric, pulling pictures off the wall.

So real had those flights been, it hadn't surprised her to hear Laurent and Shauna claiming that they'd seen a vision of a female at the window.

Well, this was Chemignac, a place of possibility. Suddenly, the branches above her shook – what was upsetting those birds now? She pushed herself up with her stick, sucking her teeth at the slowness of her legs. Then she laughed. The doves were mating. In this heat? They must be mad.

The ancient thorn tree guarding the *chai* relinquished a few desiccated leaves. The Gown of Thorns in its wardrobe at the top of the tower slept.